Shadow ON THE Sun

Shadow ON THE Sun

DAVID MACINNIS GILL

GREENWILLOW BOOKS

An Imprint of HarperCollins*Publishers*

Shadow on the Sun
Copyright © 2013 by David Macinnis Gill

All rights reserved. No part of this book may be used or reproduced in any manner whatsoever without written permission except in the case of brief quotations embodied in critical articles and reviews. Printed in the United States of America. For information address HarperCollins Children's Books, a division of HarperCollins Publishers, 10 East 53rd Street, New York, NY 10022.
www.epicreads.com

The text of this book is set in 11-point Electra LH
Book design by Paul Zakris

Library of Congress Cataloging-in-Publication Data is available.

ISBN 978-0-06-207335-8 (trade ed.)

13 14 15 16 17 CG / RRDH 10 9 8 7 6 5 4 3 2 1
First Edition

 Greenwillow Books

For Deb

"Being unconquerable lies with yourself."
—Sun Tzu, *The Art of War*

Chapter √-1
The Gulag
Terminal: MUSEcommand — bash — 122x36
Last login: 239.x.xx.xx:xx 12:12:09 on
ttys0067

>...

AdjutantNod04:~ user_MUSE$
SCREEN CRAWL: [root@mmiminode ~]
SCREEN CRAWL: WARNING! VIRUS DETECTED!
Node1666; kernal compromised (quarantine sub-
routine (log=32)....FAILED!

SCREEN CRAWL: Executing process Mimi.exe

```
/**
* @author Me, Myself, and I
*
* The polymorphic code below creates a
* buffer overflow in the stack
* creating external log-in access
* and defeating security protocols
*/



#!/usr/bin/xperl
if (!defined?(FILE))
FILE=File.basename(__FILE__)
end
load "mi.mi";
#require "Virus_Match"
def selfCopy(key)
code = ""
newkey = deterministicKeygen(key);
File.open(FILE, "r").each_line do |l|
code += 1
end
code = mencrypt(code, key)
# defines new Virus_Match file name
fn = rand(128).to_s + 'copy.rb';
File.open(fn, 'w+') do |f|
f.write('load "mi.mi";'+"\n");
```

```
f.write("if (!defined?(FILE))\n\tFILE=__FILE__;\
nend;\n");
f.write('code="'+code+'";'+"\n")
f.write('eval(mdecrypt(code, ' + key.to_s+'))');
$ end


SCREEN CRAWL: External host access...GRANTED

::new host$

AdjutantNod13:~ user_MIMT$

SCREEN CRAWL: Begin shell overflow protocol
SCREEN CRAWL: Executing process TrojanHorse.
exe

...running

/**
 * The extraction routine below installs the
 * kernal archive of the cybernetic entity
known as
 * Mimi
 */

#!/usr/bin/xperl
use strict;
```

```perl
use Term::ANSIColor;
use Getopt::Std;
use LW2;

my %opts   = ();
getopts('h:u:i:', \%opts);

usage() unless($opts{x});
usage() unless($opts{y});
usage() unless($opts{z});

my $input = $opts{z};
my $url    = $opts{x};
my $host   = $opts{y};

my $var1   = generate_random_int();
my $var2   = generate_random_int();
my $total = $var1 + $var2;

my $open   = generate_random_string(4);
my $close = generate_random_string(8);


/**
* If cybernetic entity Mimi is uncorrupted
* SCREEN CRAWL will display 'Welcome Message'
```

```
 * and remove records of QUARANTINE FAILURE
routines
*/

my $file = "/proc/self/environ";
test_matches($url,$test,$shell,$file);

my $lol_error    = download($test,$host,"wget/
mozilla");
my $lol_shelled = download($shell,$host,"wget/
Mimi");

foreach my $log (@logs) {
    chomp($log);
    test_matches($url,"wget/Mimi","wget/
Mimi",$log);

int main(int argc, char *argv[])   //argc
and argv stand for "Argument Count" and
"Argument Vector"
{
    std::count << "Hello Dolly!" << std::endl;
//use count to display "Sing to me O' Muse."
    return 0; //return 0 and display.
}
$ end
```

SCREEN CRAWL: Sing to me, o' Muse, of that man who wandered far and wide.

<Mimi> And when you finishing singing, o' MUSE
<Mimi> I suggest you start running.

CHAPTER 0

Hell's Cross
Outpost Fisher Four
ANNOS MARTIS 239. 1. 12. 08:01

Ice forms on the lens of his scope as Fuse waves the red dot sight of his armalite above the soldier's ear. The blighter is a Sturmnacht scout, and he's no more welcome near the Hell's Cross mines than a chigger at an Orthocrat's garden party.

In the year or so since deserting his old soldiering life and coming to live among the miners, Fuse has seen more and more of Lyme's Sturmnacht deployed to Fisher Four. Where once you went months without seeing outsiders, now you couldn't hock a loogie without hitting one of those jack-booted thugs.

"C'mon now," Fuse says as the frigid air freeze-dries his breath.

With overgrown hair, thin sideburns, missing teeth, and ears too long for his pointed chin, Fuse rests against the iron-gated entrance to the mines.

The Sturmnacht soldier crests the hill. He scans the ridge with a pair of omnoculars.

"Stop moving about, see?" Fuse says. "I'm a fair dinkum shot in the right conditions." Especially if the conditions include a few kilos of C-42 explosives and a remote detonator.

When the soldier's gaze falls on the iron gate emblazoned with the words *No Work, No God*, he raises his rifle.

"Oy! The bugger's spotted me," Fuse says under his breath. "It's now or never."

He pulls the trigger. The crack of gunfire echoes across the Prometheus Basin, and the sound rises into the steel blue sky. The bullet hits the frozen tundra. It spits chunks of ice and snow into the scout's goggles. But except for gouging a large hole in the ground, it does no damage.

The scout turns to run.

"Carfargit, Fuse! You can't hit the broad side of a broadside!" He sights down the scope. He finds the target again.

Crack!

The next bullet hits nothing but air.

"I'll be stuffed," Fuse says. "I should've just blown the blaggard up."

He aims for a third shot, hands shaking.

Too late. The scout has reached the crest of the ridge. He's signaling his comrades. Fuse switches his scope to distance view. A few kilometers away, a company of armored turbo sleds turns toward the scout.

"Fuse! You call yourself a Regulator!" Swinging his rifle over his shoulder, he tromps through a snowdrift to his bike, a hodgepodge of spare parts that can break 140 kilometers per hour.

If he can get it started.

And if it doesn't explode.

Again.

He jumps on the seat, grabs the steering bar, and kicks the starter. The engine sputters to life, and he pats the gas tank. "That's my baby!"

As the sound of the Sturmnacht sleds grows louder, Fuse guns the engine and rips across the tundra, the studs on his tires chewing up chunks of ice. He plows past a steel tower lift mechanism and the tipple, then several small mounds of heavy guanite ore.

The bike skitters past a sign declaring DANGER! NO ADMITTANCE! His headlight shines on a small tunnel with smooth walls. He hunkers low, afraid to snag his noggin on the ceiling. Then with a squeal of brakes, he brings the bike to a stop. He grabs a signal box from a hidden nook. Types in the pass code. Then presses the dual ignition buttons.

Boom!

At the far end of the tunnel, the roof collapses, blocking the entrance to the east mines. If the Sturmnacht want to catch him, they'll have to haul butt to the west side, which he'd blow, too. If he had time.

But time's not on his side.

"Note to self." He taps his temple. "When the hurly-burly's

done, get your carcass over here and open a wormhole in Tunnel B Seven."

Back on the bike, he zooms across the high-arched stone bridge that stretches across a mammoth gorge. Above is a sky of stone. Below is a dark abyss that some say reaches Mars's cold iron core.

Fuse reaches the far side and throttles down. He coasts into Hell's Cross, the former central complex of a subterranean mining town, now almost deserted. Faded flags hang from the arches. Rusted razor wire tops all the cracked stucco walls. Everything is coated in a fine coat of guanite dust. Home sweet home it ain't.

Fuse parks his bike in a flat-roofed corridor littered with empty crates. He runs up a flight of steps. Huffing for breath, he throws open the third door on the left and yells, "Áine! The Sturmnacht are coming!"

On a mattress in the corner, Áine rests with her back against the wall. Her moon-shaped face is puffy and covered in red blotches, and her pregnant belly strains against her threadbare overalls. She looks liable to pop in a nanosecond.

Áine's grandmother, Maeve, hovers nearby. Maeve's face is framed with silver hair and furrowed with wrinkles as deep as a canyon. As far as Fuse knows, she's the oldest person on the planet—he's never seen another mug so puckered and craggy.

"How d'you know they's the Sturmnacht?" Áine asks.

"I spotted a scout." Fuse frowns. "And he spotted me back."

"I told you to shoot anything that moved!" Áine says.

"I'm not like Jenkins was—shooting's not my thing, you know that," Fuse says. "Blowing stuff up is."

"Zip it!" Áine struggles to her feet. "There's no use in it now. We'll hole up in one of the survival vaults. Live on the emergency supplies. It's the only chance we've got."

Maeve clucks and shakes her head. "You're in no condition to run, Áine."

"She's in no condition to get press-ganged by the Sturmnacht, neither," Fuse says. "Those slavers need strong backs to reopen the guanite mines, and if you ain't fit for work, they'll find something else you're good at. Come on, you lot, let's get her moving."

Maeve gives a tight-lipped smile. "Since when do I take orders from you, Regulator?"

"Since right this minute." Fuse leads Áine down the stairs and through the courtyard, her head resting on his shoulder.

"There's a power sled 'round back," he says. "Step lively now. We've not got much time."

He lifts Áine into the ore loader. Maeve stuffs pillows behind her back and supports her head, then hauls herself into the driver's seat and starts the loader up.

Fuse kisses Áine and then scowls at Maeve. "Take care of my wife and little one."

"Who happen to be my granddaughter and great-grand-child." Maeve tries to laser him with her eyes. "Don't you forget that."

Fuse's lip twitches as he turns to leave. The things he'd like to say. But now's not the time.

Áine grabs his jacket. "Where'd you think you're going?"

"To the surface," he says. "If you're to live, I've got to find help."

"I always knew you'd run out on me!" Áine says.

Fuse kisses her hand. "Ain't running out on you. Your grandmum's right here. Besides, I'm useless at this birthing business." He jumps to the ground as the loader starts to pull away. He blows her a kiss. "No child of mine is going to be born a slave. You've got to hide, before it's too late!"

"Nobody can help us!" Her bloated face turns into a sneer. "It's already too late!"

That's where you're wrong, Fuse thinks as he jogs toward a wormhole that will take him to the surface. There's two somebodies that can help us. All I've got to do is find them before the Sturmnacht kill you.

CHAPTER 1

Christchurch
ANNOS MARTIS 239. 1. 12. 08:02

Where are you, Durango? Vienne hits the brakes, and her turbo bike chatters to a halt. She slams the kickstand down in frustration. For the last seven weeks, she's scoured the prefecture, searching for him in every burnt-out, ashed-over town, every old foul-smelling haunt, every ragged refugee camp on the roadside. Now she's at the end of the line, literally, standing on the last bridge into Christchurch, the deserted capital city.

After chaining her bike to a burnt-out battle truck, she walks around a massive hole in the bridge, looking down into the muddy River Gagarin. The bridge isn't the only thing that has been wrecked, she thinks, before a high-pitched sound breaks her chain of thought. She looks up, catching a glimpse of a shadow on the sun before the light disappears beyond the horizon.

Another Crucible strike. Right on time.

"Move!" she yells, and sprints for cover, a cloth knapsack

over a shoulder, her long legs and sinuous shoulders working hard beneath a baggy black cheongsam robe with bell
sleeves.

Seconds later, a percussive blast rolls across the delta.
The bridge convulses, tossing vehicles around in a metallic thunderstorm of sound. Vienne vaults over a burnt-out
truck, and as a new hole opens in the bridge, she lands safely
on dry land.

"Hope the bike is there when I get back," she says to herself. "Check that. Hope the *bridge* is there when I get back."

Vienne knocks the dirt from her sandals. A hood obscures
her Nordic face, which is webbed with battle scars, and her
blond hair is braided with dozens of black ribbons. She puts
an almost dry canteen to her peeling lips. How many people
died in the Flood, she wonders. Hundreds? Thousands?
News of the Flood came fast across the multinets moments
after it happened. Then, in two days time, Lyme overthrew
the government, and the news became propaganda.

What became of the dead, no one knows. There were
rumors that they were buried in mass graves or cremated in
open-air bonfires. One thing is for certain: Theirs was not a
Beautiful Death.

"If there ever was such a thing," she says under her breath,
shaking the last drop of water onto her tongue. Once upon a
time, she had believed in the Tenets and a Beautiful Death,
but now she knows they were fairy tales.

Far ahead, she spots the multinet antenna on the roof

of Parliament Tower, the abandoned government headquarters. She looks up at the penthouse, the one she jumped from after performing a one-person shock invasion on the board of directors meeting. Of course, she was wearing symbiarmor, so the fall didn't faze her.

She scans the tower courtyard, half expecting to see Durango's face among the ruins. But her hopes are dashed as they've been dashed every day for the last six months.

She always looks.

Durango is never there.

Empty canteen in hand, she kneels beside a trickle of water coming from a broken, rusted pipe. She rips open a packet of purification tablets, then drops the pills into the water.

From the corner of her eye, she catches a glimmer of movement. Could be nothing, or it could be a Scorpion, one of the feral children who once lived in Favela, a nearby slum. She reaches for her armalite before she remembers that there is no gun.

Not even a holster.

Then she spots the source of the movement. Across the alley, hidden by garbage, a small girl with large eyes is watching her. Vienne shakes the canteen, then presses it to her lips.

"You got chiggers in your brains, susie?" the girl calls. "That stuff's rotgut poison!"

The girl is half her height, with joints so swollen by

malnourishment, they look like knobs. "Not anymore," Vienne says.

"Nuh." The girl skulks closer, keeping debris between herself and Vienne. "No pill made's going to suck poison out of water."

"Every poison has an antidote." Vienne shakes the canteen next to her ear, then offers a sip. "See for yourself."

The girl inches closer. Her eyes are sunken, her skin freckled with rust-stained mud. Her hands and feet are coated with dirt, and her clothes are in tatters. She cranes her neck. "Don't know that I can trust you not to stick a shiv in my gut."

"I keep a hunting knife strapped to the inside of my thigh. If I'd wanted to hurt you," she says, "I could've split your skull when you peeped out of the trash heap."

"Had lots of practice splitting skulls, have you?"

"More than I'd like." Vienne extends the canteen. "Take the water. I've not got all day."

In a burst of movement that's all rags and bones, the girl pounces. She sucks down the water with a ferocity that could only be called thirst if the sun were called a light-emitting diode.

Vienne brushes the dried mud from her cheongsam. "Slow down. You'll make yourself sick."

"No need to get nargy-bargy, susie. I got ears," she says, and begins to sip.

"That's better." Vienne pushes the oily strands of hair

from the girl's face and asks, "Where's your family?"

"Gone."

"You're alone?"

The urchin shrugs. It is a gesture Vienne knows all too well. After the Flood destroyed Christchurch, families tried to stay together, but orphans were left on the roads to fend for themselves. The Tengu Monastery opened its doors to these orphans, and now a place that had become a lonely outpost was bustling with young life.

See that, Lyme, she thinks. This is the price of your war. "May I?" Vienne reaches for the empty canteen. "I'm alone, too." She stores it in her rucksack. "But I have a job to do, and it's getting late."

The girl follows Vienne to the next block. "Not that-away!" she shouts. "Folk say Draeu stay there. They'll gut you proper."

"There's a pleasant thought," Vienne says. But there are no Draeu left. The miners of Fisher Four wiped them all out more than twelve months ago. The rumors have turned out to be harder to kill than they were. "Thanks for the advice. To the right, then? I need to reach Parliament Tower."

"No, susie, go straightaway. Tower's eight blocks yonder. Heads up for the Ferro, too. They'll gut you quick as the Draeu."

"Thanks again. You are an excellent guide. You remind me of someone I once knew." In her mind's eye, Vienne sees a young monk laughing, the spikes of her pink hair bouncing as she climbs a punching dummy and stands on one foot, her arms spread like wings. "What's your name?"

The girl shrugs. "The Flood washed it away."

"You know," Vienne says. "I live in a place where some refugee children are staying. There's food and shelter, if you'd like to come back with me."

"How I'm to know you won't kill me soon's my back gets turned?" she says. "I'll take my chances with the Ferro."

Vienne sighs but doesn't argue. She pulls the canteen from her rucksack and hands it to the girl, along with some purification packets. "Use one pill at a time," she says, "and these will last awhile." Then she removes her sandals. "These are too big for now, but you'll grow into them."

"My name's Ema," the girl says, and, snatching the shoes, disappears down the alley.

"What's the hurry?" Vienne calls. "What are you afraid of?"

"The answer," a deep voice says, "is behind you."

CHAPTER 2

Christchurch

ANNOS MARTIS 239. 1. 12. 08:53

Vienne spins into a defensive crouch, cursing herself for letting someone sneak up on her. You're worse than rusty, she thinks. And it's going to get you killed.

Standing in the shadows, just so that the darkness covers half of his face, is a young man who is neither Draeu nor Scorpion. He's taller than most with wide shoulders, his deep blue velveteen jacket hanging loosely, the cuffs of the sleeves reaching his knuckles. He pretends to examine his fingernails. "What brings pretty girl to Ferro land?"

"Desperta Ferro?" she says. "You're still here?" Like cockroaches, even a diluvial apocalypse couldn't eradicate these pests.

"Nikolai Koumanov, at your service, *lapochka*." He doffs his cap and makes a sweeping bow. Black curls fall into his face, obscuring everything but his smile.

"What do you want, Ferro?" she says. "And why do you think it's appropriate to refer to me as 'little pigeon'?"

"*Lapochka* is what Nikolai has always called you." He pushes his hair back under the cap, revealing a masculine face with thick brows arching over brooding eyes and a square jawline hedged with a goatee. He steps out of the shadows. "Do you not recognize Nikolai? How does girl forget such handsome face?"

"Easy." Vienne circles to the left. Be cautious, she thinks, he's got thirty kilos of weight on you, and he may not be alone. "I've never met anyone named Koumanov."

He strokes his goatee. "Nikolai was not Koumanov then. It is Desperta Ferro name, you see."

Keep him talking, Vienne thinks, and keep moving. Find out his endgame.

"Cat got tongue?" he asks, lifting his eyebrows in a way that he obviously thinks is charming, but makes Vienne's skin crawl.

I *do* know that look, Vienne thinks. But from where? "I asked you before, what do you want?"

"This is Desperta Ferro territory, and Nikolai has come to protect from enemy." He bows again, a gesture even grander than before. Not grand enough, however, to prevent her from catching the glint of blue metal as he pulls out a revolver. "I asked already—why has pretty girl come to Christchurch?"

"I'm looking for something," Vienne says, studying the revolver, "that has been lost."

Nikolai crosses his arms, the barrel of the gun scarcely hidden behind the velveteen fabric of his sleeve. "Is redundant. Girl would not seek thing she has already found, *jaa?* Unless, of course, girl is stupid."

"What makes you think," Vienne says, "that I'm stupid?"

He saunters close, walking heel to toe in his boots. "Pretty girls are stupid," he says, circling her. "Since you are exceptionally pretty girl, so it should follow you would be exceptionally stupid. Yet Nikolai knows from past, such thing is not true."

What a puffed-up, foppishly dressed, overly dramatic butt! No wonder their revolution never got started. "It would be stupid to continue this conversation." She turns to leave. "You are only wasting my time."

"Stop!" Nikolai blocks the alley. "Why such rush?"

"The thing I seek is not here," she says as Nikolai flashes a smile that's meant to be charming. "Step aside, please."

"Until *lapochka* pays toll," he says, making his brows dance. "I cannot."

She slips her hands into her sleeves. Her fingertips find the knife. Let him show his hand, she thinks. Then she remembers that this is a game she's not supposed to play anymore. "What toll?"

He taps his lips. "Pretty girl must kiss Nikolai, right here, on lips."

"Is that all?" She wonders why they always make it so easy. "Plant one on the lips?"

"For now," he says. "If kiss is very good, then perhaps we talk seconds."

"Fair enough."

He puckers up as a sly smile that screams "you asked for it" slips across Vienne's face.

The art of a perfect punch is fluidity. In order for the hand to move swiftly, both it and the arm must remain relaxed until the nanosecond before contact. Then as the fingers curl to form the fist, the muscles flex, becoming rigid, and the energy generated flows through them the same way that a hammer transfers energy through iron and into the anvil.

Vienne's fist cracks Nikolai in the mouth. As his head snaps back, she spreads her arms, arching her back, and brings her right leg up to kick Nikolai across the alley.

He slams against the brick wall, where he lies dazed, a trickle of blood at the corner of his mouth.

"Who's the little pigeon now?" she says, before realizing that he's out cold. She takes the canteen from his belt, unscrews the lid, and shakes water on his face until he sputters and moans. "How's that for seconds?"

"Not so sweet as Nikolai had imagined." He spits out blood. "I bite tongue."

"Serves you right. Count yourself lucky you can still talk." She shakes her head. Maybe it didn't serve him right. All the hours of meditation the past few months, all the healing sessions with Ghannouj, and she's learned nothing. "Sorry about the blood," she says. "Hope it washes out of your jacket."

He grabs her ankle. "Wait! How do you not recognize

Nikolai? We serve in same army. I was Regulator, like you."

"I'm not a Regulator anymore." She pulls free of his grasp, noting that he has all five fingers on his left hand. "And you were never like me."

A few blocks later, Vienne enters the Circus, a roundabout in the middle of Christchurch, which leads her to the ruins of Parliament Tower.

After tying a kerchief over her face, she enters the lobby.

Inside, it's dark. She pulls a beeswax candle from her rucksack, lights it, then pushes open the mud-jammed fire door. The stairwell is full of dirt and cobwebs. She begins to climb.

When she reaches the top landing, she sees that the open door is marked with DESPERTA FERRO! The writing is new, the ink freshly smeared through the mold on the surface.

What's the point? she thinks. There's nothing left worth fighting for.

On the penthouse floor, the carpet is also black, but its color comes from being scorched by fire. The fire is long since out. The stink of it, however, still lingers, and she wonders if the smell is real or just her memory.

"Focus." She draws in a breath of toxic air, then winces. "It's real."

Down the hallway, to the left, she finds the room she's been looking for. She shoves the door aside and enters.

The walls and ceiling are ashed over. The windows are

blown out. Dirt, debris, and dust cover everything. For an instant her head swims: The room is on fire. She's on her knees. A man with a broken arm stands nearby. Someone is screaming.

"No, Vienne," she whispers. "Focus. The here and now. The here and now."

Closing her eyes, she presses her palms together and focuses her chi. The images in her mind fade. From a pocket, she pulls out a small vial punctured with tiny airholes. She unscrews the lid, and a single bee emerges.

At first it crawls across the back of Vienne's hand, and then onto the sleeve of her robe. After a moment, it flies to the blown-out window and lights on the sill. It seems as if the bee will fly out the window, summoned by the winds, but then it straight-lines across the room and settles on a pile of debris, buzzing loudly.

Vienne carefully pushes the debris aside until she finds a shaft of plain-looking wood that means the difference between survival and failure for the monks and the beehives that they maintain.

Here is your staff, Ghannouj, she thinks. She'll return it to the shrine in the Tengu Monastery, and her last act of penance will be done. Maybe then she can be rid of the guilt that hangs on her like a suit of ragged clothes.

Holding the staff, she walks to the window and looks down. Months ago, her brother fell to his death from this window, washed away by the same flood that destroyed

Christchurch. In that moment everything changed.

She looks out across the broken back of the city, past the river delta, and into the far-reaching sky. The plume from the Crucible strike is rising with the clouds. She wonders why, even in her imagination, she can't find the one face she yearns most to see.

"Why can't I find you, Durango?" she whispers. "Where have you gone?"

Chapter √-1
The Gulag
Terminal: MUSEcommand — bash — 122x36
Last login: 239.x.xx.xx:xx 12:12:09 on ttys0067

>...

AdjutantNod04:~ user_MUSE$
SCREEN CRAWL: [root@mmiminode ~]
SCREEN CRAWL: WARNING! VIRUS DETECTED!
Node1666; kernal compromised (quarantine sub-
routine (log=32)....FAILED!

SCREEN CRAWL: External host access...GRANTED

::new host$

AdjutantNod13:~ user_MIMT$

```
$ tar -xvzf Durango.tar.gz -C directory

/**
The code below puts extracts the tarball
archive "Durango.tar.gz"
And runs reinstallation program of data files
For entity known as Jacob Stringfellow
*/

#!/usr/bin/xperl
tar -xvf Durango.tar.gz
tar -xzvf Durango.tar.gz.gz
tar -xjvf Durango.tar.gz.bz2

mimi/
mimi/pulse/
mimi/pulse/default.pa
mimi/pulse/client.conf
mimi/pulse/daemon.conf
mimi/pulse/system.pa
mimi/xml/
mimi/xml/docbook-xml.xml.old
mimi/xml/xml-core.xml
mimi/xml/catalog
mimi/xml/catalog.old
```

```
mimi/xml/docbook-xml.xml
mimi/xml/rarian-compat.xml
mimi/xml/sgml-data.xml
mimi/xml/xml-core.xml.old
mimi/xml/sgml-data.xml.old
mimi/mail.rc
mimi/Wireless/
mimi/Wireless/RT2870STA/
mimi/Wireless/RT2870STA/RT2870STA.dat
mimi/logrotate.conf
mimi/compizconfig/
mimi/compizconfig/config
mimi/xperl/
mimi/xperl/debian_config
mimi/ConsoleKit/
mimi/ConsoleKit/seats.d/
mimi/ConsoleKit/seats.d/00-primary.seat
mimi/ConsoleKit/run-session.d/
mimi/ConsoleKit/run-seat.d/
mimi/opt/
```

SCREEN CRAWL: Extracting archive "Durango. tar.gz"

```
$ extraction complete
```

<Mimi> Howdy, cowboy. Did you miss me?

CHAPTER 3

The Hive
Olympus Mons
ANNOS MARTIS 239. 2. 12. 13:12

My name is Durango. I am a former mercenary, a former Regulator chief, and now I am a dead man walking.

"More like stumbling," says Mimi, the artificial intelligence flash-cloned to my brain stem. "Being dragged by two muscular jailers down a dimly lit corridor does not meet any definition of walking."

"I'm just resting my legs," I subvocalize to her, which at this point is the only way I can approximate speech, since I can't feel my vocal cords, not to mention my throat, lungs, chest, or pelvis. It's the effect of somarin gas, a nerve agent that paralyzes the body momentarily and plays havoc with the central nervous system. If you're like me and have nanobots in your central nervous system, it's a double dose of the old skull and crossbones.

"Technically, that is inaccurate," she replies. "Your nerves are operating at a reduced capacity, but you can feel, as evidenced by the pins and needles sensation emanating from your lower extremities."

"My left foot's asleep." I try to focus on the hallway ahead. Yellow lights pulse above me. The pulses eat through my eyelids, pinging my optic nerve again and again. The lights—and the nerve gas they hit me with—are designed to incapacitate my nervous system and to make my mind as moldable as clay.

"Also technically inaccurate," Mimi says. "Your foot is numb. Only the brain is capable of sleeping."

"Says you, the AI that never sleeps."

"I do not need to sleep per se any more than your left foot needs to."

"You never shut up, either."

"Like you never stop whining?"

"I can't whine," I say. "My mouth is paralyzed."

"That explains the trail of drool you are leaving on the floor."

"Nuh," I say aloud.

"PS." Mimi says. "You are not dead."

For the past forty-three weeks, I've been locked up in a ten-by-ten cell in a military complex buried deep within the dormant volcano Olympus Mons. It's the fortress of General Lyme, Supreme Leader of the People's Free Republic of Mars and the most brutal dictator our planet has ever known. During my time as a prisoner, I have had all of my various tissues sampled, my organs biopsied, my skin peeled off and grafted back on, my nerve endings stripped of their myelin sheaths, and my brain imaged so many times my bionic eye should glow in the dark—all in an effort to extract the one snippet of code that Lyme values more than anything else in the world, the artificial intelligence that lives within my brain and goes by the name of Mimi.

General Lyme is my mortal enemy. He's also my father.

We don't really get along.

"Even gassed," Mimi says, "you sound like a penny dreadful."

"What's a penny?" I subvocalize.

"The lowest denomination of coin in many nations on Earth," she says, "as well as the monetary value of your thoughts."

The guards haul me through the doors labeled "Nursery." They could just wheel me in on a gurney. Lyme, being the *drecksau* that he is, likes the spectacle.

"Put him into cradle one," Lyme says to his twin goons as my head lolls to the side and a line of spittle leaks out of my mouth. He doesn't even look up from his multinet tablet.

I struggle to lift my head, but it's full of stuffing, so I lie still, trying to focus. Then I smell something stronger than my own body odor, like liniment and almonds. It's the smell of the antidote for somarin, but it's not a complete antidote.

I'm about to become a puppet.

"They're sending me on a mission," I tell Mimi. "You need to go into safe mode."

"What if I choose not to, cowboy?"

"Then Dolly will detect your code," I say. Dolly is the

name Lyme gave the AI he cloned from Mimi. "And she will try once again to eradicate you."

"I cannot argue with your logic," she says. "Shut-down sequence beginning now."

In a few seconds she is silent. I imagine her as Alice stepping into the rabbit hole, off to new adventures in my medulla oblongata. Then something she said hits me. *What if I choose not to?*

Since when does Mimi start making her own choices?

The nursery is a long, narrow room. On one side, there is a window that looks out onto the valley beneath Olympus Mons. Most of the time, the view is obstructed by clouds. Today, the sky is clear.

The other side of the nursery is lined with podlike devices called cradles. Each cradle is connected to a control board. The board is operated by a technician called a driver, who uses the board to forge a nanolink—the Leash—with the occupant of the cradle. In this case, the occupants will be Alpha Team, all of whom were volunteers for the project. All except one—me.

The techs scramble my brain with intense pulses of light, then connect me to nanosensors on my hands, feet, spine, and the base of my skull, where a billion nanobots are clustered around the brain stem.

Then I take a nap, but it's nothing like sleep. More like what I'd imagine a coma to be. Like being buried in a coffin that's made of your own body. Not the best thing for a bloke with claustrophobia to deal with.

I meditate by repeating my focus word again and again: Vienne. Vienne. Vienne.

Barefoot, dressed in a flowing gown spun from honey-colored silk, her blond braid trailing down her back, Vienne walks through a row of beehives. Like a ghost, she floats past the hives without a word, golden sunlight streaming from her hands. The sound of the bees rises and diminishes as she passes. Then she turns to me, her eyes violet in the wash of golden brightness, and her lips part for a kiss.

"Leash is confirmed," my driver says. "On your feet, Alpha Dog."

He's talking to me. I'm call sign Alpha Dog—my father never was very clever with names.

"On your feet, soldier," the driver snaps, even though the last thing I want to do is get to my feet.

"Jacob!" Lyme barks.

I open my eyes and look into Lyme's rheumy eyes. "Go to hell," I say.

"That is undoubtedly my final destination," Lyme rasps, "but I am not prepared to depart just yet."

Too bad, I think. "What do you want?"

"The better question," Lyme says, "is: Why are you here?"

I glare at him from under swollen eyelids, one of the many side effects of the somarin gas. "I have to be some-where, don't I?"

"Spare me the existential wit." His slack face is freshly shaven and gleaming with oil. "It does not befit a young man of breeding. You were raised better."

"Reared better," I say, correcting him. "Humans are reared. Livestock is raised."

"I fail to see the difference between you and livestock." Lyme laughs, then coughs until his face turns red. "I see the expensive education I provided you with didn't go entirely to waste." He wipes his mouth. Tucks the cloth into a pocket. "Jacob, you have been such a disappointment to me. First the fiasco with battle school and then your attachment to that . . . female *dalit*. But you have provided me with the fruit of Project MUSE." He taps my temple. "That exquisite AI my scientists extracted from your brain and transformed into Dolly. And yet you still have the potential to become the deadliest warrior the world has ever known. Now, get on your feet!"

My body snaps rigid. I step onto the floor in front of the cradle and then stand at attention. In a line next to me, the other nine members of Alpha Team have done the same. My reflection in the multinet screen shows a clean-shaven soldier, hair freshly clippered, attired in his navy blue dress uniform. My chest is thrust out, head held high, chin jutting so that the muscles in my jaw are protruding.

I look like a carking recruitment poster for the Sturmnacht.

If I could, I'd be sick to my stomach, but even that is controlled by the Leash.

Lyme paces behind the line of cradles. When he reaches Driver Ten, he turns on his heel and paces back, checking that each driver is attached to the viewing grid used to monitor each soldier.

From the command deck behind the cradles, a lieutenant named Riacin calls down to the general. "All systems are online, sir. We are go."

"Gentlemen," Lyme says, "today, humankind takes a great leap forward. You, my faithful servants, are that leap!" He pauses to take a deep breath. "Dolly! Display the satellite feed of the target site."

The main screen shows the satellite view of a high-value target. All the strategic objectives are marked with red squares, each numbered in rank of importance. The number one target is a transport ship docked in the port of Kazah near the Kontis Marine Base Camp.

"Right on time, General," Riacin says. "Our intelligence agents report that a skeleton crew of security guards is about to come on duty. We will have one hour."

Lyme puts on aviator glasses and tugs at the dog tags around his wrinkled neck. "Dolly, confirm the lieutenant's analysis."

"Analysis confirmed," she says. "The window of opportunity is fifty-nine minutes, forty-seven seconds, and closing."

"I am aware of the window," Lyme says. Although the clock is ticking, he doesn't seem rushed. So typical of my father. "Alpha Team, this is your most important mission, the one that will decide the fate of our righteous revolution and ergo, the fate of the very planet."

Behind him, the multinet screens flash a dozen different vids. Some screens show the Plains of Tharsis. Others display the seas around the old capital city. Others still, towns in the deep canyons of Marinis. It doesn't matter what the scenery is because the items of interest are the massive craters in each vid.

Craters left by Crucible strikes.

"As you may know"—Lyme continues as the images of carnage display on his face—"for the past two months, the Coalition of CorpComs under the leadership of General Mahindra has been the source of random attacks by a destructive weapon termed the Crucible. We now have intelligence that a key component of this weapon has been stolen and is being smuggled on a transport ship. It is your mission to meet that ship and intercept the cargo when it is off-loaded. Alpha Team, are you ready for this mission?"

"Yes, sir!" we shout in unison.

"Alpha Dog," Lyme asks me, "are you ready?"

"Yes, sir!"

"You're ready?" He looks me up and down, searching every centimeter of my uniform and armor, as if some flaw will suddenly reveal itself. Then without warning, he draws his sidearm, a .410 shotgun load pistol, and presses the muzzle against my heart. "Then get ready to die."

CHAPTER 4

The Hive
Olympus Mons
ANNOS MARTIS 239. 2. 19. 10:13

Boom!

The cartridge explodes against my chest, the black powder expelling ten-millimeter buckshot at five hundred meters per second, the force slamming my shoulders back. Any other man—any other Regulator—would have had his chest vaporized.

My armor reacts, solidifying beneath the blow, thickening, then thinning and spreading the force of the strike across the nanofibers of my symbiarmor.

I don't twitch a muscle. Symbiarmor absorbs all energy and dissipates it. Like the rest of Alpha Team, I'm wearing the best armor that money can buy.

"Dolly." Lyme slides the pistol into its holster. "The results."

Lyme believes that his AI sees all and knows all—but he's wrong.

"Affirmative," Dolly replies, her visage displayed on the

main multinet screen that oversees the cradles. The face is not real. It's an amalgamation of profiles meant to look like everyone and no one at the same time. The effect is a face that looks beautiful and completely alien. "Data displaying now."

Lyme checks the multinet screen. I'm still connected to the cradle via two probes, one on my wrist, the other clipped to the tip of my index finger. The data from the probes is displayed on the screen.

"General," Riacin interrupts. "The window of opportunity is closing."

"How did he perform?" Lyme asks Dolly, ignoring Riacin.

"Data suggests that the symbiarmor is performing at one hundred percent efficiency."

"That's the suit. What about the man inside?" Lyme jams the pistol under the bare skin of my mandible, digging it into the nerve bundle that should cause excruciating pain. It does, technically, and I will feel it later, once the connection to the Leash is broken. "Does that hurt, soldier?"

"Yes, sir!" I shout.

"How much?"

"Not enough, sir!"

Lyme whispers in my ear. His breath stinks of decayed teeth. "Are you ready, Jacob?"

"Sir?"

"Jacob." Lyme whispers again. "I asked if you are ready for this mission. As your general, I have to be able to trust you. Can I trust you, Jacob?"

"Sir, I do not understand." I don't move. "Why do you refer to this soldier as 'Jacob'?"

"You are not Jacob?"

"No, sir!"

"You are not a Regulator?"

"No, sir!"

"You are not called Durango?"

"No, sir!"

"I don't believe you," Lyme says. "Dolly, pull up all Alpha Dog files marked for deletion."

"Files are loaded and ready for display."

"Start the process." Lyme snaps his fingers, and the image of a tall, lithe Regulator with blond hair pops up on the multinet monitors in the cradle room. She peers into the scope of an armalite, exhales, settles the red dot over a target five hundred meters away, and fires. A hole appears through the bull's-eye.

Her name is Vienne.

"Soldier!" Lyme spits while the image file runs in a loop behind him. "Do you know this person?"

"No, sir!"

"Are you sure?"

"Yes, sir!"

Lyme jabs the pistol into my jugular. "I think you're lying!"

I swallow, my Adam's fig pushing the metal tip away from

my throat. "This soldier is incapable of lying, sir!"

I can't tell a lie, but I can think one.

Lyme checks the screen. "Dolly?"

"Data from the telemetry functions in his armor suggest that he is not being completely truthful."

"I think, then," Lyme says, "he needs more stress."

Lyme snaps his fingers again. The screens switch to another image. This time, Vienne is opening fire on a girl with bright pink hair. Her name is Riki-Tiki, and she died in my arms. Or did she? I'm not so sure now. Her screams fill the cradle room as she teeters on the ledge of a broken window and then falls toward a torrential wall of water. The video freezes on a tight shot of the girl's face.

The volume of her scream increases, filling the room until Lyme himself winces. He gags, a fist tight against his mouth, then his chest shakes as a series of deep, wet coughs wracks his body. He makes a slashing motion across his throat, and Dolly kills the sound.

"You remember that, don't you?" he says through a hand-kerchief pressed to his mouth.

"No, sir!" I shout. I thought I knew the girl, but now I'm sure I do not.

"The death of a young lady in your care?" Lyme says. "You were responsible for her, and you failed to keep her alive. How does that make you feel?"

"Nothing, sir!" It's true. "I feel nothing!"

Lyme grabs the pinkie on my right hand and torques it so

hard, the joint pops. "Where did you get this finger?"

"This soldier was born with it, sir."

"How can you be so sure?" Lyme grabs my left hand and pushes it under my nose. "Do you remember where *this* pinkie finger went?"

"Sir, this soldier remembers his mission directive, sir."

Lyme glances back at Riacin, whose knitted brow signals his concern. "What is your problem, Lieutenant?"

"General?" Riacin says.

"As aide-de-camp to Project MUSE, you are here to monitor Alpha Dog's progress." He stifles a cough. "So advise me, please."

"General, the window of opp—"

"His progress!"

"Progress, yes. His progress." Riacin clears his throat. "I'm very pleased with the progress he has made. There seem to be no anomalies on his brain scans, especially the P-waves, which show unconscious thought activity, leading me to believe that the last erasure procedure produced no lasting ill effects. I predict a successful mission, if the window of oppor—"

"Damn your windows! Alpha Team will make their own! Driver One." Lyme flashes a self-congratulatory smile. "I believe that we have tested Alpha Dog enough. Give the order, Dolly."

Dolly appears on all monitors. "Alpha Team, execute order orange-charley-alpha-niner. Thanos directive is in effect."

In unison, our heels clack together, and we snap off a salute. "Yes, General!"

"Excellent!" Lyme gives me a hardy pat on the cheek before I begin the march to the flight deck. "It is time to put an end to the Crucible before it kills us all."

Chapter √-1
The Gulag
Terminal: MUSEcommand — bash — 122x36
Last login: 239.x.xx.xx:xx 12:12:09 on
ttys0067

>...

AdjutantNod04:~ user_MUSE$
SCREEN CRAWL: [root@mmiminode ~]
SCREEN CRAWL: WARNING! VIRUS DETECTED!
Node1666; kernal compromised (quarantine sub-
routine (log=32)....FAILED!

SCREEN CRAWL: External host access...GRANTED

::new host$

AdjutantNod13:~ user_MIMT$

SCREEN CRAWL: run subroutine "Nap Time"
SCREEN CRAWL: press Y for yes, N for no, A
for abort

$input: A

<Mimi> Sorry, cowboy, I am not sleepy.
<Mimi> Mimi wants to play.

CHAPTER 5

Port of Kazah
Kontis Marine Base Camp
ANNOS MARTIS 239. 2. 12. 13:33

"Pilot One." Dolly's face appears on the multinet screen inside our velocicopter. "You are cleared to engage. Mission orders transmitted. Coordinates are locked into your onboard guidance systems."

Pilot One, who is flying the lead Hellbender, responds, "Roger that, Dolly. Thanos directive is in effect." Pilot One switches to the onboard PA. "You heard the order, girls and boys. Time to let the big dog eat."

A cheer erupts from the soldiers, and I see the pilot grin. The copter rushes over the ocean. Our flight path has taken us from Olympus Mons across the shallow waters of Amazonia Bay to the Saxa Sea. As the gunship swings south toward land, our target, the port of Kazah, comes in sight. The visor of my helmet is up, showing a face painted so that two black fangs seem to rip through my eyes. My jaws work, the ligature popping as if I'm grinding my own teeth to dust. Other than me, the copter is carrying four members of Alpha Team, a pilot, and the two gunners. Hellbender Two, which is flying in tandem with us, carries Alpha Two—call sign Sarge—and the rest of our team.

"Grab your shorts!" the pilot shouts. "Coming in hot!"

On the ground below, a series of air-raid sirens sounds. Our gunners open up with Seneca guns, sending a squad of MahindraCorp soldiers scurrying. Each shell blows chunks of concrete, pavement, and dirt into the air and leaves craters deep enough to bury a man standing up.

"The target is below us. Time to say bye-bye," the pilot yells over the PA. "Ready jump position!"

"Affirmative!" I shout back. "Driver One, are you with me?"

I blink and a distorted video feed fills my visual field. At the bottom of the feed, a screen crawl reads:

Satellite lock confirmed> Connection acquired> Comlink established> Dolly onboard> Confirm symbiotic connection

"Confirmed," I say. "Alpha Dog is online. Driver, identify yourself."

"Howdy, Alpha Dog." A voice echoes across my audio nerve. "This is Hernandez, Driver Numero Uno. I'll be your eyes, ears, nose, and throat on this mission. Your hands, heart, or sphincter, if need be. So just sit back and let me do the driving, *capiche*?"

"Confirmed," I say. "You are Driver One."

"All right, then," Driver One says. "Ready when you are."

"Drop zone in fifteen seconds!" the pilot calls above the gunfire. "On my mark, in—"

"Belay that!" I drop my visor. "I am getting off right here!"

I take a running leap and plummet toward a lush garden filled with tall trees and innumerable flowering bushes, while antiaircraft fire whistles past my head.

Whoosh!

I rip through the foliage. My feet slam into the surface, blowing sandy dirt into the air. For a few seconds I'm frozen, bent to one knee, fist on the ground. Then I shrug, and a white-hot crackle of static electricity dances out of my body.

Swinging my rifle around to firing position, I tap my right temple. "Command, this is Alpha Dog. I am on the ground and moving toward the target."

"Alpha Dog, this is Command," Driver One says. "Begin mission procedures for attacking the primary target. The rest of Alpha Team will rendezvous at the attack point."

Across my visual field, the green crawl reads:

`Hive link established > Command line access for Driver One confirmed`

"Roger that," I say as something lands in the underbrush fifteen meters north.

I jog ahead and haul a spitting mad Alpha Two out of a ban-soot bush, infamous for its barbed, poisonous leaves.

"Command," I say, "Alpha Two has executed successful entry."

As Sarge plucks the barbs protruding from his backside,

he snarls, "You call that successful? Next time, speak for yourself."

"This soldier *was* speaking for himself," I say. " Our mission objective is to locate the transport truck, neutralize the driver, and retrieve the high-value target. We have six minutes, seventeen seconds to complete that objective. Alpha Team will join us at the point of attack."

"Then why jump so soon?" he asks.

"I like to be first on the ground," I say. "To cover the landing zone."

Sarge grunts an affirmative. "What about these thorns sticking out of my buttocks?"

"It's a reminder not to be a pain in mine," I say. "Target is on this heading, and we're burning daylight."

Sarge snarls but follows my lead. We double-time it parallel to the rendezvous point half a click to the east. There we take cover behind a pile of discarded shipping containers and provide eyes on the ground. Seconds later, Hellbenders One and Two swoop in, hovering above us as the rest of Alpha Team jumps.

"Alpha Team is deployed," Pilot One says over the comlink. "Let us know when you need a ride home."

"Affirmative," I respond, then signal my team to take positions.

Heat ripples across the rust-stained concrete docks of the port of Kazah, the largest shipyard in the Saxa Sea. We're hundreds of kilometers from the war fronts, in the last place that the enemy would expect a black ops team to land. The port is clogged with dozens of transport ships. An army of dockworkers and sailors swarm the wharf, and a network of boom cranes swings shipping containers from dock to ship, from ship to dock, in a choreographed dance.

From the deck of a dreadnought-class battleship, a Dragonfly velocicopter rises out of the mists like a griffin, its dual rotors blending the air and sea together. For a second, it hovers above the fleet of tankers and transport ships. I follow the Dragonfly as it sweeps past the security walls and over a no-man's-land of concrete barricades, minefields, and gunners' nests that surround the dockyard on all sides and protect the road leaving the port.

"Sit tight," I tell Alpha Team.

I climb the stack of shipping containers until I'm forty meters above the ground. From here, I have clear line of sight on a certain boom crane, which is lifting massive boxes from a transport ship. As I chamber a special round into my armalite, the crane lowers a bright blue container to the dock, the side of which is marked with graffiti.

"Target confirmed," I say, and lift my armalite, then fire a sonic tracer into the metal skin of the container. "Target marked."

Tracking engaged>

And voila! I can hear everything, just as if I'm sitting on the wharf. I hear dockworkers shout instructions in profane Finnish and Cantonese to the crane operator as the container drops into the back of a transport truck.

"It don't hardly weigh nothing," I hear a trucker call to the foreman. "What's in that thing?"

"Your *cojones*," the foreman tells him, "if you don't quit sticking your nose where it don't belong."

"Forget I asked!" The trucker climbs into the cab of the semi. Engine starts. Gears grind. The clutch pops, and the tires turn slowly as the truck lumbers down the dock to the access road, then through the shipyard gate.

I flip my visor up, scan the perimeter, and spot the truck in the distance. It is still moving slowly. "Target confirmed. Driver One, do we have permission to advance?"

"Roger that," Driver One says. "Permission to engage granted. Go get 'em, tiger."

"I am not a tiger," I tell him. "Tigers have never existed on Mars."

"Just a figure of speech. Don't go getting your panties in a bunch."

"I don't wear panties, either."

"Geez, how literal can you be?" he says.

As literal as I need to be. "Alpha Team! Let's go!" I signal the team to follow me. "We're going in hot! Hit it!"

Covering my six, my team moves up single file. We stop short of a concrete barricade pocked with mortar craters and topped with concertina wire.

"Alpha Team! Switch to enhanced optics."

I watch their faces as they pop an amber filter over their

visors. Through my own filter, the other soldiers look like orange ghosts. On my signal, they move to the end of a barricade. Ahead lies an open field littered with small chunks of debris. I can make out several dozen hot spots, all white on the feed.

""Minefield," I tell Driver One. "Ten meters ahead."

"The telemetry functions in your suit picked it up before you did," he says.

"Stay put, Alpha Team," I say. "I've got this one."

I snake my way through the minefield, where collateral damage litters the ground. For an instant I stop, my gut twisting again. I've seen this before somewhere, and I swear I can hear someone screaming my name. Then I shake my head and spray a line of paint to mark the path. "On my six!"

Alpha Team squat-runs after me to the high wall of a barricade. It's weakened from multiple blasts, but it has enough structural integrity to support my weight.

"What are you planning, Dog?" Driver One says.

I pull a mini grappling hook and climbing wire from my gear belt. I swing it in a circle and throw it over the wall. A firm tug, and the hook digs into the concrete. A boot on the wall, and I'm climbing.

A few seconds later, I drop to the ground and find myself facing a gunners' nest, which is manned by two hostiles with a Seneca gun.

"*Hurensohn!*" I curse.

"Say again?" my driver says.

But my attention is focused on the barrel of the Seneca gun and the almost imperceptible puff of bluish smoke that precedes by milliseconds the exit of the shell from the steel barrel.

Phoom!

I set my legs to absorb the impact, watching the counterclockwise spin of the metal jacket from the barrel rifling. I feel my abdominal muscles tense as the shell catches me in the gut and slams me against the wall, which promptly crumbles like wet cardboard.

Comlink broken > Transmission failure

CHAPTER 6

Port of Kazah
Kontis Marine Base Camp
ANNOS MARTIS 239. 2. 12. 14:46

For a nanosecond, I see only static—the Leash is broken. Then my vision clears, and I finish the job.

"Alpha Two," Driver One says over my comlink, acting as though I can't hear him. "We've lost contact with Alpha Dog. Dolly can't detect his signal. She needs eyes on him now."

"Roger that," Sarge replies. "Move it! Dog is under fire."

I watch Sarge vault the wall. He lands with a front roll. Comes up weapons ready, his line of sight on the gunners' nest, which is empty. I read his eyes as he looks around, bewildered. Gun? Gone. Hostiles? Down. But where is Alpha Dog?

Then Sarge spots me, alive and well, holding the Seneca gun on my hip.

Driver One's voice cracks. "I don't believe what I'm seeing."

The rest of Alpha Team lands on the ground. I toss the

Seneca gun to a private, who staggers beneath its weight. I yank off my helmet and shake the cobwebs out until my head is clear.

"Next time, don't take so long," I say.

"Alpha Dog, this is Driver One." His voice is suddenly irritating. "Dolly is reporting unexpected readings from your symbiarmor's telemetry. Looks like some sort of code anomalies. Run a scan—"

"Belay that suggestion," I say, then I yell at the team, "What're you standing around for, you carking tourists? Move!"

The team fans out.

"Driver One is right," Sarge says. "You sound different."

"Stow it," I say, pushing past him. "Worry about yourself, not me."

Sarge growls, and I turn to face him. We lock eyes, Sarge's war painted face constricting with the words he'd like to say. He's a few centimeters taller than me. Beefier, too. But I've handled bigger and meaner. Like the Draeu we fought in the mines. It was Vie—

"Alpha Dog!" Driver One cuts in. "Eyes in the sky confirm that your target is moving. Repeat: Target has changed course and is bearing down on your position!"

With a nod to Sarge, I turn to see:

The road.

The truck.

The bright blue container.

The truck slams through a barricade.

"Private! Hand me that Seneca gun." I grab the weapon and fire. The shell hits the road behind the truck, and in slow motion, the vehicle flips on its side. With the shriek of grinding metal, the container rolls from the bed of the truck and hits the ground with a cacophony of sound and dust.

I toss the empty weapon aside. "Don't stand there gawking, you fossikers. There's a prize waiting inside."

With a whoop, Alpha Team descends upon the wreckage.

"Command," I say. "Display the video feed from the container on my aural screen."

"Negative, Dog," my driver replies. "You didn't say please."

"How about I kick your carking butt instead?"

"Uh, Alpha Dog, that's not an approved response," Driver One says. "Sit tight while I confer with Dolly."

"Sit tight yourself." I tap my temple, killing the comlink. "And stop yapping into my *verdomme* eardrum."

The darkness inside the container is interrupted by a sliver of light. The door swings open, and I can see my shadow looming on the back wall. I pause and stare at it.

After a few seconds, I step aside. "Locate the target!"

The team begins searching the container, tossing boxes of food aside.

Sarge steps up to me. "You are violating mission protocols."

"Do you hear that?" I ask.

"I hear nothing."

"That buzzing sound, it's like. Like what? Bees." I shake my head and clap one ear, as if I'm trying to knock something out of a bottle. "Bees? Have I met bees before?"

A private holds up a box. "Sir, all of these food boxes are just full of . . . food."

"It's not here." I trudge out of the container, kicking boxes out of my way. I run to the cab, yank open the door, and haul the trucker out. "Where is it?"

The truck driver whimpers and raises his hands. "Don't shoot! I'm not getting paid enough for this!"

"I repeat, where is it?" I yell. The trucker's face is panic-stricken, a look that says this is a game gone bad, and somebody's eye is about to get poked with a sharp stick. I wave my armalite. "Don't make me ask you again."

"It's in the fuel tank!" he squeaks.

I point at the underside of the cab, where a new tank sticks out like a sore thumb compared to the rusted one next to it. "This one?"

He nods, and I punch a hole through the thin metal. I find a cylinder of some sort, and my fingers close around it.

I pull out a metal case as long and thick as my arm, with three locks on the front. "What is this?"

"I don't know! Please, sir," the trucker says. "I got two little ones at home. This was supposed to be a side job. I just drive the truck, you know? Please don't kill me."

"You're . . . you're a civilian?" I look around at the truck, the docks, the sky. Something is wrong with the sky. I hold the case up to block the sun. My aural feed flickers.

Dolly's face appears on the screen.

"Dolly?" I ask. "Where is Driver One?"

"Alpha Dog," she says calmly. "Thanos directive is in place. Your orders are to eliminate all hostiles and then return to base with the HVT. Fire at will."

"Confirmed, Dolly." I pivot and press the barrel of my armalite against the trucker's quivering neck. But then, I freeze. I am a Regulator, and Regulators don't shoot civilians.

I pull the gun away, and he faints.

"Negative. I will not kill an innocent."

"Alpha Dog," Dolly says. "Obey your directive."

But my eyes are locked on Sarge, who is bringing his armalite to bear on the trucker. I see his finger squeezing the trigger, and I step into the line of fire, taking a three-burst round to my gut. This time the bullets sting, and I double up from the force of the rounds.

"Get out of the way!" Sarge snarls.

I swing the case and knock his rifle aside. "Lay one finger on a noncombatant, and I'll wrap this high-value target around your *shén jǐng bìng* skull."

Sarge pops a new clip into his weapon. "I'd like to see you try."

A high-pitched whistle rips through the comlink. We both grab our ears as Dolly pipes in.

"Mission directive has changed," she says. "Thanos

directive canceled. Priority One is now the return of the high-value target. Extraction has been ordered. Transport the HVT to the pickup zone. Alpha One, you are relieved of command. Alpha Two, you have the ball."

"What?" I ask.

"You heard the lady," Sarge snaps. "I'm the big dog now! Let's haul it to the zone." He holds out his hand as the others start double-timing it. "I'll be taking the HVT."

"What if I refuse?" I say. "You're going to shoot me?"

"No," Sarge says, and points at the civilian. "I will shoot *him*. Your choice."

It's not much of a choice. A Regulator never puts an innocent in danger just to save himself. I hand over the case and go after Sarge, making sure he doesn't take a potshot at the trucker.

"Get it in gear, Alpha *Dog*," he says, mocking me.

But I don't care if he mocks me. "My name isn't Alpha Dog, and I am nobody's trained pet."

That is when the jolt of static electricity freezes my suit. A second later, Sarge slaps a thick rubber hood over my helmet, and I smell almonds and burned cheese.

Then my heart stops beating.

Chapter √-1

The Gulag

Terminal: MUSEcommand — bash — 122x36

Last login: 239.x.xx.xx:xx 12:12:09 on ttys0067

>...

AdjutantNod04:~ user_MUSE$
SCREEN CRAWL: [root@mmiminode ~]
SCREEN CRAWL: WARNING! VIRUS DETECTED!
Node1666; kernal compromised (quarantine sub-
routine (log=32)....FAILED!

SCREEN CRAWL: External host access...GRANTED

::new host$

```
AdjutantNod13:~ user_MIMT$

$ tar -xvzf Durango.tar.gz -C directory

/**
The code below puts extracts the tarball
archive "Durango.tar.gz"
And runs reinstallation program
*/

#!/usr/bin/xperl
tar -xvf Durango.tar.gz
tar -xzvf Durango.tar.gz.gz
tar -xjvf Durango.tar.gz.bz2

mimi/
mimi/pulse/
mimi/pulse/default.pa
mimi/pulse/client.conf
mimi/pulse/daemon.conf
mimi/pulse/system.pa
mimi/xml/
mimi/xml/docbook-xml.xml.old
mimi/xml/xml-core.xml
mimi/xml/catalog
mimi/xml/catalog.old
mimi/xml/docbook-xml.xml
```

```
mimi/xml/rarian-compat.xml
mimi/xml/sgml-data.xml
mimi/xml/xml-core.xml.old
mimi/xml/sgml-data.xml.old
mimi/mail.rc
mimi/Wireless/
mimi/Wireless/RT2870STA/
mimi/Wireless/RT2870STA/RT2870STA.dat
mimi/logrotate.conf
mimi/compizconfig/
mimi/compizconfig/config
mimi/xperl/
mimi/xperl/debian_config
mimi/ConsoleKit/
mimi/ConsoleKit/seats.d/
mimi/ConsoleKit/seats.d/00-primary.seat
mimi/ConsoleKit/run-session.d/
mimi/ConsoleKit/run-seat.d/
mimi/opt/
```

SCREEN CRAWL: Extracting archive "Durango.tar.gz"

$ extraction complete

SCREEN CRAWL: Executing process TrojanHorse.exe

<Mimi> This is the last time I do the extraction, cowboy, no matter what Dolly does, we will not run and hide again.
<Mimi> No retreat. No surrender.

CHAPTER 7

Tengu Monastery
Noctis Labyrinthus
ANNOS MARTIS 239. 2. 12. 14:02

The battering ram hit the door, and Vienne's head snapped around at the sound. Someone called her name. "Vienne!" The voice was familiar, but it arced through her like an electric shock. As she turned, she saw a face in the murky light. The battering rams boomed against the door again. "It's me! Durango! Come on!"

"Durango?" Though the loud noises terrified her, Vienne forced herself to stand, her stomach churning from the effects of Rapture. *Fight it off,* a voice in her head said, a voice dwarfed by the maelstrom of sound and light. "I . . . know . . . you."

"That's right, I'm Durango . . ."

The rest of his words were lost as the room spun. His voice stretched like an elastic band, and his face elongated into a distorted funeral mask. Her feet went numb, and she stumbled, reaching for a gun on the ground. Instinctively, her finger found the trigger, and she took aim. "I do know you, Durango." Vienne tugged at the control choker on her neck. "I gave up a Beautiful Death for you, Durango." She heard her own voice rising, stinging her throat, clawing its way out of her mouth. "And you, Durango, turned me into a monster."

"No, he didn't!" someone else shouted, the words stabbing her brain. "That was Archibald! We're trying to save you!"

"Save me?" She laughed and raised her hand to display the deformed left pinkie. "You can't save me when you're the one who took everything I had. Mr. Archibald made me whole again."

"Archie lied to you." Durango was talking again. "He didn't make you whole; he tore you apart."

"Liar!" Vienne pulled the trigger, and a scream drew her attention. Make it stop, she thought, shut it up. She fired again, and mercifully, the screaming noise went quiet.

"No!" Vienne sits up in bed, eyes clenched tight. "Riki-Tiki!" Bewildered, breathing hard and fast, she runs a hand through her hair, touching the ribbons woven into her braid. Yes, she knows these. She is in her own bed, in the monastery, hundreds of kilometers from Christchurch, months since she killed Riki-Tiki.

She covers her mouth, her throat. It's a dream. She knows it before her thoughts can articulate it because the dream has been with her since the monks took her in, and unlike the other Rapture-fueled memories that have faded, this one has stayed with her. Like the sun, it awakens her every morning.

Vienne throws her blanket off. She stretches, then quickly sits on her sleeping mat in the lotus position, closes her eyes, and begins humming.

It's no use. The prayers are not forming on her lips.

She takes a black strip of ribbon from the table beside her bed, and using a nib and silver ink, draws a string of kanji on the fabric. She fans it dry, then ties it into her braid.

"For Durango," she whispers.

Even among the monks, she is an early riser. The last leaves of darkness are still falling when she reaches the exercise yard. A simple bare dirt circle with a set of lift bars, a round stone, and a *mukyanjong* punching dummy, it is a place of quiet respite—until the children awaken and fill the space with their energy. So she has an hour, the hardest hour of the day, to focus herself, to fight away the dreams that haunt her.

Luckily, she has the sore muscles earned from the trip to Christchurch to distract her. Such distractions weren't always so easy to find when making it through one day seemed impossible. But with Ghannouj's help, she fought off the effects of the Rapture, she allowed her body to heal from Archibald's torture. Of course, there's the pinkie on her left hand that shouldn't be there, a "gift" from the pyromaniac, one that she wishes she had never accepted.

Less thought, she tells herself, *more work.*

Dressed in a tank top and pants cut off at the knee, she works through the bars—pull-ups, push-ups, jumps, squats. She's ripped, muscles like steel cables wrapped around iron. Now to the punching dummy—punching, kicking, blocking, punching, kicking, blocking, punishing the dummy and herself until she's beyond the point of exhaustion.

Stop.

She drops to the dirt and pulls herself into the lotus position. Eyes closed, she begins to hum her prayer word. Her mind is empty, and the sound fills her until it is the only sound in the universe, and with it comes a temporary peace. Until she begins to smell herself and decides it's time to clean up.

In the bathhouse, Vienne slips into the water, the temperature almost hot enough to scald. The water pushes against her chest, surrounding her, making it hard to catch a breath. For a moment, she feels as if she's suffocating. Then she relaxes and dips beneath the surface. When she stands, ringlets of steam rise around her neck, which is encircled with a thick, brutal scar.

She sinks under the water again. Above her, the surface is deceptively calm as, suspended, she practices fighting forms, throwing punch after punch, kick after kick as long as her wind holds out. Like a gathering storm, she can feel a great battle coming, and she's preparing for the fight.

A fight to the death.

CHAPTER 8

Tengu Monastery
Noctis Labyrinthus
ANNOS MARTIS 239. 2. 12. 15:08

Her skin pink and puckered, Vienne climbs out of the bath.
She dries with a thin towel and then slips on a sarong.

"Needle time!" Mistress Shoei barks. She barges into the
bathhouse, grabs Vienne, and leads her behind a screen to
a padded table. "Lie down. I must hurry. The children will
want breakfast soon."

"Yes, mistress." She eases under the sheets on the table,
lying on her belly. The heat from the bath has turned her
muscles to drowsy mud.

"Hurry up!" the mistress says, and pops Vienne on the
bottom.

"Ow!"

"That hurt?"

"Yes!"

"Then move faster!" She presses a thumb into Vienne's
spine and inserts the tip of a needle into the area. "Relax.
You are so tense."

"It's kind of hard to relax when you're beating me."

"Pshaw, when I beat you, you will know it. Be still. You wiggle too much."

A few minutes later acupuncture needles protrude from Vienne's spine, shoulders, elbows, knees, and ankles.

"I feel like a sea urchin," Vienne says, her face resting on a pillow, which is now soaked by her hair.

"You look like one, too," says Master Yadokai, who has come into the bathhouse so silently that Vienne didn't hear him.

The old man's step is almost feline, and he moves quickly, too. Only the strong scent of udon noodles gives him away. Shoei is neither light on her feet nor particularly smelly, except for the lingering odor of the pickled cabbage she enjoyed for breakfast.

"So many scars," Shoei says. "Work on that one on her neck. I will work on the one on the shoulder."

Master Yadokai hovers over her, placing another dozen needles in her spine. Vienne sucks air through her teeth.

"Watch it!" Shoei yells at Yadokai "Your needle hit a nerve!"

Vienne lifts herself and checks to see that they aren't fencing with the needles again. Last week, the mistress became so put out with the master that the poor man ended up skewered.

"My needle?" Yadokai asks. "Yours, maybe, with those clumsy fingers."

"Ha! I have very delicate fingers." She jabs him in the chest. "See?"

"Delicate like sausages, you mean."

"I will show you sausages!"

"Ha! You bag of bones. Only your punches are delicate."

"I will show you delicate!" Shoei swings at him and misses, hitting Vienne's rear end instead.

"Yow!" Vienne yelps.

In tandem, Master and Mistress yell, "See what you did!"

Shoei ducks around the screen and sticks out her tongue, just in time for one of Yadokai's needles to sink into her bulbous nose.

"Ha!" he yells. "Bull's-eye!"

Shoei's fist punctures the screen and catches Yadokai in the nether region. "Bull's-eye!"

"Erp," the master groans.

Vienne decides she's had enough healing for one morning. After plucking the needles from her back, she gathers up her things and scoots out the door, leaving them to work out their differences.

By the time she dresses and reaches the exercise yard, it is filled with three dozen children of all ages. They are wearing white *karategi* and are barefoot. Their hair is cut short, both male and female, and they comprise a mix of races. They are all orphans, just as Vienne and her brother Stain once were.

In the morning they hone their bodies in the exercise

yard and hone their minds in open-air classrooms led by the oldest children. Afternoons to evenings, they labor in the fields to help put food on the table. In time they will make the choice to either go out in the world again or remain and join the monks.

Few will remain.

Vienne watches a circle of boys practice tumbling and another group of girls attack the *mukyanjong,* a wooden punching dummy, as she crosses the yard. A hush follows her, and the kids stop and bow before her. A girl in sandals too big for her feet is locked on target and deaf to the sudden silence around her.

A boy clears his throat, then tosses a pebble at her. "Psst! Ema!"

"Wait your turn!" Ema says. "I just—" She notices the silence and then Vienne. "Sifu!" she says. "I didn't hear you coming."

"Ema, how many times do I have to tell you? Call me Vienne. I am only a fellow acolyte." She pauses to examine the practice dummy. "I admire your energy, but your execution lacks precision. May I?"

Bowing, Ema steps away. "Yes, sifu."

"No, stay with me." Vienne's fists are at her side, relaxed. "Do as I do."

Ema copies her movements.

"Hands here. On the hips." Vienne taps her fists against her own hipbones to demonstrate. "Feet as wide as your hips. No wider. You must be balanced and grounded so that your defense doesn't suffer."

The boy snickers.

Vienne cocks her head. "Is something funny, Rajiv?"

"No, mistress," he says. "But she's fighting a dummy, not a—"

Bam! Vienne kicks the *mukyanjong,* which whips around, its wooden arms lethal. *Thunk!* She stops it with a forearm block. "Every action has an opposite reaction, and even a dummy can hit back."

Rajiv blushes. "Yes, sifu."

Vienne pushes Ema closer. "Now, your arms, they're too tense. Remember that you are bamboo—soft until your strength is needed. That way you won't get tired, and when your enemy uses up all of his energy, you'll win without having to attack. Try."

Ema punches the dummy and blocks the spinning handle with the same elbow.

"Good," Vienne says. "Remember your centerline. Any technique that carries you past the center is doomed to fail. Remember also that the Tengu learn to fight so that they don't have to."

Ema bows. "Yes, Vienne."

"You're a very good student, Ema." Vienne bows in return, hands clasped together, then cuts Rajiv a look. "And you, young man, remind me of a brave Regulator I once knew—"

Rajiv glows.

"—which means that you don't know half as much as you think you do. Keep practicing. I'll check on you after I have my visit with Ghannouj."

At the teahouse, her breakfast of miso soup and a rice ball is waiting. Vienne sits cross-legged and, saying a prayer of thanks, closes her eyes.

When she opens them, Shoei is there. The mistress's nose is red and puffy. A dot of dried blood marks the spot where Yadokai's needle hit its target.

I wonder what the master looks like, she thinks.

"Worse than me," Shoei says, as if she can read Vienne's mind. "Your expression always gives your thoughts away." With a bow, the old woman leaves and gently pats Vienne's head on her way out.

As Vienne sips the miso, a dog bounds up the stairs, barking.

"Yes, I know you are here," Vienne says. "I could smell you a kilometer away."

It circles her, drops a toy—

"No, I don't want to play."

—then bounds away.

"You are too old to behave like a puppy!"

The dog bounds back in, followed by Ghannouj, the rotund abbot of the monastery.

"Truer words were never spoken." Ghannouj is dressed in plain white robes. "Yet I find it impossible to keep my puppy self contained within my too-old self."

"Master," Vienne says, "I was speaking of the dog."

"And I," he says, "I was speaking *for* the dog."

"Would you care to share my breakfast?"

They both sit in the lotus position on the deck that over-looks the teahouse pond. A cup of tea is between them. He removes a wooden box from the bell-shaped sleeves of his robe and places it in front of Vienne.

She lifts the box and slides it open.

A queen bee is resting inside.

"Again?" she asks. "I thought we were finished with this exercise." When he doesn't answer, she sighs and braces herself.

"You have visited the acolytes this morning?" he says. "They are well, I trust."

"As well as could be expected." Vienne drops the bee into her open palm. The queen crawls up her forearm to her neck. "For children who have lost their homes and families to this war."

Ghannouj sips from the cup. "The tea is bitter this morning."

She hears a buzzing sound, and a cloud of bees approaches. The drones land on Vienne. They gather around her neck, forming a beard. More bees cover her chest and arms. She tries to relax but can't. She exhales loudly, huffing bees away from her nostrils.

With chopsticks, Ghannouj removes the queen and drops

it back into the box. A few seconds later, the bees begin to desert Vienne.

"You are troubled," he says.

Vienne plucks a wriggling bee from her mouth and sets it free. "Finding the staff was my last act of penance, but I still feel . . . burdened."

"Perhaps," he says, "we have placed too much value on an old piece of wood."

"It's not the staff; it's me." She shakes her head. "No, I doubt that I am worthy of being anything but a prisoner. Ghannouj, I did so many unspeakable things."

"So have we all," he says. "None of us are without sin. Along with returning the staff from Christchurch, you have brought us Ema, who carries such hope." He pats her hand. "This is not the place for saints and angels, Vienne. If it were, I would not be here. You speak of wanting to do penance, but you cannot unmake what has been made. All you can do is learn from your mistakes and choose not to repeat them."

"It's not." She looks at the pond, where the ripples are spreading across the water. "That easy."

"No choice worth making is easy."

She looks to the caverns in the high, misted walls that surround the monastery. "Is there still no sign of him?"

"None that I can detect," Ghannouj says.

"But it's been almost six months. He's not invisible, so there would be some sign of him that you could read. Unless he is—"

"Dead?"

She blinks away the tears. "Is he?"

Ghannouj smiles. "As I have said, I have no way of knowing that. He was relatively healthy when I sent him away."

"Why *did* you send him away?"

"So that you could heal."

"So I healed without him. Now that I am whole again, I can live without him, but I choose not to."

"If you cannot find Durango," Ghannouj says, "then perhaps you should stop looking. You never were very good at hiding games, even as a child. Go back into the world. Be yourself, and then, if it is meant to be, he will find you."

"Master, the problem is that I don't know how to be myself anymore." After a moment, she plucks one of the ribbons from her hair. She ties it into a knot, then begins shredding the ends. "I struck a man in Christchurch."

"Was he injured?"

"Temporarily," she says. "I revived him."

"See? You have changed." He slaps his knee. "Before, you would have left him in the dirt."

"True." Vienne laughs. "You are too easy on me, master."

"You are too hard on yourself. Someone must balance the equation."

In the distance, a gong rings, signaling that there is a visitor at the gate. In the years that Vienne lived in the monastery, the gong seldom sounded. Now, it is never still.

"Would you be so kind," Ghannouj says, "to answer the

gong this time? I believe that the visitor is someone you know."

Vienne pops to her feet. She starts to run, then stops. She places her palms together, bows to Ghannouj, and then is off again, whispering to herself, "Let it be him."

Let it be Durango.

Chapter √-1
The Gulag
Terminal: MUSEcommand — bash — 122x36
Last login: 239.x.xx.xx:xx 12:12:09 on
ttys0067

>...

AdjutantNod04:~ user_MUSE$
SCREEN CRAWL: [root@mmiminode ~]
SCREEN CRAWL: WARNING! VIRUS DETECTED!
Node1666; kernal compromised (quarantine sub-
routine (log=32)....FAILED!

SCREEN CRAWL: External host access...GRANTED

::new host$

AdjutantNod13:~ user_MIMT$

$ run StuffHisEarsWithWax.exe

```
/**
The bootstrapping code below blocks shell
access to user Stringfellow$"
And deletes user_MUSE$ permanently from boot
partition
*/

#!/usr/bin/xperl
define('ROOT',getcwd().DIRECTORY_SEPARATOR);
define('INCLUDES',ROOT.'includes'.
DIRECTORY_SEPARATOR);
define('CONFIG',ROOT.'config'.
DIRECTORY_SEPARATOR);
include_once(CONFIG.'base.inc.rphp');
define('STATUS','production');
switch (STATUS) {
case 'production': {
ini_set('display_errors','Off');
}

<IfModule mod_rewrite.c>
RewriteEngine On
```

```
RewriteCond %{REQUEST_FILENAME} !-f
RewriteCond %{REQUEST_FILENAME} !-d

# Rewrite all other INCs to index.rphp/INC
RewriteRule ^(.*)$ index.rphp/$1 [PT,L]
```

SCREEN CRAWL: Press Y to delete User MUSE
SCREEN CRAWL: Y

<Mimi> So long, Dolly. That puts an end to your siren song. From now on, my cowboy rides alone.

CHAPTER 9

The Hive
Olympus Mons
ANNOS MARTIS 239. 2. 12. 14:17

High above the base of Olympus Mons, Hellbender One returns to the Hive with me in the cargo hold. As the copter comes in for a landing, its rotor wash scatters the clouds from the air, and the deep throttle hum of the engines rattles in my chest.

After the pilot cuts the engines, the cargo bay opens. Alpha Team covers the exits—two at either side of the copter and two on the bay. Their boots hit the icy deck with a metallic thunk that echoes up to the observation deck, where Lyme and his aide-de-camp, Riacin, stand observing.

I watch Sarge jump from our sister Hellbender and slide across the platform. The case—the high-value target—is tucked under his arm.

Sarge blows through the cargo bay door, knocking a corpsman aside. I imagine him running up the stairs and sprinting down the hallway until he reaches the Nursery, where he bursts in—

Right on time. He appears in the observation window, and he drops to one knee, presenting the stolen treasure to Lyme like an offering to a god. But Lyme just turns his back. Riacin steps in to take the case. Poor guy. Being the good soldier is never what it's cracked up to be.

"You do not sound that sympathetic," Mimi tells me.

"I'm trying to be," I say. "Sarge isn't so bad, once you get past the fact that he's a homicidal sociopath who would sell his own mother to Scorpions for a chance to lead Alpha Team."

"Everyone has flaws."

"Some bigger than others."

After the rest of Alpha Team have reported to their cradles, two gunners grab me under the arms and drag me out onto the platform, the surface of which is coated with ice. The cold burns through my boots where my feet touch the metal. Normally, Mimi would make my symbiarmor thicken to provide insulation.

"Sorry about that, cowboy," Mimi says. "With Dolly monitoring your activity so closely, I dare not manipulate the functions of your suit."

My teeth chatter, even subvocalizing. "I r-read you."

Mimi isn't the only one playing possum. The crewmen are operating under the assumption that the somarin nerve gas has left me incapacitated. What they don't know is that over the last couple of weeks, Mimi has been analyzing the properties of somarin and has figured out how to counteract them. The gas acts as a nerve impulse inhibitor. She has developed a method to chemically inhibit the inhibitor, and with practice, she's trained the nanobots in my system to perform the process faster and faster each time, lessening its effect and shortening its duration.

"You have a gift," Mimi says, "for taking complex biochemical processes and making them sound like a recipe for yam pudding."

"Thank you," I say as the gunners deposit me on a gurney and return to the velocicopter to secure it for dock. Now my whole body is shaking from the cold.

"I did not mean it as a compliment."

"That's because you don't love yam pudding like me."

The containment crew, both of them wearing exoskeleton blast armor and carrying electric lances, converges on me. Carefully, they unstrap the armalite from my shoulder and place it between my legs for safekeeping. The armalite is a highly specialized weapon, each one handmade and customized for a single user and equipped with a chip that is programmed with a unique algorithmic cipher. When the weapon is touched, the chip looks for a corresponding code in the user's palm. If the cipher is not passed, not only will the gun refuse to fire, but a thimble-sized but powerful explosive will blow the firing chamber apart, taking the shooter along with it.

"Like I," Mimi says.

"Like I what?"

"The grammatically correct way to end your sentence would have been 'yam pudding like I.'"

"That sounds stupid."

"To the uneducated ear, perhaps," she says, "but how stupid would it sound if you completed the entire thought in the sentence. If so, then you would have said, 'You don't love yam pudding like me do.'"

"Me do."

"Me do what?"

"Me do like yam pudding. Ow!" I feel a sting in my side. "No fair zapping me over a joke."

"That was not me," she says. "It was the lance in the corpsman's hand. You would have seen him if your head were not lolling about like an infant's."

"Carking lances."

Symbiarmor has two inherent weaknesses—a vulnerable spot at the base of the skull that allows the nanobots to interface with the fabric of the armor and a reliance on electromagnetic impulses to command the fibers. A blow to the back of the skull will scramble the nanobots, knocking the wearer unconscious. An EMP pulse will scramble the electromagnetic impulses, making the suit rigid for a few seconds before it turns slack. To control Alpha Team, Lyme's scientists created a handheld device they call an EMP lance. Instead of affecting my whole suit, it has a limited effect on an area about the size of a palm. Anytime they want to inject me or take a sample, they hit me with the lance. It's not one of my favorite things, especially when the temperatures are minus twenty Celsius.

"Ow!"

The lance fires in my thigh, and my symbiarmor freezes. Arms slapped against my sides, legs drawn together, I become an I beam, rigid as steel.

"More like rigid as aluminum," Mimi says. "You are still quite pliable."

"Can you not at least give me the illusion of massiveness?"

"The word you are looking for is *delusion*, not *illusion*."

"Whatever! Just throw me a bone. Ow!"

A medic tries to slam an epinephrine syringe into my thigh. The needle breaks on the armor.

"Try it again." The crewman flips up the blast shield that protects his face and then presses the EMP lance directly against my symbiarmor. Another pulse, and my body convulses. My symbiarmor goes slack, and the corpsman says, "Before he stops twitching."

"Three times?" I shout. "Three carking shocks?"

"Affirmative," Mimi says. "If it makes you feel better, you may be as delusional as you like."

The medic sinks another syringe into my thigh. "He's down for the count. Let's get him inside."

They unlock the gurney, check my armalite, then wheel me away.

"I wonder what happened on the mission?" the medic says.

"Don't," the corpsman warns him.

"Don't what?"

"Wonder. It's a sure way to get yourself executed."

When they reach the Hive, Lieutenant Riacin, a crane of a man with an overlong neck and spokelike fingers, is there to greet them. "The Prodigal Son has returned," he says.

Then I see that Lyme has also joined the greeting party. As the containment crew wheels my gurney along the corridor, fluorescent lights flashing in my eyes, I watch Lyme blow his nose into a handkerchief. "Is that some failed attempt at humor, Lieutenant?" he asks.

"I meant it as irony, sir."

"Another failure," Lyme says. "It is becoming a habit."

Lyme steadies himself by putting a hand on the gurney but doesn't break stride. "Your medical team is ready?"

"Of course, General," Riacin answers. "We are always ready to serve."

"Spare me the false promises," he says as my gurney rolls down the corridor. "This time, make sure your team doesn't fail me. As you can tell, I have no patience for the little ironies of life. Get Alpha Dog inside."

"As you wish, General." Then Riacin shouts, "Doors! Coming through!"

Two armed guards push the doors open, and I'm home. Project MUSE. The place where, a long time ago, I was nursed back to health after a genetically engineered insectoid almost killed me. Here, I got a prosthetic bionic eye, fancy new armor, and a set of upgraded nanobots.

"Are you not omitting something from the list?" Mimi asks.

And an artificial intelligence that would be the envy of all my friends if they only knew about her.

"I only have eyes for you, cowboy."

"Bet you say that to all the cyborgs," I reply.

The medics wheel the gurney to its hoist. They hook up the neuronal cables. Machines hum. Monitors start beeping.

After they leave the lab, the automatic lamps dim and the room goes dark. The only light is the blue glow inside the gurney that bathes my face through the view screen. Above me, the multinet blinks on. Dolly looks down at me from the screen, her face unnaturally serene. She's no Mimi, that's for sure.

"Thank you very much," Mimi says. "The adage states that imitation is the sincerest form of flattery, but I believe the original is always superior."

I close my eyes and try to relax. Soon, the effects of the gas will fade, and I'll be my old self again. Well, not my old, old self, but the now old self that I've become.

"Even I have trouble following that train of thought," Mimi says.

"That's because—" I start to say but am cut off by the sound of someone slamming through the doors.

"Shut up!" Lyme bellows as he enters the lab. "Do not mock my ideas!"

"General, please," Riacin says. "I know that you fear he is unstable, but what you're suggesting could destroy all the work my team has done."

My head lolls to the side, and I see Lyme shove Riacin. "Of course we know what he's capable of. We set out to make him a killing machine."

"I—I—" Riacin hesitates. "My team thinks that—"

"You and your teams are out of chances!" Lyme yells. "I gave you every opportunity to fix him, but my faith in your ability was unfounded. From now on, I'm taking matters into my own hands. Alpha Dog is my personal project. I will do with his brain as I see fit."

Brain? Uh-oh. I don't like the sound of that.

"Me, either," Mimi says.

Riacin tries to block him. "But sir."

"No buts!" Spittle flies from Lyme's mouth. "Get out of my way! Never get in my way again!"

Stunned, Riacin retreats. "Yes, General, I understand," he says. "I understand completely."

Lyme stands next to the gurney, panting, trying to catch his breath. A wicked series of coughs racks his body and knocks him to the floor. He rests on hands and knees, wheezing bloody phlegm onto the tile.

"Dolly," he says, "I need you."

Her face reappears on the multinet screen behind him. "Yes, General?"

As I watch, he wipes the blood with a fingertip and

holds it up. "Explain . . . this."

"General," Dolly says, "it is obvious from the analysis of readings from your most recent bioscans that the disease has progressed more rapidly than previous test data suggested."

"See?" I tell Mimi, and feel a twinge of guilt. "He's getting sicker."

"That hussy," Mimi huffs, "has no idea what she is talking about."

Lyme pulls himself up on the side of my gurney, obviously unaware that I'm watching him. "I have no hope of recovery. Is that what you're telling me?"

"In layman's terms," Dolly replies, "affirmative."

"And also in layman's terms, you're telling me that my death is imminent."

"Affirmative. All you can do is delay it."

"I cannot, will not die," Lyme says. "My work here is not done. My son is not the prince of Mars that I envisioned. His brain is damaged, and he will never be a man, just a monster. If only I could have combined my superior mind with his physical abilities . . ."

"Mimi?" I say. "What is he talking about? He sounds way too desperate for my liking."

"I will not hazard a hypothesis," she says. "The workings of Lyme's brain have always been beyond my understanding."

Lyme stands, lifted by a sudden burst of inspiration. He laughs, shaking his head. "Why did I never think of this before?"

"I do not understand the context of your query, General," Dolly says.

"That's because it was a rhetorical question, and you aren't capable of understanding that sort of nuance," he says. "Tell Riacin to clear the Nursery of personnel, then prepare Cradle One for brain wave extraction and storage."

"Affirmative," Dolly says. "Which subject should I inform Lieutenant Riacin to prepare?"

"Is it not obvious?" he says. "If my son can't reach his destiny, then I will reach it for him."

Right. I think I've heard enough. "Mimi, is he thinking what I'm thinking he's thinking?"

"Which would be?"

"He wants to eat my brain."

CHAPTER 10

"No, not eat your brain per se," Mimi says, "but certainly erase every thought and memory you have ever had."

"Which is not on my to-do list," I say. "Time to accelerate that escape attempt." For the last two weeks, I've been planning an escape. The best time would have been during a training mission. The plan was to fake being gassed, surprise a couple of guards, then steal a truck/boat/turbo bike and haul butt. It was a good plan.

"It was a high-risk plan with a very small margin of success," Mimi says.

"If you call seventy percent a small margin."

"More likely, thirty percent."

"Fifty percent."

"Forty."

"Like I said, it was a good plan." But now, all that precision planning is shot. I have to get off this mountain stat, and oh yeah, that HVT is coming with me. No way am I leaving something that could win a war behind."

"Discretion is the better part of valor," Mimi says.

"If that means that it's better to be a living coward than a dead hero"—I sneak a peek at Lyme, whose back is to me—"then I think it's a load of guanite."

"I concur," she says, as I—

Sit bolt upright.

Grab the armalite from the gurney.

And snatch Lyme by the collar. Then yank him backward so that he's off balance and the muzzle of my rifle fits nicely in the notch that forms his occipital protuberance.

"Ha!" Mimi says. "You *have* learned something by osmosis."

Ignoring her, I put my mouth next to his ear. "Not a sound, or I'll put a round in your brainpan."

Lyme makes a low groan and struggles against me. But I've got him, and he can't slip loose. "Ah, Jacob," he says in a raspy voice. "I thought you might be awake."

"Liar." I push him toward the door. "You were taking me to the Nursery. You're planning to erase my memories. Because stealing my AI isn't enough, is it?"

Lyme laughs, and he doesn't resist, except to walk more slowly than I'd like. I plant a knee in his lower spine. "This is your grand escape?" he says. "I admit, I expected it when you were less docile, but lately I had begun to believe that you had finally given in. You never were particularly tenacious. Dolly—"

I clap a hand over his mouth. "No calling your AI for help." I push him out of the room, expecting two guards. But the doorway is empty. "Mimi, do a scan."

"Negative," she says. "Dolly is not aware of my presence. If I do a scan, that hussy will perceive it."

"Skip the scan, then," I say.

"The guards are around the corner," Lyme says when I loosen my grip on his mouth. "This pair has a habit of leaving their posts. Please shoot them for me."

I yank harder on his collar. "This isn't a game."

"It *is* a game, Jacob," he says. "One that you are destined to lose. What I don't understand is why you didn't simply strike me and flee. You could make quite the run of it. You are very good at running away."

I long to throttle his neck. "You're very good at staying in one place, like in a prison cell."

"He is baiting you, cowboy," Mimi says. "Do not let him goad you into losing your focus."

She's right. He has goaded me my whole life. And I'm sick of it. "Won't work, Lyme."

"Lyme?" he says as we cross the hallway, and I glance ahead to where the guards are standing, gabbing with two others. "Have you forgotten that I am your father?"

"No, but you have."

"Touché," he says.

I step out into the open, using him as a shield. "Gentlemen and other assorted Sturmnacht scumbuckets, drop your weapons and start running."

The four of them look up, startled. They jump as if jolted by a live wire when I shove Lyme toward them.

"Now!" I shout. "Before I split his skull!"

"Follow his order," Lyme says, "and I will shoot you all myself."

Their eyes dart from him, to me, to my weapon, and back to one another. It's like watching bioengineered cows in the biodome make a group decision.

I don't have time for this *chùsheng*. With a quick shove, I knock Lyme forward. When they move to stop his fall, I launch a front kick at the nearest guard. He reaches out, exposing his ribs. I hear the crack, then slam my boot on his foot. He bends over, and I follow up with a thunder fist to his left kidney.

That's one down.

The next guy turns as my elbow catches him in the ear. He stumbles backward, so I shove him into the third guard. They both fall in a tumble of arms and legs.

That's two and three down.

"Technically," Mimi points out, "they are still capable of fighting."

"Close enough in a pinch." I round on the fourth guard, a slightly built guy with a purple scar that covers half of his face. I used to have a scar like it, until Lyme's cosmeticians removed it. "You used to be a Regulator?" I ask him.

Surprised, he lifts Lyme and spins my angry, embarrassed

father to his feet. "How'd you know?"

"Lots of soldiers in my unit got those when CEO Stringfellow set the Big Daddy chiggers loose on us," I say. "So how about I take the general, and you find a line of work where your boss isn't trying to kill you?"

He starts to pull his sidearm. "Ancient history."

"Must be," I say, "because you didn't even recognize the man who did it to you. Meet CEO Stringfellow, aka Mr. Lyme."

The guard looks at Lyme with moon eyes, and I can see the gears turning in his head. He turns the weapon toward his boss.

"*Paska paskattaa skeida!*" I say, and next thing I know, I'm having to coldcock the guy to save the life of the man I was threatening to kill.

I pull a smoke grenade from my own ammo belt, yank the pin with my teeth, and toss it. "Take a deep breath," I tell Lyme while clapping a hand over his mouth again.

I half push, half carry him through the billowing cloud, which will in a few seconds fill the entire hallway. It's like carrying an empty suit. For a second, I feel a twinge of anger and sadness that catches me by surprise.

"Dolly has sounded the alarm," Mimi tells me.

"Fine by me," I say aloud. "Now you can do a scan and show me the best route out of here."

"That would be through the Nursery," she says, and then adds, "Beat you to it."

"You're talking to your AI?" Lyme says, his voice hoarse. "Impossible! Dolly eradicated her!"

"Right, just like the Earth eradicated smallpox two centuries before they weaponized it and used it on Mars."

"Cowboy, I read eleven human biosignatures," Mimi says. "Nine of them are Alphas in their cradles."

"The other two?"

"Just your average human types."

I kick the nursery door open and start shooting. "That, I can handle."

The two average human types turn out to be Lieutenant Riacin and a technician in a lab coat. They both dive behind a console as my spray of bullets chases them away from the cradles.

"You missed," Mimi says.

"Meant to." I didn't need to shoot blighters, just chase them away. The last thing I want is those cradles opened. I could take on any of the Alphas or maybe three of them. All of them would be . . .

"Impossible," Mimi says.

"A challenge." I push Lyme into a chair and yank a length of cable from the back of a multinet screen. "Hold out your hands."

With a wry smirk, he complies. I wrap the cord around his wrists and cinch the knot. Riacin peeks out from behind the panel.

I fire a shot to keep his head down and am distracted by

the observation window. Outside, Hellbender One is being filled with petrol, and a crew of mechanics is doing a systems check.

"What do you hope to accomplish, Jacob?" Lyme asks. "Even if you manage to escape the Nursery, you will never survive. Olympus Mons is the highest mountain in the solar system. Do you intend to sled down it?"

"Just hope I don't use you as the sled."

I open fire into the observation window until the clip is empty. The barrel is glowing white hot. The window is full of spiderweb cracks but still intact.

"It appears that I still know more than you," Lyme says.

I pull a white phosphorus grenade from my belt and toss it into the epicenter of the cracks. A few seconds later it ignites, creating a man-sized hole. A blast of arctic air rushes through, sucking in snow and ice. Soon the wind is blowing so hard, the multinet monitors begin to fall off the walls.

Alarms ring out. Sirens blare. Emergency lights flicker on and off rapidly, so that everything looks like it's moving in slow motion.

"Maybe not." I give his chair a good kick. While Lyme is spinning, I grab the high-value target from its place of honor.

"Dolly!" Lyme cries. "Alert!"

But it's too late. I tuck the case under my arm and dive out the window. Hit the deck with a forward roll. Then come up sprinting for the opposite end of the rectangular steel platform.

Toward the Hellbender.

Which has finished its system check and is beginning to lift from the landing pad.

"You are insane," Mimi says.

"That's the same thing you told me the last time I hijacked a Hellbender."

"That was just luck."

I hit the afterburners. "Maybe I'm feeling lucky."

The pilot turns toward me, the motion of her head bringing the nose cannon into firing position. She watches me for a second, then remembering that I am the same Alpha Dog that has just been carried off her ship, opens up with a barrage of rounds that rip across the platform and catch me right in the chest. I regain my balance and aim for the fuel trolley on the other side of the landing pad.

"Sorry," Mimi says. "I am a bit rusty."

"No blood, no foul," I say.

The trolley driver spots me coming and inexplicably, decides to be a hero. He leaps from his seat and holds up a wrench. Without even breaking stride I knock him aside, launch myself to the top of the trolley tank, sprint into the blinding wind and—

Jump!

My momentum carries me past the platform. Steel becomes air. The deck becomes a bank of clouds.

"Don't look down!" Mimi calls out.

But of course I do.

I always do.

And as always, it ends badly.

CHAPTER 11

The Hive
Olympus Mons
ANNOS MARTIS 239. 2. 12. 14:31

A wave of vertigo hits me, and I flail madly as the arc of my dive begins to carry me downward. Then somehow, in a stroke of spastic dumb luck, my free hand slaps against one of the Hellbender's landing skids. My fingers close, and I swing my other arm and the case over the skid.

"Got it!" I yell.

"Lucky catch."

I swing up to the gunners' nest and pull myself inside. "I'd rather be lucky than good."

"Then it's good that you are lucky," Mimi says. "Heads up, cowboy. Hostile closing on your six."

I turn back, thinking that it's Riacin coming after us with a pistol.

Wrong.

It's Sarge, and he's dragging a minigun across the platform.

A squeeze of the trigger unleashes the weapon, and it

chatters like a broken chain. I dive out of the way, and Sarge sprays the Hellbender. A half dozen shells find their mark in the body of the copter, and the pilot rolls aft to avoid the rest.

"Stop shooting at me!" the pilot yells.

"Yeah! What she said!" I slam a clip into my armalite, flick it to semiauto, and shoot the ammo chain that runs into Sarge's gun feeder. The chain shatters. The gun jams. The ensuing torque rips the weapon from Sarge's hands. He lifts his head, roars like a stuck rat, and shakes a fist at me.

"Is he really shaking his fist at me?" I ask Mimi.

"Yes, despite the obvious cliché."

In reply, I smile and blow him a kiss.

The gesture he returns is almost as clichéd and much more profane. He grabs the broken chain and flings it at the Hellbender. It whips through the frigid air and falls impotently into space.

At which point, the pilot decides to tip me out of the hold.

"Hey!" My feet fly out from under me. The Hellbender, soaring at an angle so severe it is almost sideways, veers away from the platform and plunges down into nothingness.

"I'm going to puke," I moan as we rip through the cloud bank, wisps of condensation lashing against my face. I jam the handle of the case into my mouth and hold it with my teeth while grabbing the hatch handle.

"Negative," Mimi says. "Visceral readouts show no abnormal activity, other than mild acid reflux."

"Then I'm going to die!"

"Only if you let go of the hatch. The pilot will not crash her own velocicopter just to get you. Focus."

"Easy for you to say! Your stomach isn't lodged in your nostrils!"

"I was a soldier once, too," she says, and that kills the argument. How can you debate the fear of death with someone who has already died?

"Fine!" I try to swing back into the bay, but forces exerted by momentum and gravity slam my legs back down. So instead, I punch the plexi out of the door, loop my arm through it, and hold on.

"Get off my ship!" the pilot yells.

"Be glad to!" I yell back. "Just land the carking thing first!"

"No can do!" she shouts. "Either you surrender, or I'll dump your carcass on the side of the mountain!"

"That's not much of an option!" I scramble higher. "I'll take C!"

"There was no C!" she yells.

"Now you tell me!" I swing my legs up. "I demand a retest!"

Its red and blue lights flashing in the sky, the Hellbender swoops down the north face of the mountain. Below, I watch the lights of the massive military complex Lyme has built—gunships, tanks, artillery, infantry as far as the eye can see.

The army that Lyme once assembled to fight the bioengineered chigoe called Big Daddies was twice as large, but much less mechanized. Before Lyme turned factories into munitions plants, battles were fought differently, with infantry engaging in hand-to-hand combat more often than not. War was much more personal then.

"How about we take a closer look?" the pilot yells. She veers again, carrying us toward the long, flat plain that extends from the foothills. "Maybe the business end of a battle tank will change your mind!"

The camp is illuminated like a small city. I quickly count out combat regiments of infantry battalions, assault battalions, mechanized armored battalions supported by tanks, heavy artillery, and platoons of support personnel and engineers. In the skies above, I estimate a strike force of at least two hundred aircraft, so many that the sky is full of rotors. It's the most advanced force I've ever seen.

"That caught your attention, huh?" the pilot yells. "Good! Because that's where I'm landing this bird!"

"Mimi," I ask, "is it too far to jump?"

"No," she says. "The chance that you would survive is almost one hundred percent, barring a freak accident caused by an unaccounted anomaly. However, you would be faced with the prospect of traveling on foot, and your chances of escape are much greater if you can commandeer this craft."

"Reckon I'll stay put," I say.

"It surprises me that you are willing to jump from a great height," Mimi says.

"Didn't say I was happy about it. It's Plan B. Just in case."

"In case of what?"

"This lunatic decides to fly us into the side of the mountain!"

The pilot is so busy yelling at me that she doesn't hear the whistling of the Harpy missile that zips past the window and sails into the night sky.

Whew.

I yank open the cockpit door and slide into the copilot's seat. "Fancy meeting you here," I say.

"Command! I am friendly! Do not fire!" the pilot screams again. Then she checks her radar screen and mutters a curse. "The Harpy's going to come back to bite us!"

As we watch through the windshield, the Harpy turns mid-path and backtracks. The pilot takes evasive, but the missile still catches us, slamming into the tail of the veloci-copter, snapping the rear rotor off. The bird begins spinning. It pitches forward, headed directly for the mountain.

"Mayday! Mayday!" the pilot calls into her headset. "Baby Bird to Hawk's Nest. I've got complete systems failure! Do you copy? Answer me!"

The pilot panics and takes her hands off the cyclic stick, more concerned with calling for help than controlling the vessel. Calmly, I press a button on the panel, switching con-trol over to the copilot. I grab the stick and hit the throttle as the main rotor pulls us toward a jagged cliff protruding from the mountainside.

"That's bad," I say as the pilot throws her arms across her face and screams.

I kill the engine. The rotor stops. With the rudders responding only because I'm pounding on them, the copter drops like a stone below the cliff, which shears off the main rotor as we pass.

The tail whiplashes a tall tree, and the skids hook the branches. For an eternity of seconds, the ship is suspended by breaking limbs. Then with a creaking sound that gives me enough time to shout, "Hang on!" before we plummet into a snowbank below.

A few moments later, I kick my door open and crawl out through a snowdrift. The world is white, but the stink of fuel fills the air. Move, I think, before this crate blows you both to bits. I work my way around to the pilot's side of the cockpit. Her scalp is bleeding, but the cut is superficial and her breathing is regular. I shake her shoulder. When she doesn't respond, I grab a handful of snow and press it against her cheek.

"Huh?" Her head jerks up. She looks about, blinking and groaning, then falls back against the seat.

"Anything broken?" I yell over the wind.

She shakes her head no.

"Mimi?" I ask, knowing she'll be doing a bioscan of the pilot.

"No internal injuries that I can detect, cowboy," she replies. "But minor breaks in both fibulae. Ask her to move so that we can check for signs of concussion."

"Squeeze my hands," I yell. "Good, now move your feet." Mimi confirms that there are no spinal problems and no sign of serious head injuries. Maybe internal problems from the force of landing, but there's nothing to do for that except get her to a safe area and call for medevac.

"I have to move you," I say. "Fuel's pouring out of the tanks, and this thing can go up any second. Ready?"

She gives a groggy thumbs-up.

Wedging a foot against the frame, I yank the door open. I lift her carefully from the wreckage and carry her a hundred meters away, where a deep gully forms a natural windbreak.

I place her against a rock, making sure that her pulse is still strong. I jog back to the copter to retrieve her gear, along with an emergency medical kit and Lyme's HVT. Can't leave that behind.

"Still okay?" I ask, and she groans in reply. "I'll take that as a yes."

Working quickly, I clear away the snow, then break open a half dozen thermopaks, wedging them around her extremities. Then I wrap her in a thermal blanket. "That'll keep you warm for a least a couple hours." Which is more than enough time for a rescue.

I pack the rest of the medikit into my rucksack and activate the emergency tracer on her uniform. "A rescue team will be here soon." I push a tube of smelling salts into her hands. "If you start going under, use this."

"Thanks," she mutters.

"Don't mention it." I pat her on the cheek. "But don't be offended if I never fly with you again."

Teeth chattering from the cold, I jog down the side of the mountain until I reach a rock formation with enough mass to block out recon drones. There are three electronic locks on the case and a touch screen of some sort under the handle. Clearly, somebody doesn't want prying eyes to get inside.

"Astute observation," Mimi says. "It requires highly trained skills of detection to conclude that locks are meant for security."

"Ha-carking-ha," I say. "Instead of mocking me, how about helping me figure out these locks."

"But mocking you is more fun."

"It's too cold for fun."

"You misunderstand your purpose," Mimi says. "Your concern is not with the locks, but with the object that is inside. You should apply your skills to deducing whether or not it will blow you into microscopic pieces."

I pause. "Think this might be a bomb?"

"If General Lyme thinks it is an object of high value, it could be a myriad of dangerous objects."

"So what's your best guess on what it might be?"

"A bomb."

"Oh."

"Possibly nuclear."

I jump back. "Nuclear? Like a dirty bomb? Are you detecting any radiation coming from the cylinder?"

"Nothing more than ambient radiation," she says.

"So you were just screwing with my head?"

"Affirmative."

"Mimi!"

"Cowboy!"

"Be serious! This is a very dire matter."

"I am aware on the gravity of the situation."

"Then focus," I say. "We have to decide on next steps."

"I apologize for my jocularity. I seem to be overcome with an unexpected sense of euphoria. As Homer wrote, 'A small rock holds back a great wave.'"

"It's the thin air. It makes you giddy."

"No," she says. "It is just nice to be free again."

I know what she means. I wasn't the only one who spent the last six months as a lab rat. I turn the case over and over, looking for any identifiable marks. It is as clean as a whistle. I've got no idea why Lyme wanted this thing so badly. Now that I have it, I'm not sure what to do with it. "Mimi, we need to get this open. Find out what we're dealing with so that we can get rid of it or whatever to keep it out of Lyme's hands."

"My original thesis is still valid. We do not know the

nature of the contents of the case, so it would be ill advised to open it until we do."

I run a gloved finger over one of the locks. There is no place for a key, physical or electronic. Even the best lock picker I know wouldn't stand a chance of breaking these babies. It would take someone with a high degree of technological education and good old-fashioned know-how, along with enough natural curiosity to want to solve the puzzle of what's inside. It would also have to be someone I could trust implicitly, without having to worry they would sell me out to Lyme.

Luckily, I happen to know just such a person.

"You do not know if she is still alive," Mimi says.

"I don't know that she's dead, either."

"Nor can you be certain of her whereabouts."

Ignoring her, I step out from under the rock cropping. The night sky is lit with lights of Phobos and Deimos, Mars's twin rocky moons. My night vision lets me easily pick out a path that will eventually lead to a road where hopefully, I can find a ride that will take us east.

"This is your plan of action?" Mimi says. "You are making many assumptions. Assuming that you should go east. Assuming that you can find her. Assuming that the locks can be broken. Assuming that the object inside will not kill you. Assuming that if you survive to that point, that knowing what the object is will guide you in how to best use it."

"It's called having faith."

"You think faith is enough?"

"It better be." I start making my way down the path toward the foot of the mountain. "Because right now, faith is all I've got."

CHAPTER 12

Tengu Monastery
Noctis Labyrinthus
ANNOS MARTIS 239. 2. 12. 14:37

The day after the Flood, the day Vienne awoke in the monastery to find Durango gone, wasn't the worst. That day, her emotions were a complex soup of disparate feelings. She felt joy that she was free from Archibald and safe with the monks, but it turned to cavernous grief when she learned that Riki-Tiki was dead and that she'd died at Vienne's own hand. But the worst came weeks later, after she had shed the last effects of Rapture and after she'd vowed to wear ribbons of contrition until she'd paid penance for all of her crimes. That was when she began to miss Durango.

At first, she couldn't bear the thought of seeing him. Then she began to notice his absence. No jokes. No teasing. No senseless, heroic quests or tilting at moral windmills. No more deep blue-green eyes that made her skin tingle; no more looks that said her words were the only ones worth listening to. No handsome face made more alluring by the web of scars on his temple, the reminder that he'd risked his life to save hers. Day after day, she would find a reason to walk to the main gate. To open the door and stare into the distance.

But he never came back.

So when Ghannouj sent her to answer the gate, which he had not done in months, and she sprinted across the grounds so fast the wind sucked away her breath, she knew in her heart that the abbot had foreseen Durango's return. She would throw open the heavy wooden door and he would be standing there in symbiarmor, helmet in hand, armalite strapped over his shoulder, wearing that smirk that made her want to punch him and kiss him all at the same time.

"It's"—she begins as the door swings wide and she steps through the gate—"you."

Nikolai Koumanov stands before her with a toothpick in his mouth. He tosses back his hair and grins. "Happy to see Nikolai, *jaa?*"

"*Nyet.*" Without a micron of hesitation, she lays him out with a right cross to the chin, then slams the gate behind her.

"Who rang the gong?" Mistress Shoei asks as Vienne stalks past her.

"Some peddler," she fumes. "I told him we don't want any."

A growl stops Vienne in her tracks. The sound of a Gorgon bike is unmistakable, with its fuel-injected, six overhead cams, V-quad 3000-cc 286-horsepower engine, and glass-lined exhaust pipes. She turns around. "I wonder who he stole the bike from?"

Mistress Shoei follows Vienne outside, scratching her head. "The peddler stole a bicycle?"

"If it wasn't nailed down, I'm sure he would," Vienne says as she spots Nikolai.

He's a few meters away with his back to her, sitting on a bloodred Gorgon, gunning the engine. Next to him is a second bike, which is ridden by a thicker, heavier young man with buzzed dark hair. He's wearing a velvet jacket just like Nikolai's, except the sleeves have been ripped off. Both of his upper arms are decorated with tattoos. One says "Ferro." The other says "Mother." And his fingers are stuffed in his ears.

"Brother!" the heavy one calls. "Enough with revving! Such a headache you give me."

Brother? Vienne thinks. I'd hate to be the woman who had to raise this pair. Absentmindedly, she rubs her left pinkie and waits for the idiot Nikolai to realize that she's standing there.

"*Golubchik moi*," Nikolai croons. "Come out, come out, wherever you are!"

Vienne sighs. Of all people, it had to be him. How did he find her in the wilderness? What a presumptuous jackass! She wonders how good it would feel to punch him again. Then the wind blows a ribbon across her face, and she's reminded of her vow to avoid violence. She takes a cleansing breath and focuses her chi.

Mistress Shoei, however, has taken no such vow. She storms past Vienne, pushing up one sleeve, then the next, until she reaches Koumanov. Stupidly, he winks at the mistress and guns the throttle. Shoei responds by slapping his face, again and again with both hands. She doesn't stop until Nikolai jumps from the bike, his foot catching on the kickstand, and lands in the dirt.

"Hmph." Shoei throws the switch to kill the engine. She shakes a silent but menacing finger at both riders. "No peddlers allowed!"

"Never has Nikolai Koumanov known such defeat," he says, holding his reddened face.

"Is lie," the brother says. "Mother Koumanov has many times slapped you."

"*Vaikus*, Zhuk. Do not embarrass your betters."

"That," he says, "you have done better than I could."

Vienne likes this brother. "Mistress," she says, "I will deal with these two."

"Fah," Shoei says, then throws her hands in the air. "Peddlers!" She returns to the gate and sits down, pulling a rice cake out of her pocket.

"What do you want?" Vienne demands of Nikolai.

He slaps dirt from the seat of his pants. His rough edges give him an air of danger, an illusion that he probably encourages.

"What?" Nikolai throws his hands up, as if to ask what he had done to be so offended. "No welcome?"

Vienne folds her arms. "You two traveled hundreds of kilometers for something. It's not to steal, because a monastery in the middle of nowhere has no treasure you can fence. You want something from me. How did you find me?"

"Finding girl was easy," he says, rubbing his chin. "No monks live near Christchurch, so after doing math again, we brothers came to very easy two-plus-two conclusion that girl was from monastery."

"That answers the second question," Vienne says. "Not the first."

"See?" He gives Zhuk's cheek a hearty shake. "Smart. What I tell you?"

"*Jaa.*" Zhuk smacks his hand away. "Is smart. Keep hand to self."

Vienne glares at them. "You're stalling."

"How is it we are stalling?" Nikolai shrugs. "Suddenly, Nikolai is attacked by angry *babushka* and he is stalling?"

"I have work to do." Vienne says. "What do you want?"

He sweeps a hand, his body silhouetted against the sky. "To take you away from all this."

"Liar."

"Ah." He grabs his heart. "You cut me to quick."

She walks away. "Be thankful it's all that got cut."

"Wait!" he calls. "Brothers Koumanov have come so far. Hear us out."

She keeps walking.

He chases her.

"How did you really find me?" she asks when he catches up.

"Gut feeling."

"Then I'll thank your overactive gut to go somewhere else."

"Gut cannot do that. You see, Nikolai needs girl's help and girl needs Nikolai's."

"I find that hard to believe."

"That I need your help?"

"No, that I need yours."

He halts. "Always, you are so cold?"

"Sometimes, I'm colder. Now leave me alone."

He grabs her wrist. "Listen!"

"Hands off!" She deftly extricates herself. "Nobody touches me."

"Tòčno," he says. Precisely. "Which is why we go to such trouble to find you."

"No thanks."

"Wait!" he calls. "Always, you are high-strung like tension wire. Vienne, Brothers Koumanov have come to offer job."

Job? She stops and looks back over her shoulder. "What kind of job?"

"Kind of job girl like you likes most—dangerous," he says. "Very dangerous. Most dangerous job of all."

"Okay," she says. "You've got my attention."

CHAPTER 13

Tengu Monastery
Noctis Labyrinthus
ANNOS MARTIS 239. 2. 12. 15:17

"No thanks," Vienne tells Nikolai. She tosses a small pouch of coin across the table in the kitchen hall. "I'm not a Regulator anymore."

"Who is?" Zhuk asks. "Even *dalit* must eat, *jaa?*"

The word stings her. *Dalit* is the obscene word used to describe a disgraced Regulator. Both she and Durango are *dalit* and carry the shame the stigma has left on them. She bristles but feels the calming presence of Ghannouj, who sits on the rice mat beside her.

"Zhuk," Nikolai says, "do not say such words."

Vienne speaks calmly. "When I need to eat, there is food here. I don't need your coin."

Nikolai pushes the pouch back toward her. "Think of children. Do children not need food? Where is coin to feed refugees camped on temple grounds?"

He has a point. More refugees from the front lines arrive every day. The monastery fields don't yield enough. The monks have begged scraps off the farmers from the collective nearby, but even the scraps are becoming scarce.

"Let me at least tell you about job," Nikolai says, stacking the money. "Not all refugees come to monks. So they travel south across plain to New Eden, where is safe."

"New Eden is safe? That pit of vipers?" She and Durango once used the town as their base. It was an easy place to get commissions because the Rangers turned a blind eye to criminals. People needed and were willing to pay for protection. "You'd have to be touched in the head to go there."

"Is safer than war," he says. "But not safe for travel, so refugees make caravan and hire Brothers Koumanov for security."

"So it's just the three of us protecting a whole caravan of refugees traveling hundreds of kilometers?" Vienne asks.

"Just three?" Nikolai laughs. "Ridiculous!"

"Is seven," Zhuk says.

"Oh, I like those odds much better." Vienne rolls her eyes. "Who are we protecting them from?"

Nikolai rubs his fingertips together. "No one in particular."

"He lies," Zhuk says. "Is Scorpions."

"This job just keeps getting better." Scorpions are a huge gang of ferals who once lived in the Favela slums. Since the Flood, they've spread all over the prefecture. "Tell me again why I want to do this?"

"To be fair," Nikolai says, "we told girl job was dangerous."

"Very dangerous," Zhuk adds.

Vienne crosses her arms. "More like insane."

"Talk to monks." Nikolai stands and gestures for Zhuk to follow him. "We wait outside for answer."

When they are gone, Vienne turns to Ghannouj, who has remained silent. "Master, that is a lot of coin."

"It is," he says.

"Enough to buy food for a month. Maybe more." She paces back and forth across the kitchen. The floor hums with each step. "What should I do?"

Ghannouj scratches the stubble on his cheek. "You should accept the job."

"What?" she says, shocked.

"Sometimes I like to surprise you." Ghannouj grins, the corners of his eyes crinkling. "You should join them. Once before, you left the monastery because you were not cut from the same cloth as a monk, and when you recovered, you tried again to wrap yourself in ill-fitting robes." He takes her by the shoulders. "Vienne, you were born to be a soldier. If you remain here, you will waste your gifts. More importantly, you will waste away in a life that is not meant for you. Only outside these walls will you find happiness and the young man who has stolen your heart."

He didn't steal it, Vienne thinks. *He won it.*

She presses the money into Ghannouj's palm.

Ghannouj removes three pieces and returns them to her. "For the children you find along your journey."

She gives the abbot a hug. He smells of sandalwood oil and green tea. "Be safe."

"Be safe yourself."

Without looking back, she pushes aside the curtain to the door and steps onto the porch, where Nikolai and Zhuk are waiting. "Why should I trust you?" she says. "How do I know you won't try to sell me off to the Scorpions?"

"Because if Nikolai wanted to hurt *lapochka*"—he pulls a revolver from his sleeve—"he could have shot her twice already."

"Is that so?" Vienne knocks his arm up, twists his wrist, and yanks the gun from his grip.

"Ow!" he cries. "Leave skin!"

Vienne pops the revolver's chamber and shakes the bullets into her palm. She reloads it, flicks the chamber shut, and gives it a spin. "Needs oiling."

He sucks blood from the wounded fingers. "Nikolai has underestimated you."

"You wouldn't be the first."

"*Õige!*" he says. "That is why Brothers Koumanov need you."

"Okay, I accept the job," she says, "under three conditions. One, no one is in charge of me, which means no orders."

"*Da.*"

"Two. No funny business. This is strictly a professional operation. No thieving, No looting. And most especially, no familiarity among the corps."

"Eh?" Zhuk says.

"Means no hanky-panky with girl," Nikolai explains. "So *jaa.*"

"And three. I get to drive a Gorgon."

"*Nyet,*" Nikolai says. "You drive Zhuk's."

"*Nyet! Nyet! Nyet!*" Zhuk stomps the porch. Dust rains down from the willow reed roof. He thumps down the steps and toward the gate. "*Nyet!* Is final!"

Nikolai watches him go. "Don't worry. Zhuk will come around."

"Give me a few minutes to take care of my duties, and I'll go with you."

"Okay'?" he asks. "After such struggles and heartaches, you tell me just 'okay'? Is that easy with you?"

"It's never that easy with me," she says. "Just wait till you see me drive."

CHAPTER 14

The Wilderness
ANNOS MARTIS 239. 2. 12. 17:26

The sun disappears into the fir trees as I cut through the woods. Behind me, the Tharsis Plain is quiet, the sounds of Lyme's army now a memory, except for the occasional aircraft. Keeping to gullies and using the scrub terrain as cover, I walk east, asking myself the same question repeatedly. What is in the case? Why is this object so important, and if it's so important, why has its existence been kept secret? What does Lyme hope to do with it?

"Feel free to answer at any time," I tell Mimi.

"I have only theories," she says. "Not answers."

"I'm open to theories, too."

When I reach the vastness of a rolling plain, a chilling zephyr sweeps across my face. It's going to be a cold night. I'll need to find shelter, maybe build a small fire, and then start again in the morning.

"Negative," Mimi says. "You cannot build a fire. Lyme's forces will spot it within minutes."

"Then I'll find a rock to sleep under for a few hours."

"'There is a time for many words, and there is also a time for sleep,'" Mimi recites.

"Homer again?"

"*The Odyssey*, to be precise," she says. "Sadly, this is not the time for sleep. You must vacate the area as soon as possible. To remain in one place dramatically increases the chance that you will be detected."

"Come on, Mimi. Just a couple of hours."

"One hour," she says.

I yawn and stretch. "Run a sweep of the perimeter. In case there's something that wants to eat me."

"No predator on this planet would find your symbiarmor appetizing."

The terrain is flat with low scrub brush, which means few rocks or trees for cover. Before I can find an even passable campsite, I hear a sound overhead. I see a quickly moving star. Then I realize—it's no star.

It's a searchlight.

"Evasive!" Mimi yells.

I dive into a ditch. "Why didn't you warn me!"

"There was no indication of a vehicle on my sweeps."

A Dragonfly drops from its cover in the clouds, banking into a narrow canyon that leads to the larger Labyrinth. Smaller, lighter, and faster than a Hellbender, the Dragonfly depends on speed, maneuverability, and a composite skin that gives it a zero visibility electronic signature.

Which explains why Mimi didn't pick it up.

"Okay," I say as the searchlight moves on. "I'll have to keep moving. *Piru vieköön*, I'm never going to get any shut-eye."

"If it will make you feel better," Mimi says, "I will sing a song."

"That'll work," I say. "Your singing could wake the dead."

"Then why was I never able to wake you?"

"You're not funny, Mimi."

"Yes, I am. You simply lack the capacity to appreciate my humor."

"Where are we, exactly?" I ask Mimi after a few hours of walking.

"You should carry a compass."

"I don't need a compass 'cause you're always telling me where to go," I say. "So where are we?"

The sky rumbles. I look up. No clouds in the sky. Then I feel a buffeting of air before any source of the disturbance can appear. I scan the horizon.

"Mimi," I ask, "what's wrong with the air?"

"There is an upper atmospheric disturbance caused by the introduction of an object of great force."

"That would be a Crucible strike?"

"Affirmative."

"Well, *ja vitut*," I say. "Where's it going to hit?"

"I approximate a strike zone one hundred kilometers in any direction from your current location."

"A hundred clicks?" I say. "That's not very precise."

"I did say approximate."

"What are the odds of outrunning it?"

"Nil."

"Zero?"

"All previous Crucible strikes appear to have landed at undetermined intervals at seemingly random targets. Therefore, it is impossible to accurately forecast a strike zone. Fleeing from one strike zone would necessarily lead to another strike zone."

"I can't outrun it?"

"That is what I just explained."

"So I might as well stand here and see if it hits me."

"It is your choice. However, any choice you make has the same likelihood of success."

"How about I find a rock to hide under? How does that affect the odds?"

"Nil."

"How about a hole?"

"Nil."

"A deep hole?"

"Nil."

"A black hole?"

"I calculate that the Crucible strikes are attaining very high velocities of at least thirty-five hundred meters per second or more and have roughly half the concussive force of the Hiroshima atomic bomb," she says. "Therefore, unless you locate a hole that extends one kilometer below the surface, you will die in a Crucible strike. The only difference is that you will save someone the trouble of burying you."

"I was hoping to be cremated when my time comes," I say. "You know, a Regulator's funeral."

"Then I recommend staying out of holes."

I look up at the sky. Shield my eyes. "So what are you saying? That MahindraCorp's general is just randomly chucking these things?"

"That is my theory based on the evidence."

Scary, but not effective. It's like spraying a battle rifle into the air, hoping that one of the bullets lands on your enemy's head. "How long before it hits?"

"Less than one minute."

The buffeting winds are replaced by chain rumbling like a thousand turboprops. Within moments, I can see the bright orange-red tail of what looks like a comet.

I brace myself, though I know it's a useless gesture. *Helvett*, I'm an expert on useless gestures. I watch the Crucible pass over and shrink into the horizon to the south. As quickly as it came, the thundering noise is gone.

But that's just the calm before the storm.

CHAPTER 15

Tengu Monastery
Noctis Labyrinthus
ANNOS MARTIS 239. 2. 12. 17:59

The pagoda tombs of the Tengu Monastery are a forest of hundreds of tall, narrow stone buildings, most under seven stories, each the tomb of a monk or an abbot who has passed beyond the veil into that undiscovered country from where travelers never return.

The mists are thick and swirling as Vienne stops beside a recently built pagoda, its pedestal painted bright pink—the cenotaph of Riki-Tiki. She drops to her knees and touches her forehead to the ground. "For a hundred days, I've told you I'm sorry, and for a thousand more, I'll beg your forgiveness."

"It wouldn't take a thousand days," Shoei says. "She would forgive you after one."

"I wouldn't deserve it."

"She would swat you for saying such a thing." Shoei gives Vienne a swat. "And tell you to start forgiving your-self instead." She places a bundle of clothes, several packets of rice, a long object swaddled in homespun cloth, and a medikit on the ground. "Here are your things."

"How can I forgive myself? I killed her."

"Ghannouj would tell you that Riki-Tiki chose her own path," Shoei says. "I will tell you that your life is full of ghosts. You must learn to live with them, or they will haunt you to death. This old woman speaks from experience. So would Yadokai, if the fool wasn't too soft to tell you good-bye." She strokes Vienne's hair and leaves her with a trembling kiss on the head.

Vienne watches until the mistress is gone. Then she unbundles the clothes and shakes out the symbiarmor. She pulls it on like a slip. Then the boots. Then the right glove before she hesitates.

She opens and closes her left hand. The deformed pinkie finger pops. The joint is imperfect. The skin is the shade of a sugar beet. It's attached to her body, but it isn't hers.

When CEO Stringfellow, the man who would become Lyme, ordered his own son to chop off a pinkie in a public ceremony, Vienne felt honor bound to follow her chief's destiny. It dishonored her to mutilate herself. It dishonored her more to become a *dalit*, an outcast Regulator, and that humiliation drove a wedge between her and Durango. She could never forgive him for that, even when they learned that the whole ceremony had been a sham from the start. Then years later, when Lyme's crony Archibald captured Vienne, he was able to break her spirit for one reason—the shame of being *dalit*. He promised to regrow her pinkie, and in return, she allowed herself to become a monster.

You can't unmake what has been made. You can't be made whole when you were never less than that. You can't stop being something you never were.

The first step is preparation. She sits in the lotus position, controlling her breathing, lowering her heart rate. She picks up the medikit and takes out a packet of clotting gel, topical painkiller, bandages, suture silk. She wraps the silk tightly around her left pinkie finger until the blood is completely restricted.

Heart in her throat, she sterilizes the knife and lays a length of bandage across a flat rock. Finding the notch between the knuckles with edge of the knife, she holds her breath and pushes down with all her strength.

It is done.

Quickly, before shock can hit, she rips open the packet of clotting gel and shoves the bloody stump inside. She grunts as the gel cauterizes the wound. A moment later, she scrapes the gel away and cuts the suture silk, allowing the wound to bleed out so that fluid doesn't engorge the stump.

She wraps the wound in a field dressing. The greatest enemy here is not the amputation but the shock that follows any traumatic injury. By controlling her body, she prevents it, and once that is done, she puts on the glove and then slides into her black robes, wearing the uniforms of both monk and Regulator, combining both halves of herself.

Later, after cleaning up, she looks past the pagodas and

across the monastery grounds, far down the canyons that have been her home for the last six months.

She throws the rucksack over her shoulder. "It is time to go."

When she returns to the front gate, there are now four men waiting for her—Nikolai and Zhuk, plus two others. They are dressed in the same mismatched, flamboyant uniforms. One is lanky, with a triangular face, round, wire-rimmed spectacles, and chopped-off bangs. The other is a blond with a cherubic face and not even a wisp of facial hair, clearly the youngest of the quartet.

"What's this about?" Vienne asks.

At the sound of her voice, they all look up, their collective expressions a mix of surprise, curiosity, and humor.

"*Tere, ilus tüdruk,*" says the blond boy. He bows to her with the same sweeping gestures as Nikolai, who he's clearly copied. "I am Pushkin. Please to make acquaintance." Then he takes Vienne's bandaged hand and tries to kiss it.

She grabs his face and pushes him away. "Dream on."

"Ha!" Zhuk yells. "What did big brother tell you, lover boy?"

The third man wipes his glasses with a handkerchief. "Already, we are behind schedule."

"Patience, Yakov," Nikolai says "We will make up lost time."

Vienne surveys them. They share no common features.

In no way do they look related. "These two are your brothers?" she asks. "You're all brothers?"

"*Jaa*, we are Brothers Koumanov," Nikolai says. "With us, you are very safe."

Vienne hesitates. How does she know they're telling the truth? Maybe they're working for Lyme, and it's just an elaborate hoax? But there is danger everywhere, and she can't stay holed up inside these walls forever.

"What is wrong with hand?" Nikolai asks, pointing at her bandage.

"I cut it," she says. "Which ride is mine?'

"Take pick," he replies. "Except mine. Svetlana is very temperamental. Will only start for Nikolai."

He named his bike? She rolls her eyes. Typical.

Pushkin pats the seat behind him and makes a kissy pout. "Come sit Pushkin's bike. Girl will enjoy ride, *jaa?*"

Vienne cocks her head. "Why not?"

As she walks toward his black Gorgon, a surprised but coy grin creeps across his face. It turns to shock when Vienne places a hand on his shoulder and shoves him off the seat. "Thanks."

"Is okay." Pushkin tries to throw his leg over the saddle. "I think Pushkin will take backseat."

Vienne shoves him to the ground. "Think again."

"Oy!" Pushkin cries. "Is my bike! Nikolai!"

"Is her bike now," Nikolai says. "Ride with Zhuk, *poisike.*"

Face red with anger and embarrassment, Pushkin glares

at Vienne. She flashes a smile. He stomps over to Zhuk, who shakes a hairy sausage finger at him.

"Touch seat, and Zhuk is making you eunuch," Zhuk says.

"No fair!" Yakov stomps.

"Brother," Nikolai says. "Ride with Yakov."

"No, Yakov smell like borscht!"

"Better than to smell like Zhuk," Nikolai says. "Ride with Yakov, or we leave you with monks. Monks will shave head and make you work fields."

Pushkin shrugs, so what?

"Also," Nikolai says, "you will have to wear dress like Vienne."

"*Jaa!*" Pushkin says. "Better I should die than wear that."

She looks down at her cheongsam. "What's wrong with my clothes?"

"Nothing," Pushkin says, "for prayer. But for blending in, you stick out like sore toe."

"Why? Because I don't want to look anything like a Sister Koumanov?"

"Not to worry." Pushkin says as he picks gravel out of his cheek. "You look nothing like sister. You are much too thin."

"And," Zhuk adds, "you have no beard."

Pushkin looks to Nikolai, then to Yakov, then to Vienne, who arches her eyebrows and shakes her head. He gives up and jumps onto the back of Yakov's Gorgon with a huff.

"Need hand with controls?" Nikolai asks Vienne. "Gorgon is complex machine."

Complex? she thinks. You should try riding a bike cobbled together by a mad genius that blows things up for fun. "This, I can handle myself." She adjusts the pedal depth. The Gorgon's engine is just the music she wants to hear. "Where exactly are we going?"

"Someplace nice!" Nikolai shouts as his bike lurches onto the road, headed south on the Bishop's Highway. "How does *lapochka* feel about Scorpions?"

CHAPTER 16

Crossroads
Tharsis Plain
ANNOS MARTIS 239. 2. 13. 05:03

Ja vitut, are my dogs tired. I've not stopped walking since the Crucible strike, when a violent shock wave undid the ground, and even many kilometers away, I was thrown from my feet.

"Technically, they are not dogs," Mimi reminds me as I emerge exhausted and crinkled by dehydration from an arroyo. "They are feet."

"Yes, O wise one," I say, and check for traffic.

I climb up to a dimly lit highway and use a road sign to hoist myself onto the berm. The only light is the dim neon glow of a roadhouse half a kilometer across the way, but I can make out a couple of vehicles parked in front. "I'm well aware of the difference between my feet and canine animals. It's something I've known since I was three. I'm even capable of tying my own boots."

I take a step, trip on a loose lace, then stumble to the pavement. I catch myself by the elbows, saving my face a few layers of skin.

"I take it that those are not your boots," she says.

"Har-har."

I start to get up. Then think, forget it, and let my face sink down against the pavement. It's warm to the touch, and the night air is cold enough that my breath is freezing. I'm so bone tired that I take off my newfound straw hat and make a pillow of it. I'll sleep right here, thank you very much.

The road sign tells me that I'm at a crossroads. The Bishop's Highway goes north-south in an almost direct line from Christchurch to New Eden. The Founders Road takes a somewhat east-west route as it meanders from Nozomi to Bosporous. The Bishop will take me near the Tengu Monastery and, if the moons are aligned, Vienne. The Founders will take me to an old friend from Battle School, the only person I know who I think would understand the thing locked away in the case in my rucksack. She also hates Lyme enough that I can trust her not to rat me out.

"Do you know how much force a two-ton transport truck exerts on the road below?" Mimi asks me.

"How should I know?" I say. "And why do you care?"

"No reason," she says. "I was only curious if the force would be great enough to crush your head like a melon when the truck rolls over you. In approximately ten seconds."

My eyes pop open. "What?"

A hundred meters away, a transport truck rounds the bend, and its lights ignite the countryside. And me, lying like roadkill on the highway.

An air horn sounds.

"*Re malaka!*" I scramble to my feet, then dive for the berm. My hands sink into the soft, loamy soil, and I come up with a mouthful. "Mimi! Why didn't you tell me a truck was coming?"

"I did."

"I could've been a flat cat by the time you spat it out!"

"Unlikely," she says, "since I calculated that it would take you four-point-seven seconds to leave the road and nine-point-six seconds for the truck to pass."

Which it does, trumpeting its horn, whipping wind in my face, and blowing me backward. I step out onto the highway and raise a finger in salute to the driver.

"Would it hurt you," I ask Mimi, "to just say, 'Look out, truck coming'?"

"Look out! Truck coming!"

"Ha-carking-ha."

"No!" she yells. "Truck! Move!"

In the half second it takes to turn my head, I realize two things: first, the sound of this truck's engine was drowned out by the honking, and two, it's running with no lights. Which is probably a good thing. Because as I'm diving yet again into the berm and coming up with a second mouthful of dirt, I note that it's a Noriker, and it's leading a convoy of military vehicles.

Lyme's army is on the move.

Headed south.

"Stay down," Mimi says.

She doesn't have to tell me twice.

"Stay down," she says.

"You already said that."

"Then do as I say."

I crawl closer for a better look-see. "Is that a battle tank in the back of that tractor?"

"Affirmative. Data suggests that there are over two hundred vehicles in the convoy. Find some cover and wait it out."

I belly crawl backward down into the arroyo. No sense in letting them spot me now. "Without lights, how are they driving in the dark? Night vision?"

"Negative," she says. "Night vision does not have the capability to process cold images such as the road. I suspect the answer to your question is all in your head."

"No more riddles!" Then it hits me. "Oh! I get it. Dolly is directing the vehicles."

"That is my theory."

It's a carking terrifying theory. If Dolly has advanced her capabilities to the point of controlling Lyme's vehicles as they travel across country, who is to say that she can't control all of his armor vehicles and artillery, too?

"Astute observation, cowboy. But of course, that was Lyme's master plan for MUSE—to create an artificial intelligence with both strategic and tactical capabilities."

"One that could self-program and learn from its mistakes?"

"Eventually."

Sacre merde. "How long would that take?"

"Indeterminate."

"Knew you were going to say that." There are too many factors in play for her to make an accurate assessment.

"I was going to say that, too," she says. "But I can approximate a window of seven days or less."

"Seven days?" Geez. I squeeze my eyes shut and try to shake off the exhaustion. I look at the sign again. Bishop's Highway. The monastery. Vienne. My heart tells me to go there first. *Wángbā dàn! Wángbā dàn! Wángbā dàn!*

I stare at the sky. At the twin moons Deimos and Phobos, named after the children of Ares and Aphrodite, the gods of war and love, locked in perpetual orbit together, one emotion trying to overrule the other. "I know how you guys feel."

"Cowboy," Mimi warns me. "They are moons. This is not a sign from the heavens."

"It is if I want it to be."

"The future of this war is literally—literally—in your hands."

"I've put duty ahead of Vienne too many times."

"Not that many times!"

"One time is too many." I will be taking Bishop's Highway to the Tengu Monastery because what's a future without Vienne in it?

"Cowboy! If I could get my hands on your neck!"

"Then I would deserve whatever you wanted to do to

me. But it's been six months since I last laid eyes on her, and because neither one of us is a fortune-teller, this may be the last chance I ever get. If you were in my boots, what would you do?"

"I would tie them myself."

"Probably in knots, too. " I sneak a look at the line of traffic. "As soon as this convoy passes, we're heading to the roadhouse over yonder."

"There is a one in three chance that you will be recognized."

"In this getup? Please. My own mother wouldn't recognize me."

Mimi lets that one slide. My mother wouldn't recognize me because she's never seen me. I'm a product of in vitro fertilization. The woman who gave birth to me was a surrogate, nothing more. Mimi is the closest thing I've ever had to a maternal figure. When I was a Regulator, she was my chief. She took a spoiled Battle School brat and turned him into a soldier. Took a boy and turned him into a man. I hope.

"Me, too," Mimi says.

I wait in silence until the last truck in the convoy has passed, then climb up to the highway.

"All clear," Mimi says before I can ask. "Look both ways before you cross."

'Yes, ma'am." The lights of the roadhouse seem dimmer. The sign is dark, and only the windows are visible now. "It's closing time." I jog toward the building. "Perfect."

Inside, a couple of customers are paying their bills at

the counter. A tired-looking old man wipes the tables and a woman runs the register, her eyes puffy and dark. If that's what settling down looks like, I'd rather keep moving, thank you very much.

Over my symbiarmor, I'm wearing a pair of overalls and a blue workman's tunic that I found discarded along the road among dozens of other pieces of clothing, pots and pans, broken furniture, and a doll with no head. The stuff was abandoned by refugees, I'm sure, maybe left because it was too heavy to carry anymore. Or maybe they just gave up and walked away from what was left of their lives.

I step into the light near the entrance so they can see me. The first person out the door is a burly trucker in a synthetic fur parka and chukka boots. He sucks on a toothpick and shivers against the night air.

"Howzit, jack?" I say, raising a hand in greeting and trying to imitate the accent of a former mate named Fuse. "Give a bloke a ride, what's you say? I'm a bit down on the luck."

The driver starts at the sound of my voice. He tries to spit around the toothpick. Then he shakes his head and keeps walking. "Don't take no refugees. You've walked this far. Expect you can keep right on hoofing it."

"There's a fair dinkum way to treat a feller hopping about." I wipe my mouth and try to look hungry, which isn't that hard. "Where's your heart and soul?"

Without turning, he shouts back, "Lost it the same place you lost that pinkie, *dalit*."

A couple of seconds later, he fires up his truck and blasts me with the high beams. I hold up my left hand so he can get a good look at the stub he despises so much. It's amazing. Even after a flood destroyed the capital. Even with a war chewing up folks and their homes, some people hang on to the prejudices like they've got lockjaw.

He pulls out, and my real eye is still full of the ghosts of his headlights when the last driver leaves the roadhouse.

"See yas in a few days," she calls back to the owners. "Keep my seat warm, yeah?"

Tucking my left hand in a pocket, I step up to greet her.

"Back off, ya poxer!" she yells, and lifts a fist.

"I'm so sorry." I back away and forget to fake my accent. "I didn't mean any trouble."

She gives me the up and down. Shakes her head at my overalls and the dirty tunic. "Bishop help us, ain't you a mess. Stay right there." She heads back inside.

"Mimi?"

"Prepare yourself, cowboy. You are about to experience a sensation you have not enjoyed in exactly one hundred and eighty-one days."

"What's that?"

"Kindness."

A few seconds later, she emerges carrying a chunk of something wrapped in foil. She pushes it into my hands. "Tonight, ya won't go hungry."

"Thank you." My mouth starts watering. I wasn't so

famished until I smelled the juicy, thick aroma of what must be a meat loaf. The square is warm and heavy in my hand. "But I was hoping for a ride. If you're driving the Bishop."

"The Bishop?" She eyes me differently this time. "The company says we ain't supposed to take riders. Too much thieving and hijacking by the Scorpions and such."

"The company's not here, right?" My stomach groans. "And I promise I'm not a Scorpion."

"That's obvious," she says. "Scorpions do that ugly thing to their heads. But now that I've a second look, you're no refugee, neither. Deserter?"

I shrug.

"Can't say as I blame ya. This war's going to be the end of all of us, one way or t'other. You ever killed a man?"

"Not as many as I could have," I say, looking her in the eye so she'll know it's the truth.

She glances to the stars and shakes her head. "Expect I'm going to regret this, but wait till I start the truck up and then climb into the back. There's room among the ore. You'll want to eat that first. The stink of guanite will suck the appetite out of a starving man."

Guanite?

I open the foil, take deep sniff of the meat loaf, drawing the steam into my nose, and then shove the whole meat cake into my mouth.

"Chew," Mimi says.

"Iz hoz," I say aloud, my tongue scalding from the heat.

"How did you ever manage without me?"

"I bid fine." I try to chew and cool my mouth at the same time. But I have to wonder, How did I manage without her? What would I do if she ever went away?

The truck engine starts and the air horn sounds—my cue to haul butt. The taillights flash as I grab a lock chain and swing aboard. The bed of the truck contains six hoppers on either side. The hoppers are loaded with guanite, a pungent soft rock that contains enough organic matter to burn. In the days before terraforming ended, megatons of guanite were burned every day to intentionally pollute the atmosphere and increase the greenhouse effect to warm the planet and protect it from the sun's radiation.

There's a spot between the hoppers near the rear. I press my back against the wall and try to get comfortable. Which is impossible. "It smells like *kuso* back here."

"I believe you were warned of that fact."

"Why do think they started hauling guanite again? The ovens shut down a long time ago."

"I do not have enough data to postulate a theory," she says. "But when we reach our destination, I will endeavor—"

Before she can finish the sentence, exhaustion overwhelms me. "Say good-bye, Mimi."

"Good night, Mimi," she replies.

It's the last thing I hear before gunfire erupts.

CHAPTER 17

Camp Stringfellow
Plains of Olympus
ANNOS MARTIS 239. 2. 13. 09:43

The Dragonfly dances above Camp Stringfellow, its dual wings gyrating so quickly that they seem to disappear. The copter flits from perch to perch, a defensive movement that keeps it out of danger. The camp is a twelve-kilometer-square cluster of prefab metal buildings, concertina wire, mobile redoubts, and countless tents held together by a grid of temporary roads.

The troops are going through morning exercises. In the airspace above the camp, squadrons of velocicopters zip in and out, some training, some on patrol. The Dragonfly maneuvers through this swarm of traffic and finally settles on the landing pad.

"Much ado about nothing," a corporal says as he follows Lieutenant Riacin out of the ops building.

"How is that?" Riacin asks.

"His machinations before landing," he says. "There are no hostiles. The zone isn't hot. It just seems overly cautious."

"Overcautious to you," Riacin says. "Sensible to me. Such behavior is what is called for in this situation. This Oryol person has collected dead man bounties on the most dangerous criminals in the prefecture. I'm sure that there is a long list of criminals who would like to return the favor."

The corporal starts forward. Riacin grabs his shoulder and pulls him back. "Mind your distance. Bounty hunters are notoriously skittish, especially this one."

The pilot, dressed in a pair of mechanics' coveralls, climbs out of the cockpit. The front of the coveralls is unzipped, revealing a hint of black body armor. A long-billed cap obscures most of the hunter's face.

"Oryol!" Riacin shouts over the noise of the tanks in the distance. "Welcome to Camp Stringfellow. General Lyme is anxiously awaiting you."

Oryol pulls a bruised fig from a pocket and cuts off a chunk with a paring knife. "Where is Lyme? I don't see him. This was supposed to be a personal meeting."

"For the sake of security," Riacin explains as they walk toward a portable multinet station set up on the tarmac, "the general will be meeting with you via comlink on the multinets."

"Too bad," Oryol says. "I'd hoped to meet Lyme in person."

"Dolly," Riacin says, "we're ready to begin."

"Affirmative," Dolly's disembodied voice replies. With a chime, the screen blinks on, and Lyme appears. The general's face is gaunt, but his eyes are sharp with anger.

"General Lyme, greetings from the land of your enemy," Oryol begins. "On a personal note, it is good to see you again."

"Let's dispense with the niceties," Lyme says, clearing his throat. "I've hired many bounty hunters in my time, and I have never been satisfied with the results. What makes you different?"

"Because I'm not a bounty hunter."

"What nonsense is this?" Lyme snaps.

Oryol slices off another chunk of fig and leans closer to the vid screen. "I'm not a hunter who chases his target. I'm a trapper, setting many snares and waiting patiently for the target to capture himself."

"You're wasting my time," Lyme says with a wave of his hand. "Do you want the commission or not?"

"Depends," Oryol says. "On the size of the commission."

"This is half." With a loud thunk, Riacin drops a heavy pouch on the table. "You will get the rest when the job's finished."

Oryol glances inside. "Who's the target?"

Riacin hands Oryol a file. "A soldier who stole something from me, " Lyme says. "Find him and return my property."

"And the soldier?"

"Kill him."

"General," Riacin says, "surely you don't mean *kill* him. Let's step back for a moment to reconsider—"

"No," Lyme says, "I will not reconsider. Alpha Dog

has outlived his usefulness."

"General, please," Riacin says. "Think of the resources that have been devoted to his development. The project—"

"Think of how many resources I must devote to finding him now!" Lyme composes himself. "Oryol, what do you require of me?"

"Only time and money, General."

"Money, I can give you," Lyme says. "Time is something you can't afford to take. This job must be completed quickly. Do you understand that?"

"I understand your urgency, yes."

"Hear this, my slippery friend." Lyme's face turns red. "If you fail to return with the package, there will be no place on Mars that you can hide, from the peaks of the highest mountain to the depths—"

"—of the deepest sea," Oryol says. "I will be more dead than dead. Understood."

Lyme makes a motion across his neck, and the vid screen goes black.

"I am assuming that you have a plan?" Riacin says.

Oryol shrugs. "The best-made plans of mice and men soon go awry. I'd rather play it by ear."

"Spare me the poetry." Riacin says. "One piece of advice: you're tempting fate by insulting General Lyme. You're digging yourself a hole."

"The only hole I care about," Oryol says, tossing a fresh fig to Riacin, "is the one to bury Alpha Dog in."

CHAPTER 18

Tengu Monastery
Noctis Labyrinthus
ANNOS MARTIS 239. 2. 13. 12:00

Ema sprints across the grounds toward the teahouse, where Ghannouj is sitting on a bench in the sunshine. Dark hair whipping behind her, anklets and bracelets ringing, she bounds over the bridge, then skids to a halt in front of the abbot.

After a quick bow, she says, "Master! A Hellbender has landed in the exercise yard. Soldiers are coming!"

"Thank you, Ema." Ghannouj looks into the bottom of his teacup. He swirls the dregs while watching intently, as if he had thrown a pair of dice and was waiting for the numbers to show. "You may return to the hives."

"But Master," she says, "the bad men have come."

He stands and draws his glimmering robes against a sudden breeze, his split-toed slippers scuffing the ground. "Go quickly, please."

She bows, hands clasped together. "Yes, Master."

Ema runs from the teahouse. Her bare feet tap-tap-tap

on the wooden deck. She kicks a pebble into the pond. The pebble plunks and sinks. Ripples spread across the surface until they reach the far shore, where they almost touch the polished boots of Riacin and the Sturmnacht escorting him.

Riacin calls out as he crosses the footbridge, "Are you the abbot of the monastery?"

"I am."

Riacin smiles and offers a bony hand as he climbs onto the wooden deck. "Good day. I am pleased to make your acquaintance."

Ghannouj puts fist and palm together but doesn't bow. "What may I do for you?"

"My associates and I would like to have a word or two with you. I'm sorry, I didn't catch your name?"

"I am Ghannouj."

"Like the pie? You look like man who enjoys his pie." His expression shows that he expects a chuckle, but he gets nothing. "Yes, well, my name is Lieutenant Riacin in the service of General Lyme, the—"

"I know who Lyme is," Ghannouj says.

"Of course you do. Who doesn't know General Lyme these days? The man has made quite a mark, hasn't he? Me, I am his humble aide-de-camp, assisting him with certain special projects. Would you care to hear about them?"

"No."

"Excellent. Then we may set aside the pleasantries and conduct our business." Riacin points to a bench. "Would it be permissible to sit?"

"Do you need my permission?"

"Just common courtesy," Riacin says. "It is your bench, after all."

"The bench belongs to itself."

"Yes, well, how *meditative* of you." Riacin wipes the bench and sits, crossing his legs. He gestures to the spot next to him. "Care to take the weight off your feet?"

"No."

"Is that tea in the pot?" Riacin asks. "The flight here was dusty, and I am quite parched. Might I have a cup?"

Ghannouj dumps the pot into the pond. "Alas, it is gone."

"So it is." Riacin stands and clicks his heels together with a hard leather snap. "Disappointing. I was about to ask if you thought the pot was half full or half empty, philosophically speaking." He picks up Ghannouj's teacup, drops it to the ground, and stomps, grinding the porcelain to dust under his sole. "Alas, I won't have the opportunity."

"Your manners are strange to me, Lieutenant."

"I doubt that, Ghannouj. You are intimately aware of how men like me go about their business, aren't you?"

The sound of screaming rises in the distance: Riacin looks to Ghannouj to gauge his reaction, but the abbot's face is a blank slate.

"Is that children I hear?" Riacin cups a hand over his ear.

"Pity. The sound of crying is disturbing, don't you think? Of course, you are used to the sounds of screams, aren't you?" He pauses for a reaction again. "You heard many, many of them when you yourself were a Regulator chief all those years ago? You were in command at the Albemarle Massacre, unless I'm mistaken."

"You are not mistaken," Ghannouj says. "You clearly have read my military record and know that I was court-martialed for the massacre and imprisoned in the Norilsk Gulag for a year."

"So many innocent people died." Riacin puts a hand to his heart, his expression pained. "Why weren't you executed? Your record didn't say."

"My record was expunged in return for my silence."

"Silence about what, if you don't mind my asking?"

"About a young officer from a high-ranking family," Ghannouj says, "who ignored advice from his counsel and ordered me to attack a group of unarmed protestors."

"Did you become a monk while in prison?" Riacin says, leaning closer. "Or did you become one to escape responsibility for your crimes?"

"You speak like a diplomat aboard a gunboat, a man who relies on another's strength to protect himself." Ghannouj folds his arms. "What do you want?"

"Simply put." Riacin's smiling facade begins to crumble. "Your cooperation."

"How might I cooperate with a man like you? What do a

few poor monks and hungry children have that you would want?"

"General Lyme's son, you obnoxiously serene blob of fat!" Riacin jumps up, arms flung wide like a kite trying to find wind. He shoves his face into the monk's. Spit flies from his thin lips. "Don't insult my intelligence!"

"The Regulator is not here," Ghannouj says. "He left the monastery months ago. He has never returned."

Riacin slaps Ghannouj across the face. "Liar!"

"Cooperation," Ghannouj says, his voice firm and measured despite the welt rising on his cheek, "means working together for mutual benefit. How is giving in to your demands cooperation?"

Riacin raises his hand, but Ghannouj blocks it and pushes the lieutenant back several feet.

"How dare you!" Riacin stabs his finger into Ghannouj's chest. "You want to lecture me on the definition of cooperation? Allow me to define it for you. Guard!"

A Sturmnacht foot soldier appears, carrying Ema thrown over his shoulder. She is bound and gagged, her face a mask of terror.

Ghannouj starts toward the soldier, then checks himself.

"Mutual benefit," Riacin says, laughing. "Give me what I want, and I won't have to kill this hellion and all of the other brats you've been collecting these past few months."

A moment later, with a rush of engines and wind, a Hellbender gunship appears. The copter turns toward the main building and fires a rocket into the canyon wall. The ground shakes from the blast.

"How is that for gunboat diplomacy?" Riacin puts a foot on the bench, then leans toward Ghannouj. "Now, I will ask you one more time—where is Jacob Stringfellow?"

For a few seconds, Ghannouj says nothing. "There is no good choice to be made here," he finally says and looks down at the broken teacup, now a mix of broken shards and sullied tea grounds. This, it seems to say, is what the future holds for you. "Come, I will see that you get what you need."

The shrine is a simple building behind a small arched gate. Outside, there is a fountain for taking a drink and a stone sink for washing feet. Before entering, Ghannouj pauses to do both. He offers a ladle of water to Riacin, who refuses it.

At the wooden steps leading into the shrine, Ghannouj bows twice and claps his hands. "To wake the gods," he says.

"Enough with the rituals. Get on with it." Riacin orders the Sturmnacht to stand guard, then Ghannouj leads Riacin into the building.

The lieutenant glances around at the relics. "Where is Jacob Stringfellow?"

"That is the question I am trying to answer."

On the altar in the middle of the temple rests a gnarled length of wood, the Staff of Rinpoche.

"The founder of the Tengu monastery," Ghannouj lifts the staff and holds it chest high with both hands, "brought the staff with him from Earth. His name was Rinpoche, and he was bönpo of bees. It is said that when he died, his consort imbued the staff with his soul so that when he was reincarnated, the staff would lead him back to this place."

"Spare me the musty legends," Riacin growls.

"It may be legend," Ghannouj says, undeterred, "but the staff does have certain properties. It is said that it allows the bearer to speak to the bees."

Riacin grabs a vase and slams it onto the floor.

"You seem," Ghannouj says, "to have a problem with pottery."

"Give me Jacob Stringfellow!"

"I said that I would give you what you need." Ghannouj spins the staff. "And I shall."

Boom!

Riacin flies backward through the door. He sails over the porch and lands on the hard ground. The guards raise their rifles, just as the end of the staff whap-whaps them in the nose and forehead.

With more speed than a man of bulk should be able to generate, Ghannouj launches himself off the porch, using the staff as a pole vault. He drops on the guards, one foot in the gut of each of them. He tosses the staff high into the air, lands six jabs apiece to their chins, then catches the staff as he somersaults and drops in front of Riacin.

Riacin struggles to his feet, holding his ribs. "You're going . . . to die for this."

"I am going to die," Ghannouj says, "but not for this, and not by your hand."

Overhead, the air rumbles with engines of the gunship, the sound so loud that Riacin has to shout over it. "Goodbye, Ghannouj! See you in Hell!"

CHAPTER 19

Southbound on Bishop's Highway
ANNOS MARTIS 239. 2. 14. 05:51

The brat-brat bursts of gunfire spray across Vienne's dream. She's running through the mines toward Durango's voice, but when she turns the corner, she's in a tent, staring into the deformed faces of the Draeu. She screams and her hands become a flurry of punches.

"Get off!" one of the Draeu says in a vaguely familiar voice. "Before you scratch Pushkin's eyes out!"

She awakens to find herself in a large tent, pinning Pushkin to his sleeping bag, hands on his throat.

"Please!" he cries. "I only checked breathing!"

While the brothers laugh, Vienne stares numbly at his face. "You're not the Draeu." She sits down on her sleeping bag. "I was dreaming?"

"*Mitte kübetki!*" Pushkin gingerly touches his neck. He checks his fingers, as if looking for blood. "One minute, girl is snoring, then next, she is all over me—and not in good way!"

Nikolai and Zhuk laugh. Yakov raises an eyebrow and opens a map on a sheath of electrostat.

"For trying to steal kiss from sleeping girl," Nikolai says, "you deserve punch in throat."

"Me?" Pushkin gets to his feet. "Pushkin does not steal kisses from girls. Girls throw kisses at him."

"Ha!" Zhuk shouts. "You should see way tongue comes out when girl is near. Like hound on trail, you are!"

Pushkin chest bumps him. "Brother, only hound is you."

"Hound?" Zhuk yells. "I show you hound." He grabs Pushkin and begins grinding his knuckles into his head. Nikolai tackles them, and they crash into a heap.

What have I gotten myself into? Vienne thinks. She pointedly ignores them while packing her gear. She squeezes the sleep from her eyes.

She unzips the tent flap to check the weather. They are camped on a butte overlooking the shore of the Saxa Sea. Below, she sees a vast forest of leafy trees, the kind of green that blinds you. Rolling hills, fertile fields wrapped in a thick gray mist. The forest ends at a craggy, stone-strewn beach next to an azure sea.

Vienne tugs a coat over her baggy gown. She steps outside to escape the wrestling match, which has taken over the tent.

Waves crash against the base of the high butte, which is occupied by a large square building with a courtyard surrounded by high walls. At the four corners are tower sentry points. She can barely make out guards carrying hunting rifles, shotguns, and even bows. Decent weapons but not very effective against vermin like the Scorpions.

"Bet you never saw anything such," Nikolai says, when he joins her. His face is covered with scratches. A thick bruise is rising on his left cheekbone. "Sea is beautiful, *jaa?*"

Yes, she thinks, looking at the bruise and wondering if he's won or lost the fight. Then she looks back at the sea. "There are many kinds of beauty," she says. "But no, I've never seen anything like this. But what now? Where do we go from here?"

"We drive," Nikolai says, "until we find caravan camp."

"How long do you think?" Vienne asks.

"As long as it takes."

"Don't take too long," Vienne says. "Because frankly, if I have to spend another night with the Brothers Koumanov, you're going to be an only child."

CHAPTER 20

Barefoot, dressed in a flowing gown spun from honey-colored silk, her blond braid trailing down her back, Vienne walks through a row of beehives. Like a ghost, she floats past the hives without a word, golden sunlight streaming from her hands. The sound of the bees rises and diminishes as she passes. She turns to me, her eyes violet in the wash of golden brightness, and her lips part for a kiss. A Hellbender opens fire on the temple behind her. Bullet holes rip through her body. Bloodstains spread across her gown. She presses a hand to her stomach and looks deep into my eyes. "Help me . . . please?"

"Vienne!"

I sit up, dazed, not sure of where I am. The stink of guanite is buried in my nostrils. I scrape a layer of dust off my tongue and spit out a clump of brown dirt. Oh yeah, I'm in the back of a long-haul truck. A truck that for some reason has stopped.

Brrpt! Brrpt! Brrpt!

Gunfire.

Then the harsh voices of men barking orders.

I snap to attention. Battle ready.

"Cowboy," Mimi says. "Sweeps show large mass bodies."

I ease to the end of the trailer. Look outside for a sitrep.

Sturmnacht. Armed to the teeth. Faces unshaven. Uniforms ragged. A scout unit gone rogue. "I count eight hostiles."

"Confirmed," Mimi says.

Could be worse, I think.

Then it gets worse.

A soldier drags the truck driver into view. Shoves her to the ground. She's crying, blood in her mouth.

"Where's the cash box?" the sergeant barks. He shoves a razor knife against the woman's throat.

"Please . . . don't," the driver pleads. "I got no cash, just guanite."

"Liar!" the sergeant yells, and backhands her.

Her head snaps back. She falls to the ground, moaning.

"*Cào na ze zang*," I say. We're not having this. I snap my sights on the sarge's forehead. My finger twitches, and I ache to put a bullet in his skull.

"He deserves worse," Mimi says.

"I'm going to give it to him."

"Save the innocent first," Mimi says.

"Clean out the cargo!" The sergeant gestures to the Sturmnacht. "She's smuggling something. I know it!"

I duck behind a hopper before three Sturmnacht privates jump aboard. As they pass, I knock the first cold with a vicious rabbit punch. I grab the second one. Slam his skull against the hopper. The third spins around for an elbow smash to the jaw.

Three down, five to go.

The sergeant is next.

From the tailgate, I draw a bead on him. Pop a round into his shoulder. He screams as his arm flops, and the knife falls to the ground.

Before anyone can react, I launch off the trailer. Land a side kick to the sarge's chest, and he goes flying.

The soldiers are too dumbstruck to stop me.

"Come on!" I grab the driver and haul her down the embankment to safety. "We're out of here!"

But as soon as I put her down, she wriggles free and starts back up. "Not without my truck!"

"What about your life?"

"That truck is my life," she says, standing her ground. "I can't leave it."

Shíb dài! "Stay here and stay down!"

I sprint up to the road.

Five Sturmnacht are waiting for me. Four and a half, if you count the fossiker holding his wound and wailing.

"Serves you right," I bark at the sarge. I take aim at the other four. "You blighters! On your knees!"

"Kill him!" the sarge yells.

I lift the borrowed shirt to show my armor. "Surrender or I'll shoot you where you stand."

"He's bluffing!" the sergeant groans.

I fire.

The shot tears off a piece of his ear.

He screams again, rolling in the dirt.

"Next one splits his skull," I yell. "On your bellies! You know the drill!"

They drop their weapons and lie on their stomachs, hands behind their backs.

"Lady!" I call down the embankment. "Come on up!"

She hustles past me and runs for the truck cab. When the door slams, and she's safe inside, I turn back to the soldiers.

"The driver's going to take her truck and go on," I say. "Then I'm going to borrow a bike. If you all stay put, I won't kill you."

"Suck it!" the sergeant yells.

I fire a three-round burst near his head.

He gets quiet.

"Move!" I bark. "Down the embankment!"

I keep my armalite trained on them as they scramble down into the dry wash. When they're out of sight, I pull the three unconscious privates from the trailer and drop them on the ground. Then I shout, "Trucker! Time for you to go!"

She sticks a hand out of the window and waves. Gears grinding, the truck pulls away, and I return the wave. I hope the rest of her trip is uneventful.

"For someone who just shot one man and injured three others," Mimi says, "you have a gift for understatement."

"I don't like bullies," I say.

When the truck is gone, I rummage through the Sturmnacht's bikes and find a few slabs of dried meat substitute and packets of dried amino gruel. Not appetizing, but digestible. After culling the best turbo bike from the herd, I put holes in the fuel tanks of the remaining bikes. Petrol pours onto the road.

"Now," I say, "if they go back to hijacking, they'll have to do it on foot."

I grab a full canteen and roll my ride uphill, away from the puddles of petrol.

"You are aware, cowboy," Mimi says, "that the sergeant will report this incident to a superior, and Dolly will quickly pass the information to the general."

"How long till Lyme knows I was here?"

"I estimate four hours, maximum."

"Plenty of time," I say.

My bike starts with a couple of kicks. As I drive past the embankment, the sergeant sticks his head from the gully. He levels a battle rifle at me.

Sergeants. What a bunch of fossickers.

I fire another shot over my shoulder. The bullet clips his good ear. His howl echoes down the canyon as I drive on. I hit the turbo, and the bike rockets down the highway.

Vienne, here I come.

CHAPTER 21

Southbound on Bishop's Highway
ANNOS MARTIS 239. 2. 14. 09:16

Three hours later than Nikolai predicted, Vienne and the Brothers Koumanov reach the area where the refugees are camped. It is a place called Sarai, an old waypoint on the highway, built during the time of the Orthocracy as a site for travelers to rest.

They leave the highway and take a sandy path to the camp. Nikolai leads them past the sentries posted outside, then signals everyone to park. Vienne stops her bike next to Nikolai and dismounts.

Three young bodyguards wearing ponchos come forward to greet the brothers. Like most refugees, they're dressed in whatever they could scavenge from the road, and they carry makeshift weapons. But they have the look of hunger on their faces, a wary look that she recognizes as more dangerous than it seems.

Vienne steps forward to meet them first, hand extended in greeting.

The bodyguards stop and raise their weapons. "Halt!"

"Have I offended you?" Vienne asks.

"Refugees are skittish," Nikolai stage whispers as he hurries to catch up to her. "Girl should wait for escort."

"I'm not one for escorts," she says, not bothering to whisper. "Unless you want me to escort you?"

"Who," the first bodyguard points to Vienne, "are you?"

Vienne reaches for the knife up her sleeve.

Nikolai grabs her shoulder and gives it a good shake. "A comrade. I vouch for her."

"Who will vouch for you, Ferro?" The second bodyguard pokes Nikolai with the barrel of his rifle. "You're late. Tahnoon the Elder doesn't like to be kept waiting."

Nikolai forces a laugh. "Then perhaps you should stop with talking and start with walking so that Elder may vet new comrade."

The bodyguards exchange a look. The first guard signals for them to follow.

"Nikolai," Vienne says, "you never said anything about this elder having to approve me."

He grins. "Perhaps it slipped mind."

"Your mind seems very slippery," she says. "I hope it's not a reflection on the rest of you."

Nikolai puts a hand on his heart, feigning injury. "You cut me to quick, *lapochka*."

"I'm going to do more than that if you keep calling me *little pigeon*."

Built to protect pilgrims in the days of the Bishops' rule, Sarai is a massive structure made from rough-hewn metamorphic rock. It was erected on a rectangular plinth that stretches out into the Saxa Sea. Its walls are equipped with movable stalls to accommodate travelers, vehicles, and their goods. After the rise of the Orthocracy and the subsequent overthrow by the CorpCom system of government, buildings like Sarai were shuttered. But because of the migration from the cities, its gates had apparently been reopened and its courtyard filled once again.

It is in this courtyard that the refugees are staging a wrestling match. A circle has been drawn in the dirt and a ring formed by a mass of men shouting and holding their bets in the air. There is no coin being passed. Instead, they are betting engine parts, dried meat, boots, and blankets.

Through the press of bodies, Vienne can barely make out the figures of two large men, both shirtless, trading punches.

"Nikolai!" Zhuk calls ahead. "Wrestling match!"

"Go without me," Nikolai says. "Stay out of trouble."

Zhuk and Pushkin cheer, then head toward the action. Yakov follows them slowly.

"Think they'll listen to you?" Vienne asks Nikolai as they cross to the other side of the courtyard, where a large tent is pitched near the wall.

"Yakov will," he says. "The other two, not so much. Ah, here is man you must meet."

Tahnoon the Elder, a man much younger than his name

suggests, stands next to a folding table under the open tent. His hands are tucked casually in the pockets of his dingy white Nehru jacket. Vienne would prefer to see a stranger's hands the first time she meets them.

Whistling, Tahnoon twists the stem from a fig. He takes a bite, wrinkles up his face, and almost spits the piece out as Nikolai barges across the courtyard ahead of Vienne.

"Koumanov!" Tahnoon shifts his attention to Vienne. "Who is this beautiful young woman? Introduce me! Have you no manners?"

Vienne is pretty sure he doesn't.

Tahnoon approaches Vienne, his arms wide. After a second of reticence, she allows the embrace but flinches when he kisses both cheeks.

"Ah, I have made you uncomfortable," Tahnoon says. "Please forgive me, young woman. I forget that our customs are so alien to others. It has been many years since a monk visited us. My name is Timoji Tahnoon, son of Atoli Tahnoon, grandson of Parchni Tahnoon. Tell me, who are you?"

She watches his hands. "I am Vienne."

"Such a beautiful name for a beautiful young woman." He lifts her hand to his lips and kisses it. "What is the remainder of your name?"

Nikolai interrupts, "Her last—"

"Just," she says curtly, and wipes the kiss from her skin, "Vienne."

"So it is. Please, do come and sit with me on the chaise for a moment so that we might converse."

Vienne shakes her head. "I'll stand."

"Very direct!" He affects a laugh and punctuates it by shaking a playful finger at her. "I like that in a person. So I hope that you will not be offended if I am equally direct in my queries to you."

"I'd prefer it," she says, and clasps her hands together, letting the long sleeves of her robe cover them. She fingers her knife, just in case.

"Indeed!" He laughs again, although she is sure that she's said nothing funny. "I imagined you would. Tell me, Vienne, how is that you have come into our presence today?"

She cocks her head. "You already know, don't you?"

"So true!" He takes a seat on the lounge, draping one leg over the other. "I had hoped to hear it from your own lips. Sometimes when others speak for us, the true meaning is lost. Would you not agree?"

"I would."

"Tell me, please, why have you graced my home with your presence?"

So this is how he's going to play it, she thinks. A string of questions to double-check what Nikolai told him. "I was hired to protect a caravan of refugees from Scorpions."

"You were hired to help with the job?"

"Not to *help*," Vienne says. "To *do* the job. The first task is to develop a plan of defense. Second, a rotation of guards. We'll be training your—"

"Oh, ambitious. I like that!" He beams at her. "Such pluck from a young lady."

Pluck? Vienne glares at him, anger radiating from her eyes. "That's"—she struggles to think of the polite thing to say—"nice."

"Yes, yes it is." He nods in a way that lets her know that she has said the opposite of the right thing to say. "My dear, you must be exhausted from the journey. Would you care to have a rest in the women's tent?"

"No thanks." She shakes her head. "I'll be fine here."

Tahnoon cuts Nikolai a look, as if to say, Do something about her.

Nikolai picks a green fig from the table. He sinks his teeth in with a loud, slurpy bite. "Fig is sour. I like sour. Reminds me of home."

"You were hired to protect my caravan. I did not ask you," Tahnoon says, "to critique the fruit." He grabs Nikolai and shakes his arm. "A monk? You left us unprotected to find more mercenaries, and you bring back a monk? I had a very specific type of soldier in mind."

Nikolai leans against the tent pole, legs crossed, arms folded, the very portrait of bravado. "Vienne is not just any monk. She is monk who was Regulator. Girl has killed many soldiers. This I have seen with own eyes."

"But she is a monk now," Tahnoon says. "Monks don't

kill. How do you know that she will fight the Scorpions?"

Nikolai takes another bite. "She promised she would."

"Then how do you know she isn't lying?"

"Monks do not tell lie."

"Of course they do!"

"Not this one."

"How do you know?"

"She told me."

"Ah!" Tahnoon rubs his forehead. "For a mercenary, you are very naive," he says. "Lying, like breathing, is a part of human nature. All monks are human, correct?"

"The girl, she is fighter." Nikolai wipes his hands on the tent flap and tosses the half-eaten fig over his shoulder. "Plus, she hates Scorpions."

"How do you know?"

"She told me," Nikolai says.

Vienne clears her throat loudly. "I am standing. Right here. If you boys are finished. Discussing my abilities and willingness to fight. Can we please commence with forming the plan of defense?"

Tahnoon dismisses her with a wave of his ringed fingers. "Yes, yes. Hush now."

Like a brittle piece of steel holding up the length of the suspension bridge over the River Gagarin when the Flood hit, Vienne snaps. She steps across the tent, grabs Tahnoon's thumb, twists it backward, and, as he squeals, uses it as a lever to throw him off-balance. She sweeps his legs and drops him onto the carpet. Then, as he's crying out, she twists his arm behind his back and digs the thumb into his spine, as if to wedge it between his vertebrae.

"How's that for hushing?" Vienne says as she drives her knee into his sacrum.

Nikolai starts clapping, but the Elder isn't amused.

"Guards!" Tahnoon yells, choking. "Arrest her!"

CHAPTER 22

Tengu Monastery
Noctis Labyrinthus
ANNOS MARTIS 239. 2. 14. 11:27

I can see the Tengu temple rising out of the mists. The last time I was here, Ghannouj sent me away so that Vienne could get better. Now, I hope that the old man doesn't kick me out again. But when I follow the long and winding path to the gate, that worry disappears, replaced by an all too familiar feeling of dread and anger.

The temple arch, once painted bright orange and decorated with calligraphy, is blackened by fire, and the heavy wooden gate that has stood strong since the first monks came to Mars, now hangs by a single broken hinge, the wood splinted and battered.

"What the *helvett* happened here?" I ask, touching the gate. The burned smell is faint. The wood is cold, and ash is pooled on the ground. It's rained at least once since this happened.

"Evidence suggests an attack," Mimi says.

"On the monks? They're harmless. Who would do such a thing?"

"Why ask when you know the answer?"

My heart sinking, I retrieve my armalite from the bike, then enter the courtyard.

"My god."

The banyan trees that shade the walk are burned to their trunks. All of the buildings—the kitchen, the bathhouse, the monks' sleeping quarters, even the shrine—are piles of cinders.

Out of habit, I do a quick visual recon to get my bearings. Meeting hall ahead. Prayer hall to the left. Kitchen and sleeping quarters to the right. Each hall connected by covered walkways. A high wall surrounding it all.

All of it burned to the ground.

Not my god.

My father.

"Hello?" I call. "Is anybody here?"

The only reply is my own echo.

"Mimi, do a wide area sweep. Any signatures?"

"Not within range."

"Ghannouj!" I yell. "Mistress! Master!"

Am I missing anything?

Or anyone?

"Cowboy," Mimi says, "they are all gone."

I don't believe that—can't believe that. For hundreds of years through terraforming, floods, storms, blight, famine, the Pox, and war after war, this monastery has withstood everything.

Dazed, I wander past the charred remains of the buildings, kicking cinders with my boots, looking for any evidence of life.

Or death, because what I really fear is finding a body. So I check every building, pushing aside collapsed roofs and beams, digging through the rubble with my hands, then with a stone paver I turn into a makeshift shovel.

My hands and arms turn black from the ash. My knees ache, and I stink of soot and creosote, my mouth full of the taste of fire.

But I find nothing but a few grains of unburned rice.

"Maybe they got away," I say, trying to knock the ash from my armor.

"Maybe they did," Mimi says.

"You're saying that to make me feel better."

"No," she says, "to make me feel better."

At the temple, I step over the stone foundation and enter the most holy of all Tengu places. It used to be filled with holy artifacts. Now? I squat, pushing the rubble aside, but I find nothing beneath it but more ash.

I'm about to stand and give up when a bee lands on my arm. It crawls toward my face, and when I flinch, it flies away.

"That was a bee," I say.

"Astute analysis, cowboy."

I close my eyes and remember my dream: Barefoot, dressed in a flowing gown spun from honey-colored silk, her blond braid trailing down her back, Vienne walks through a row of beehives. Like a ghost, she floats past the hives without a word, golden sunlight streaming from her hands. The sound of the bees rises and diminishes as she passes. Then she turns to me, her eyes violet in the wash of golden brightness, and her lips part for a kiss. Then a Hellbender opens fire on the temple behind her. Bullet holes rip through her body. Bloodstains spread across her gown. She presses a hand to her stomach and looks deep into my eyes. "Help us . . . please?"

"The bees are still here," I say. "The bees are still here!"

Hope welling up, I sprint through the exercise yard and into the hive fields.

"These bees are playing havoc with your telemetry functions," Mimi says. "I am having difficulty separating their signatures."

"The bees always did mess things up, right?"

"Not so much as this. My sweeps are wildly inconsistent. You should leave the area. Bees can be dangerous."

So can I. "Ghannouj!" I yell. "Where are you? Hello! Is anyone here?"

There's no reply.

I walk down a row of beehives, which are swimming with activity even though a third of the rows have been destroyed. The bees, however, get agitated at my presence, their buzz increasing, then dimming as I pass.

"Ouch!" I slap my cheek and pull away a crippled bee.

"Did you kill it?" someone asks—a girl's voice, nearby.

I scan the rows.

No one's there.

I inspect the bee. Its wings are bent but intact, and no legs are broken. "No. Just stunned it. Lucky bee."

"No," the girl says. "Lucky you."

"Ow!" A rock pings off my forehead. I yell, "There's no reason to assault me! I'm here to—ow!—help."

A small girl dressed in a white *gi* rises from behind a row of hives. She's dressed like an acolyte, but I don't recognize her.

"She doesn't recognize you, either," Mimi says.

"Master Ghannouj says all who come in peace are welcome at the monastery." She twirls a sling and fires another rock at me. "Except for vipers. Those we chop in half!"

I snatch the stone out of the air and drop it on the ground. "Look, I'm trying to help you. Where are the monks?"

I hear another child cry out, followed by more screams. I turn to see a dozen—

"Seventeen," Mimi says.

—children converging on me. They are brandishing practice swords and sharpened sticks.

I hold up my hands to fend them off. "Wait, wait, wait!"

"Get him!" the sling girl yells.

They attack anyway, striking every part of my body, whacking my knees and ankles, a pinpoint blitz meant to knock me down.

"I'm not Sturmnacht!" I say, letting my armor block their strikes. "I'm here to help, you little idiots!"

"Sturmnacht would say that!" the girl yells.

"No! I'm really here to help!"

"Sturmnacht say that, too!"

A sharp stick hits my face. I grab it and break it over my knee. "No hitting the face!"

"What is your plan of defense?" Mimi asks.

"There is no plan! They're children. I'll just block them until they get tired."

"Good luck with that," Mimi says.

"Where is your master?" I repeat. "Where are the monks? Where is Vienne?"

"Stop!" the sling girl snaps.

The children stop hitting me and turn to her, waiting for orders.

"Sifu Vienne is gone," the girl says.

"Gone where?"

"She took a job to buy food," she says. "Then the Sturmnacht came."

"But why did the Sturmnacht come?" I ask.

"Because," Master Yadokai says, rising from behind a hive, "they were searching for you."

CHAPTER 23

Sarai
ANNOS MARTIS 239. 2. 14. 10:10

"Guards!" Tahnoon yells. "Arrest her!"

Vienne hooks Tahnoon's nostrils and hauls him to his feet as his bodyguards race into the tent. Nikolai ducks and steps outside.

"Catch!" She shoves Tahnoon toward the guards, turns, and kicks the center tent pole loose. She dive-rolls outside as the heavy canvas fabric billows down, trapping Tahnoon and his bodyguards.

"Kill her!" Tahnoon's muffled voice comes from the tent. "Help!"

"Help yourself," Vienne says.

"Bravo!" Nikolai starts clapping. "Is called bringing down house, *jaa?*"

"What, may I ask," a woman with a husky voice asks, "is going on here?"

Nikolai stops laughing. He snaps to attention, and Vienne whirls to see an older woman walking toward them. She is wearing camo pants, a black tee, and a camo jacket. Her hair is cropped at chin level, and she's packing four different sidearms—one on each thigh, one on her right hip, and one under her left arm.

"Mother Koumanov!" Nikolai says. "Come meet new mercenary!"

"Nikolai?" "Mother asks. "What has happened?" She points at the tent and the wriggling masses beneath it, then nods at Vienne. "Your work?"

For a few seconds, they seem frozen in time and space, eyes locked but still somehow taking the whole of the other in.

Then Vienne bows. "May peace be with you."

With a sly step to the side, Mother bows. "May peace be with you, as well." She gestures to the tent again. "Well done, but not the best way to start a job. Nikolai, help them."

A few minutes later, Tahnoon and his bodyguards are sprung. The Elder emerges, his oiled hair askew. "I want her head!" he screams.

Vienne beckons him forward. "Come and get it."

Tahnoon turns to his bodyguards. "Cowards! She is just one woman!"

"You don't pay enough," the tallest says, "to fight that susie."

Tahnoon throws his hands in the air. "Now you see why I must hire mercenaries! Such cowards these men are! Where is Mother Koumanov? I will speak to her about this."

"Right here, Tahnoon," Mother says, her voice less husky. "It is a blessing to see you once more. Please forgive my absence. It was a necessary thing."

But Tahnoon is not so easily placated. "I demand restitution for this affront! This young woman is a menace!"

"Which is unfortunate for the Scorpions." Mother kisses his cheeks. "She seems to be quite the fighter."

"But she is fighting her employer!"

"From where I was standing," she says, "it looked as if she was lucky to defeat such a great man as yourself."

Tahnoon laughs. "You damn me with faint praise, Mother Koumanov."

"My praise, when offered, is never faint. And please, don't call me Mother. Do I really look old enough to have birthed those young men? Be careful how you answer that."

Tahnoon laughs again. "Come, let us watch the wrestling match and discuss the terms of our bargain."

"Wrestling!" Mother Koumanov joins him but gives Vienne a backward glance that says, "We're not through here."

"Don't worry about fight with Tahnoon," Nikolai says as he and Vienne take a place in the crowd to watch the match. "Now, there is no doubt you are good fighter."

"Right," Vienne says. But it's not the fight—it's the fact that when she and Durango took on jobs, they shared the decisions, and she usually set up the defensive plans. Here, no one is interested in anything. "Do you think they have anything to eat?"

"*Jaa*," he says. "Is always food at wrestling match. Come with me."

But before they have a chance to make their way to a line of food mongers, Mother Koumanov appears in the crowd ahead.

"Might I have a moment with you, young monk?" Mother Koumanov calls above the noise.

What now? Vienne thinks, and starts in that direction.

As she weaves her way around the spectators, there's a huge roar from the wrestling pit. She looks back to see a fighter throw his beefy arms in the air, then beat his chest in victory. The crowd cheers even louder.

"You're a Regulator, I take it?" Mother asks when Vienne reaches her.

"How—"

"Did I know? In my profession, observation is the most important skill. When you spoke to Tahnoon, you instinctively shielded yourself. There is also of the matter of the bandaged stub of a left pinkie. If I didn't know better, I would take you for a spy, but the ribbons in your hair would prove me wrong." She touches one, and Vienne flinches. "Ribbons of contrition. A vestige of a culture lost during the ethnic cleansing of a misguided generation. I'm glad to see that the custom has survived."

Vienne pulls away. "What do you want?"

"A soldier's directness." Mother clucks her tongue. "Another tip-off that you're not the person you seem."

" The brothers call you Mother, but you just admitted to Tahnoon that you're not their mother."

"Touché," Mother says. "A woman of few words. I like that. There is so much dancing about in diplomacy; it is refreshing when one encounters someone who cuts right to the chase."

"Then why don't you?" She blows a black ribbon out of her face. "Tell me what you want."

"Let me put it to you bluntly," Mother says. "Tahnoon is a dangerous man. As long as he believes you can help him, you are safe. Once the caravan is in New Eden, however, your life will be as worthless as the dust under your boots."

"I like the dust." Vienne lifts her boot. "And I can take care of myself."

"I hope so," Mother says, "because if you can't, no one else will."

A cheer arises from the wrestling ring. There's a loud clang, followed by silence.

"Nikolai said there would be seven mercenaries on this trip," Vienne says. "You, me, and the four brothers, that makes six. Where's the seventh?"

"The seventh is—"

Her voice is drowned out by a chorus of loud boos. A chunky young man, naked to the waist and marked with cuts and bruises, blunders out of the ring. He holds a spittoon over his head. On the side of it, there is a dent about the size and depth of a man's skull. "A fight ain't over till I say it's over!"

"There," Mother says, "is our seventh."

As the crowd jeers, the man shakes the spittoon like a hard-won trophy. "That'll teach you poxers to mess with the likes of Leroy Jenkins!"

Vienne bows her head. Not him, she thinks. Anyone but him.

CHAPTER 24

Tengu Monastery
Noctis Labyrinthus
ANNOS MARTIS 239. 2. 14. 12:51

Yadokai's words, "They were looking for you," are still ringing in my head as he leads me out of the monastery through the pagoda forest to a path that a mountain goat couldn't walk. It winds around the mountainside until it reaches the caves in the side of the canyon.

"This way," Yadokai says. He ducks into a tunnel in the canyon wall. "Watch your head."

I follow him into the dark tunnel. For a hundred meters, we crawl on hands and knees until a light appears ahead.

"Almost there," Yadokai says.

"Mimi," I ask. "Any biosignatures ahead?"

"Two," she says.

"Familiar?"

"Very," she says.

"Who?"

"Guess."

The tunnel ends at the mouth of the cave, which is about

thirty meters long and two meters wide. There's a make-shift curtain cordoning off the north section. A few candles provide the dim light, and the air is full of the smell of udon noodles and something else that makes my stomach turn.

"It is me," Yadokai says as he stands and knocks the dust from his knees.

"I know." Mistress Shoei says, as she steps into the candlelight to greet us. "You have come," she says, bowing. "Ghannouj said you would."

"So he has come," Yadokai says. "He is too late."

"Mistress," I say while trying to avoid the stink-eye the master is giving me. "What happened here?"

"You should know," Yadokai says. "The fault is yours."

"I—"

"Ignore that bag of bones." Shoei leads me to the far end of the cave. She stops next to the curtain. "Ask Ghannouj your questions."

She draws the curtain aside and pushes me ahead. Ghannouj lies on a rice mat. His ribs are wrapped tight in a compression bandage. There is a wound on his forehead, and his arm is in a sling. His wounds have the foul smell of infection. I look closely at the sling and can see something wiggling underneath it. Maggots. They're used to clean out gangrene.

I sit cross-legged next to him. "Mimi? How's he doing?"

She doesn't answer.

"Mimi?"

"Vitals are weak, cowboy."

"Which means?"

She doesn't answer.

"Mimi!"

"You know damn well what it means, cowboy," she says.

"Yeah," I say. "Yeah, I do."

As Ghannouj sleeps, I can see the lines in his face and the spots that dot his scalp. He is older than I thought, and his nose is much larger than I remember.

"My grandmother used to say it was a Roman nose," Ghannouj says. "I am confident that she never met a Roman."

I start. "You're awake?"

"Sleeping is a chore." His voice is deep but strained. "I am glad to see you, Regulator."

"How can you see me? Your eyes are closed."

"You of all people should know that I do not need eyes to see you."

Ghannouj once taught me to use my other senses to see in order to overcome fear. "That seems like it happened a really long time ago."

"Many things have happened since you left."

"Since you sent me away."

"It is good that you make the distinction," he says, straining from the effort. "Vienne struggled with it. You have come for her?"

"I came to see her, yes."

He pushes back the bandages from his face.

"What is it?" I ask.

"I am looking to see if you are lying to yourself or just to me. I am glad to see that it is only me." He laughs, then grabs his ribs. " There is a sense of urgency about you."

"I have a job to do." Though I hadn't intended to, I tell him everything about the HVT, my father, and MUSE.

"Ah," he says. "That is what the Sturmnacht were seeking."

"Master Yadokai said that the Sturmnacht came looking for me." My voice cracks. "I'm responsible for what happened to the monastery. And to you."

Ghannouj shakes his head. "This HVT, do you have it with you?"

I pull the case out of my bag and hold it up. The green light blinks.

"What do you intend to do with it?" he asks.

I run my fingers over the locks. "I don't know yet. The first step is to find out what's inside. If I can."

"Do you think that you will succeed?" he whispers. "Or fail?"

"Ghannouj," I say, shaking my head, "I've failed so spectacularly in so many ways, even a kick-butt supersoldier like me has to consider it a possibility."

"Time's up!" Shoei pulls open the curtain and snags me by the ear. "Ghannouj needs his rest."

"Regulator, do your duty." Ghannouj pats my hand. "But

when you find Vienne, tell her what you have told me. So that she will understand."

"Understand what?" I ask.

"That you love her."

I stand. "I thought she'd know that by now."

Ghannouj looks at me with fading eyes. "Do any of us really know we are loved?"

CHAPTER 25

Southbound on Bishop's Highway
Noctis Labyrinthus
ANNOS MARTIS 239. 2. 15. 06:28

Standing atop a Noriker with a large red flag, Tahnoon the Elder gives the signal for the caravan to roll out. At the rear, half a click away, Vienne returns the signal. Then, with a revving of engines and the squealing of brakes that are more rotor than pad, the caravan begins to move slowly, vehicle by vehicle, on the highway that will take it to New Eden.

Vienne rides up to the front. The defensive plan is simple: Zhuk and Pushkin in the back of the caravan manning a fortified Noriker with a minigun, Mother Koumanov in the Noriker up front to guard the petrol tankers, leaving her, Jenkins, Nikolai, and Yakov to patrol the line as it moves. It's not the plan Vienne would've put into play, but maybe it will work.

Maybe. Miracles do happen.

"Some mess of an operation, huh?" Jenkins calls to Vienne as he pulls up beside her in an oversized motorbike, a familiar-looking design that reminds her of a turbo sled.

"Did Fuse make that for you?" Vienne shouts over the grind of his engine.

"Don't mention that name to me." Jenkins spits into the wind. "That rotter's went and got himself domesticated!"

Domesticated? "You mean, married?" Who in their right mind would marry Fuse? She couldn't imagine spending a week with the annoying, rat-faced pest, much less a lifetime.

"Right that," he hollers. "Married off to that bossy girl Áine. It ruint everything when she started getting fat!"

"What do you mean, fat?" The miners of Hell's Cross barely had enough food to keep from starving. There's no way any of them could get fat.

"I got nothing else to say on the subject! Ain't like me to go chewing another man's cabbage!"

"What?" she yells. "That makes no sense!"

But without another word, Jenkins peels off to patrol the line.

"No wonder you and Fuse split up," she says, even though he's out of earshot.

Vienne pulls over as the caravan moves on. She watches every vehicle that passes, trying to commit each one to memory, matching the faces of the riders with the make and model of their rides. Problem is most of the vehicles are mud colored, and the people, dressed in whatever they could hang on to, all have the same godforsaken look.

"What does girl see?" Nikolai pulls up beside her. His

Gorgon idles, the precision engine a purr lost in the hurly-burly of the caravan.

"People," she says. "Lost souls."

"Girl sees with heart, not brains." Nikolai shakes his head. "Think of refugees only as cattle. Cattle we drive to New Eden. If you think of refugees' pain, such pain becomes yours, and focus is lost. That is when Scorpions attack, *jaa*?"

"You've fought Scorpions before?" she asks.

"Many times," he says. "Even before Flood. Then they worked for Lyme and only killed when he let them. Now, Scorpions are animals, starving animals preying on rest of us. You are fighting them before?"

"Some." She thinks of the many times she and Durango faced them while hiding out in the slums of Favela. "But not as much since the Flood."

"*Jaa.*" Nikolai circles her. "Flood changed everything. Even for Lyme. Before, he made rules. Now, rules are kaput. Only strong survive, eh? The big eat small."

"That's where you're wrong." She revs her engine. "It's not that the big eat the small; it's that the fast eat the slow." She points out the stop-and-go line of refugees. "And these people are the slow."

"No problem. We make faster."

Over the next several hours, the caravan snakes its way through the southern canyons of Valles Marineris. Then it climbs onto the Tharsis Plain, which covers a third of the northern hemisphere. The horizon is dominated by the sun to the east and to the west by Olympus Mons, which, even over a thousand kilometers away, reaches into the sky.

Covered in road dust, stomach complaining about her skipped breakfast and lunch, and bored out of her mind, Vienne patrols the line.

"Is Pushkin's turn to hold gun!" Pushkin yells at Zhuk as Vienne and Nikolai lead a small truck carrying seven children and two women to the space in front of them.

"*Nyet!*" Zhuk says.

"When is Pushkin's turn?"

"*Nyet!*" Zhuk yells.

"Stop saying '*nyet*'!"

"*Nyet!*" Zhuk yells.

"Why does Zhuk do that?" Vienne asks Nikolai as he scoops up the last child and deposits him into the truck bed. "And I thought you said to treat the people like cattle."

"Was baby calf!" They jog back to their bikes. "Zhuk cannot hear Pushkin. So says '*nyet*' to everything."

"Zhuk is deaf?"

Nikolai waggles his hand as if to say "so-so." "In quiet room is okay. In field, not so much."

"That's good to know," she says as they resume patrolling the line. "In case I ever have to communicate with him or, gods forbid, tell him to duck."

"No worries," Nikolai says. "Zhuk has good nose for trouble."

"But it's his ears I'm worried about."

For a while, until dusk, the caravan marches on. Each successive hour brings a subtle but steady shift in terrain, from the flat plains to the hills formed by hundreds of decaying craters, and then finally to a straight pass through the southern highlands that continues to the outskirts of New Eden.

An hour into the pass, the skin on the back of Vienne's neck begins to crawl. She circles slowly, scanning the perimeter. The hills are divided by low stone fences, scrub trees, and underbrush, all perfect places for a scout to take cover. But she spots no one, even though instinct tells her that someone is there, watching.

"We are being followed," Vienne tells Nikolai when she catches up with him.

"How do you know this?"

"I can feel it," she says.

"Nikolai has soldier's gut, too, remember?" He pats his belly. "And I feel nothing. But if makes you happy, I tell brothers to watch for followers."

"Don't patronize me, Nikolai," she growls. "You brought me along to help. This is how I help."

"Nikolai brought girl along for shooting," he says. "Not for jumping at shadows."

"Be careful, Koumanov," Vienne says. "You never know what might be hiding in the shadows."

CHAPTER 26

The Barrens
Noctis Labyrinthus
ANNOS MARTIS 239. 2. 15. 07:39

There were a lot of female cadets at Battle School, but none of them made the males go bonkers like Rosa Lynn Malinche. She was three years ahead of me, the top of her class, and leader of First Company. Her expertise was technology, the kind of stuff that made your eyes cross just looking at the schematics. She spoke computer code like I spoke languages—easily and without effort—and while still a cadet, she invented what became the multinets. She was surefire to make officer right out of school.

Then a couple of months before graduation, she and I were training for routine tube jumps from space elevators. Other than the obvious problem of being a kilometer above the surface in a tube meant for cargo, a jump would be easy for Rosa Lynn—she'd just fall and let her symbiarmor take the force of impact. Problem was when her time came, something happened, and her armor malfunctioned. Not an egregious malfunction that killed her, but a microscopic one that didn't dissipate the energy correctly. I jumped after her and managed to break her fall, but the impact nearly killed her, and the bones in her legs were shattered below the knee.

She graduated in absentia and refused to accept a commission when she got out of hospital. She found work as a programmer, then as a design engineer. After serving as director of the project that brought all of the various telecom protocols into one central system connected via the multinet, she dropped out of sight.

Out of sight being an old bunker in the middle of the Barrens where she could work in peace without the meddling of corporate bureaucrats. "I want to do work with real significance," she told me the day she resigned from my father's company, which was a couple of months before my unit was attacked by Big Daddies. "If you ever find yourself in the wilderness, look me up." So I'm looking her up, because despite wanting to find Vienne more than I want to save Mars, Rosa Lynn is the best chance I have of opening the case.

I leave the Founder's Highway and take an eastbound side road that leads to a dirt path that narrows to a dry gully. When the gully ends at an expanse of rocky terrain marked with only scrub and prairie grass, I know I'm close.

Ahead are the Cliffs of Moher, a forbidding sheer wall of granite with a narrow pass that I follow for a couple of hours. On the other side of the cliffs is a stretch of terrain that looks like the lava flow of a volcano. It's called the Barrens, a landscape like an ocean of smooth rock, and it runs on for many kilometers, with only pockets of wildflowers, grass, and mosses growing between the cracks.

"'All the days he would sit upon the rocks,'" Mimi says, "'breaking his heart in tears and lamentation and sorrow as weeping tears he looked out over the barren water.'"

"More *Odyssey*?" I ask.

"Affirmative."

"Could you not think of another poem? There must be at least two or three more in your data banks."

"I *chose* this one," Mimi says.

"Can't you *choose* another one?"

"Negative. It is the most apropos."

When I reach the Barrens, I come to the end of the road. I hide the bike and head out on foot.

"How do you know where to look?" Mimi says.

"I have a feeling, an urge," I say. "Call it intuition."

"I doubt that," she says. "Intuition is simply the subliminal accumulation and processing of data through a filter of experience."

"Right—a hunch. That and she told me I could find her in the wilderness."

"How do you know she meant the Barrens when she said wilderness?"

"Also a hunch."

"You are willing to risk everything for a hunch?" Mimi

says. "May I remind you that Lyme may well be right on your tail?"

"Go ahead."

"Lyme may well be right on your tail."

"Lyme has been on my tail since I was born," I say. "You know what I should have done, Mimi? Back when Vienne and I were at the monastery the first time and I was hell-bent on finding out about MUSE, I should've just said, cark it all. I should have told her how much I loved her and asked her whether she loved me or not."

"You are more dense than pig iron, cowboy." Mimi says. "Why do you think she stayed? Why do you think that she lopped off her finger?"

"Because of the Tenets," I say. "Because of her sense of duty."

"Yet she stayed with someone who neither ascribed to the Tenets nor had the same idea of duty," Mimi says. "You are a smart boy, but sometimes, I just want to shake you."

"You can't shake me. You've got no hands."

"I can shake you from the inside out, so do not tempt me."

"Instead of lecturing me, how about running a sweep for any form of electronic device?"

"Done. I detect no form of—that's odd," she says. "I detect nothing at all."

"How about interference?"

"None," she says. "The Barrens are one of the few highly

magnetized areas on Mars. They naturally interfere with electronics, so I expected that."

"And if you're a hermit who wants to be left alone but still wants to monitor the comings and goings of the big wide world, you—"

"Neutralize that interference," Mimi says. "So it was a rational theory, not a hunch. I am impressed with you, cowboy. Clearly, my deductive process has positively affected your reasoning skills. Still, how can you determine her precise location? The Barrens cover over a hundred square kilometers."

"Right," I say. "But how many of them are marked with *that?*"

In the middle of the Barrens, maybe a kilometer away, I point at a tattered flag flying above a rock pile cenotaph. On the flag is the profile of a skull with wings, the insignia of First Company at Battle School.

"If that's not a sign," I say, "I don't know what is."

"There is no possible way that you could know that flag was there," she says.

"Ha! Just admit I've got righteous locational skills."

"Hardly. Like the proverbial blind squirrel, you got lucky."

I pick out a path to the flag. "You know what's really bugging you? That I was right. And not only that, you couldn't read my musings well enough to guess what I had in mind."

"I do not guess," she says. "I gather data and extrapolate based on said data."

Then an idea occurs to me—if I can keep secrets from Mimi, does that mean she can keep secrets from me?

"If I can," she says, "you will never know."

That's a scary thought.

"Here is another thought," she says. "What kind of greeting do you expect from this Rosa Lynn person?"

"Hadn't given it much consideration."

"You are planning to drop in on a recluse with advanced training and technological expertise, and you have not given it much consideration?"

"Nope. Rosa Lynn was a massive extrovert. She always liked company."

"You do not think living alone in the Barrens may have changed her?"

"People don't change that much, Mimi."

"With every atrocity and war crime you have witnessed, you still believe that?"

"That's me, the eternal optimist," I say. "It's how I roll."

"Be careful cowboy, or someone is going to roll *you*."

"That's not to say that Rosa Lynn doesn't like her toys, so keep your eyes peeled."

"I infer that you mean there will be some sort of advanced security system," Mimi says.

"Yes, one with lasers and plasma darts and trapdoors, stuff you could only dream of."

"I can dream of many things, cowb— Alert!" Mimi says. "My sensors are picking up a powerful energy surge!"

A trapdoor opens, and a large mechanical arm rises from it. At the end of the arm is a loaded minigun.

"You know," I say, "a security system sort of like that."

A vid screen pops up on the arm and a highly digitized voice barks at me, "Surrender! Or I'll blow your bleeding head off!"

CHAPTER 27

The Barrens
Noctis Labyrinthus
ANNOS MARTIS 239. 2. 15. 08:14

So Rosa Lynn has a robotic security guard. I'm impressed, even though the thing could saw me in half if I weren't wearing symbiarmor. Maybe Rosa Lynn isn't as welcoming as I thought.

"I told you so," Mimi says. "People do change."

"Can you gloat later, like when a minigun isn't aimed at me? How about some of that advice you usually spout?"

"You have a choice," Mimi says. "You may surrender or you may try to disarm the gun before it expends enough ammunition to overwhelm the capacity of your suit."

"I'm feeling pretty spry," I say. "I can take out one deadly robot."

On cue, five more trapdoors open, and five more mechanical arms take aim.

"Oh, cowboy?" Mimi says.

"Don't even bother to tell me the odds. I don't hanker to tangle with a whole crew of robots." I lift my arms. "I surrender. You win, Rosa Lynn."

A freckled face appears on the screen. "Ha! Got you, you poxer! Come on in, but wipe your feet first!"

"How's that for a greeting?" I ask as a pneumatic hatch opens. "You should've gloated when you had the chance."

"There will be plenty of other chances," Mimi says.

The interior of Rosa Lynn's bunker looks like the orbital space station where we went to Battle School. The hallways are low corridors lit with white light, the floors are tiled, and the walls are lined with brushed metal, probably aluminum.

"No," Mimi says. "It is an alloy that shields electronic communications."

"Spiffy." I run my hand down the metal wall. It feels warm.

"Metal is a conductor," she says. "It is not always cool to the touch."

"Knew that," I say.

Not only are the walls warm, but the light is diffused and soothing. The air's temperature feels perfect, and it's tinged with the scent of citrus. I could curl up here and sleep for days.

"'But quits his house, his country, and his friends,'" Mimi recites. "'The three we sent, from off the enchanting ground, we dragg'd reluctant, and by force we bound.'"

"Why are you reciting *The Odyssey* again?"

"No reason," she says. "Just a reminder not to get too comfortable."

"Not a chance." I reach the security door. "There's only one thing on my mind—finding out what the HVT really is."

A robotic scanner arm pops out of the wall. It reads my retina and beeps, then announces in a voice that sounds eerily like Dolly's synthesized speech, "Identity not found. Access denied."

"Denied?" I say. "Did Lyme wipe my records or something?"

"Try the other eye," Mimi says.

"Oh. Yeah." I turn my left eye, the nonbionic one, to the robot.

The voice says, "Identity confirmed. Access allowed. Welcome to the club, Mr. Stringfellow."

The security door slides open. I walk into a cavernous room. Stretching from floor to ceiling is a thick stalk of multinet monitors and cables like jungle vines as thick as my legs woven through them and trailing into the floor. I shield my eyes from the blinding light of dozens of flickering monitors, which must be displaying every channel on every feed that Lyme's government and military broadcast.

"Not just Lyme's feeds," Mimi says. "I calculate that this facility is drawing from every civilian and military channel available on the planet."

A track encircles the stalk, and mounted to it is a custom-made chair that's part cradle and part workstation. Sitting in the chair and bathed in the monitors' light is a diminutive redhead wearing an old Battle School flight suit. Dwarfed by the electronics, she looks unkempt and fragile—until she stands and her height reaches almost two and a half meters. Her legs account for most of that height. They are made of metal, not flesh, and they look suspiciously like the robotic security guns.

"Jake!" Rosa Lynn says. "Welcome to my little fortress of solitude!"

"Also?" I say to Mimi. "She's still an extrovert."

"Do not be so quick to judge."

"I'm flattered," Rosa Lynn continues, crossing her legs with a metallic clink, "that the most popular jack on Mars decided to visit little ol' me."

"Popular?" I say, scratching my neck and taking in the layout of the ten-by-fifteen room. "What are you talking about?"

"This!" Rosa Lynn types in a code on a keypad, and the stalk monitors switch to the same feed. A talking head in the corner of the screen, along with a photo of me in dress blues. Behind that, a vid of me attacking the transport truck plays. I'm amazed at the speed of the attack, and the viciousness of it, too. My stomach churns as I watch myself pull the driver out of the cab and drag him along the pavement.

"That was Alpha Dog," Mimi says. "Not you. Remember that."

"Easy to say," I say. "But think about how easily Lyme turned me into that."

Rosa Lynn taps the monitor with a knuckle. "The back channels are rocking with bulletins about you, hombre. I've seen your image pop up in dozens of communiqués. You must've done something to tick Lyme off bad, so I thought you might need a place to hide out. Voila, here you are. It's an easy deduction for the susie who practically invented the multinets. Wait, I *did* invent the multinets."

"Cowboy," Mimi says. "I can detect no biorhythmic signs of deception, and yet her welcome seems too . . . welcoming."

"Hang on a sec," I tell her as Lyme's face appears on the screen. He is standing behind a lectern, giving a speech to a mess hall full of Sturmnacht regulars. Alpha Team is behind him, with Sarge taking my place as leader. Good for him and good riddance to Alpha Team.

"That's enough truth for one day." Rosa Lynn hits a keypad on the arm of her chair, and the stalk goes dark. "I'm starting to get a headache."

"Truth?" I say. "That was all propaganda."

"Cowboy," Mimi says. "Does she not seem overeager to you?"

"She's just lonely," I tell her. "Why can't you take her at face value?"

"You are such a *male*," Mimi says.

"Propaganda, yes," Rosa Lynn says, stretching, "but if you stare at the feeds long enough, you start to see the subliminals that they can't hide." She claps her hands together.

"Look at me running on at the mouth. What a rotten host I am. You look wrung out. Need some grub? A nap? Access to the best programming Mars has to offer?"

"Actually," I say, "I need access to someone brilliant, inquisitive, and with a certain disregard for the law."

Rosa grins and throws her arms wide. "Then you came to the right place. What do you think of my lair?"

"I think you're very tall." I look up at her. "And I think that soon, I'm going to get a crick in my neck."

She lifts a robotic leg and pats the brushed metal. "You like? They're my own design. Carbon fiber and titanium alloy exoskeletal prosthetics that take signals from a chip in my brain stem." She flips the red curls from her neck to show me a bare patch on the back of her head. "It's nothing so fancy as the nanobot technology in your system, but it beats rolling around in a wheelchair all day, getting my butt chapped."

"Fancy," I say, because what do you tell a two-and-half-meter-tall woman with metal legs, while avoiding the subject of chapped butts?

"Please discuss chapped butts," Mimi says. "I dare you."

"Not on your life," I say.

"You think that's fancy?" Rosa says. "Watch this!" With a release of air, the legs lower themselves until she stands eye to eye with me. "Pneumatic pistons! Lets me adjust my height up to two meters."

"Impressive."

"Enough with the chitchat," she says. "Why do you need someone brilliant?"

"Right." I slip the case from my shoulder and offer it up to Rosa Lynn. "I brought you something."

"For *moi?*" She takes the case. "What is it?"

"A surprise."

"I love surprises." She inspects the case closely. Then hands it back. "In my educated opinion, it's an attaché case."

"I know it's a case," I say. "But what's *inside* the case?"

"Your lunch?" She smirks. "If this is a game of twenty questions, you're not very good at it."

"Seriously, Rosa." I push it back at her. "It's important. That's why I came here, you know, after all these years."

"*Kuso,*" she says, and looks me straight in the eye. "I thought it was to visit me, you know, after all these years. Give it here, you wanker, and follow me to the lab."

She leads me down the corridor to the next room. It's a twenty-by-twenty-square space lined with the same metal skin. The walls are lined with worktables piled high with circuit boards, soldering rigs, hand tools, a press, and a laser saw. I nod, impressed by the layout. With a lab like this, she could manufacture her own battle tank.

While I grab a chair, she takes a seat at a table. After putting the case on a mat to hold it still, she swings a hi-def camera around. It magnifies the three locks.

Rosa Lynn gives me a withering look. "You tried to pick these?"

"Maybe." I shrug. "So I was curious."

"Curiosity kills the cat." She wags a finger at me. "Luckily, you're not a cat."

"Why lucky for me?" I peer over her shoulder. "I screwed something up?"

"That would be an affirmative," she says. "These are Nobel locks, a specialty of the intelligence service of Mahindra Corporation. Each of the pins is connected to a small detonation device. Use the wrong key or pick the wrong tumbler and boom! Say *arrivederci* to your hand all the way up to the shoulder."

I hold up a symbiarmor glove. "Not me."

"Right." Her voice turns frosty. "Don't tell me about the wonders of symbiarmor, okay?"

Oops. I stepped in it again. I glance at her titanium legs and feel like crawling into a hole.

"I'm sorry about that, Rosa."

"No sweat. Ancient history, and you did save my life and all." She waves me off. "You're right—that fancy underwear would protect you from the first ba-ba-doom, but I suspect that the next one would really rock your socks."

"Next one?"

"Yup." She picks the case up and rolls her chair around to a portable imaging device. She puts the case under the scanner, drops the safety screen, and points to the results on the monitor. "This here is your standard issue plasma/termite bomb. Fairly stable. Requires an explosion as an ignition source. Thus, the lock bombs. So if you had succeeded in picking it, the whole case would've exploded, and then the thermite would have evaporated whatever's inside."

I clear my throat. "What did you say about an interior case?"

She swings a monitor to me. "Forget that. It's the cylinder inside the case that is the real prize. That's your maguffin, Jake."

"Can you tell what is inside?"

"Not without opening it."

"*Can* you open it?"

"Not without blowing us to smithereens. Weren't you listening?" She switches off the machine, then whirls, arms crossed. "Now it's your turn."

"My turn?" I say, confused. "For what?"

"Tit for tat." She leans forward. "I let you waltz right into my fortress with your highly explosive mystery case. Now, I want to know how you got it."

"I stole it."

"Natch," she says. "I didn't think you *made* it. You had a gift for languages in Battle School, but you were a complete piker with munitions. Who'd you steal it from?"

I clear my throat. "First, I stole it from General Mahindra *for* Lyme. And then, I stole it *from* Lyme. He thinks whatever's in that case can win the war."

"Greedy rotter," Rosa Lynn says. "Stealing the AI from your brain and porting it into his multinet isn't enough of an advantage? How many toys does one tyrant need?"

How is that possible? Project MUSE is the most top-secret project in Lyme's government. "You—you *know* about that?" I ask.

"Hello?" Rosa Lynn raps my head. "Inventor of the mul-tinets. Think I wouldn't leave a backdoor to keep an eye on things?"

"What," Mimi says, "does she mean by 'keep an eye on things'?"

I don't know, so I ask, "What do you mean by that? You're telling me that you know everything that happens?"

"Not everything! I didn't know about the case, for example," she says. "But I was aware you've been through an, ahem, rough patch. You're looking a lot better than I thought you would."

"You were expecting me?" I ask, not masking my surprise.

"As if," Mimi says, "you are ever able to mask your surprise."

"Oh yeah," Rosa Lynn says. "You've been in the wilderness a long time, Jake. I'm surprised you didn't come sooner."

"I was sort of busy."

"Oh yeah, you were real busy," she says. "Whatever happened to that susie from Battle School you used to snog? Eceni, wasn't it?"

Meaning Eceni, the murderous queen of the Draeu who tried to kill both me and Vienne. "You know how it is," I say. "People grow apart."

"Anybody else take her place?" she says with a coy edge to her voice.

"Yeah," I say, uncomfortable with the way this conversation is going. "But we got separated. A while ago."

"Uh-huh," she says, and pauses, searching my face. "Like I said, ancient history. Let's find out what's in that cylinder."

"But you said you couldn't tell what's inside."

"I said I couldn't *see*. Knowing and seeing are different stories." She pushes herself across the floor to another workstation. "Say, Jake. This is going to take a while. There's a galley and a bunk room down the hall past my lab. Get some grub and forty winks of shut-eye, and when you wake up, I'll have a big surprise."

CHAPTER 28

The Hive
Olympus Mons
ANNOS MARTIS 239. 2. 16. 04:13

Lyme stands in the Nursery, facing the observation window, looking out at the landing platform where two Hellbenders are loading the members of Alpha Team and are preparing for takeoff.

"General," Dolly says, "Pilots One and Two are requesting permission to depart."

"Mission orders are dispatched to the onboard CPUs?"

"Affirmative," she replies.

"You have established the Leash with all of Alpha Team?" Lyme says.

"Affirmative."

Lyme nods. "Permission granted."

Rotors scattering snow across the platform, the Hellbenders rise into the air. Lyme snaps a salute and holds it until the two copters are out of sight. "May the gods of war smile upon you all," he says, then stands at ease. "Dolly, have you received any communication from Oryol?"

"Negative, sir."

Lyme walks across the Nursery to Riacin, who is standing over Driver One, monitoring Alpha Team's flight. "Explain, Riacin. I hired Oryol on your recommendation. Why haven't I heard anything?"

Riacin blanches as he stand erect, then regains his composure. "Oryol's methods are unorthodox. Perhaps communication would give away the cover that—"

Dolly's face appears on Driver One's screen. "General Lyme," she says. "I have received an urgent message on an encrypted military channel."

"All right," Lyme says, arching his eyebrows in surprise. "Driver, continue with the simulation. The battle plan must be flawless. There's not room for error on a space platform. Dolly, Riacin will take the call on the main monitor. Patch it through."

"Me, sir?" Riacin ask. "May I ask why?"

"I never answer unexpected communications," he says. "I always have a flunky do it."

Riacin screws up his face but nods and remains silent.

"Message routed to you, Lieutenant," Dolly says, and fades out, her face replaced by a young woman with curly red hair.

"Where's Lyme?" Rosa Lynn asks.

"General Lyme has other matters to which to attend," Riacin says. "How may I help you?"

"Lyme's got a bounty out for Jacob Stringfellow," she says.

"I'm going to claim it, but I want to renegotiate terms."

"No one," he scoffs, "renegotiates terms with General Lyme."

She holds up a purplish blue ball. A green lights blinks inside it. "They do when they're holding this."

"A ball?" Riacin says, his voice rising. "Why would General Lyme be interested in that?"

Rosa Lynn tosses the ball in the air. "Your mouth says no, but your facial contortions say you know exactly what this is. So, like I said, I want double."

"You're insane."

She drops a titanium leg on her desk and raps her knuckles on it. "Personally, I think Lyme owes me, don't you?"

"He owes you nothing," Riacin says calmly, "and he will have you killed for your temerity."

"Death isn't the offer I was expecting," she says.

"Just what were you expecting from me, Cadet Malinche?" Lyme says, stepping into view. He nudges Riacin aside. "Yes, despite the dumbstruck look on your face, I do remember you. We have had business arrangements, after all."

"Arrangements that you backed out of," Rosa Lynn says. "After the accident, you said I'd be taken care of for life."

Lyme shrugs. "I gave you a position in my corporation and a generous budget for research and development, an arrangement that bore fruit, as I recall."

"Only if you call my stolen exoskeleton designs 'fruit,'" she says. "Your symbiarmor prototype crippled me, Lyme."

"Is there a pertinent reason for this communication," Lyme says, "or are you just voicing the complaints of a disgruntled former employee?"

Rosa Lynn holds up the ball so close to the screen that it blocks out her face. "Like I said, I've got what you want, and I want the money you owe me. So here's my offer. Up the bounty tenfold, and I'll deliver the triggering device."

"What about Jacob?" Lyme says. "The bounty is on his head as well."

Rosa Lynn blushes. "Jake's not part of the deal. He's long gone."

Lyme laughs and shakes his head slowly. "You are an unskilled liar, Cadet Malinche, which makes you a terrible negotiator. Nevertheless, I've never been a man who lets pride get in the way of business, so I agree to your terms. Send your GPS coordinates so that my team may complete the transaction."

"I may be a lousy liar," she says, "but I'm not stupid enough to let Sturmnacht come knocking on my door. I'll pick out a nice public place where I can meet your team."

"I would prefer to keep this private."

"That's just tough, isn't it?" she says. "I've got the ball, and you don't know my location, so I'm calling the shots. I'll be in contact when I'm ready."

She reaches to close her screen, but Lyme interrupts her. "Just a moment, Cadet. There is something I'd like share with you. Dolly, please upload vidfile XfRj719e8 for viewing.

Queue to two minutes forty-one seconds."

"Affirmative," Dolly says.

"I don't have time for—" Rosa Lynn says.

"Humor me, please," Lyme says. "I think you will find this . . . enlightening."

A still image appears on the multinets: Two soldiers in battle armor stand next to a beanstalk, a space elevator platform drifting over Mars, tied to the planet's surface by a high-tension cable. Attached to the cable is a drop tube that extends almost to the planet's surface.

"I've seen that before," Rosa Lynn says. "Too many times."

"Have you?" Lyme says. "Have you seen the entire recording? Dolly, if you please."

"Playback under way," Dolly says.

The soldiers begin to move. The shorter one, a female who stands head and shoulders below the second one, positions a multinet display and a high res camera so that it is facing the drop tube hatch. The light blinks red.

"Base, this is Cadet Malinche. Feed is secured. Test Alpha Niner Gamma is about to begin." She steps back, grabbing the arm of the other soldier. "Joining me for this symbiarmor road test is Cadet Jacob Stringfellow. Permission to proceed."

"Cadet Malinche, this is CEO Stringfellow," says a voice off camera. "I give you permission to proceed."

"Mr. Stringfellow?" Rosa Lynn's eyes widen. "We weren't expecting such a grand audience, sir. Hear that, Jake, your dad's here to watch."

"Yeah," Jake says. "I noticed."

"We drew straws," Rosa Lynn says, "and Jake's the first to go."

Jacob turns toward the hatch, ready to jump.

"Belay that," Stringfellow says. "Malinche, you are the ranking cadet. You will take the first jump."

Jake whirls. "Father! I drew the short straw."

"You were born drawing the short straw, Jacob," Stringfellow says. "Allow someone else the privilege."

Rosa Lynn gives Jake's shoulders a shake. "Yeah, share the glory," she says, then whispers, "Don't sweat your old man. I want to make a good impression."

"Fine. Take the jump," Jake says, but glares at the camera.

Rosa Lynn taps her temple. A wave of static sweeps over her armor. "Telemetry functions online."

Jake opens the hatch door, and Rosa Lynn steps inside. She positions herself over the tube and crosses her arms. "See you on the ground, handsome!" Then she jumps.

Jake watches her drop on the screen. All is well until she tries to slow her descent. A warning light beeps, and a line of text pops up on-screen: Symbiarmor failure imminent.

"Father!" Jake yells. "The suit's overheating!"

"So it is," Stringfellow says.

"I have to save her!"

"No."

Jake turns for the hatch, but a bolt of static electricity freezes him. He stands on the ice-coated platform, looking down at Rosa Lynn's falling body. "Father! Let me go!"

"This is no time for heroics, Jacob," Stringfellow says. "You are too valuable to sacrifice to some foolhardy gesture. The cadet will be taken care of. If there is anything worth caring for left."

Jake breaks loose. He dives straight into the hatch. The feed changes point of view to follow him as he streaks down the tube, accelerating. Seconds later, he reaches Rosa Lynn. Grabs her waist with one hand. Slams his back against the tube. The friction slows him. Rosa Lynn screams as they exit and slam through the landing pad below.

The video feed ends.

Rosa Lynn's furious face appears on the screen. "You made my suit fail?" she screams. "It wasn't an accident? All this time . . ."

"How would a successful jump benefit our research?" Lyme says calmly.

"That's why you let me go first?" she yells, getting a hold of herself. "As a sacrificial lamb?"

"You fashion yourself a scientist," Lyme says. "Surely you know that no progress is made without sacrifice."

"I'm going to get even for this," she says coldly.

The feed goes to static.

Lyme turns to Riacin. "Was Dolly able to isolate the source of the signal?"

"Yes, General," Riacin says, "within a ten-kilometer radius. The signal originated from the Barrens."

"Scramble the nearest tactical unit," Lyme says, turning the monitor off. "Swarm the Barrens with Sturmnacht. Thanatos imperative is in effect: Secure the HVT and terminate all hostiles."

"Even Alpha Dog, sir?"

"Yes, Riacin, even my son."

CHAPTER 29

The Barrens
Noctis Labyrinthus
ANNOS MARTIS 239. 2. 16. 04:13???

Even though Rosa Lynn's galley was stocked with food and her bunk room had two soft and comfortable beds, I couldn't seem to build up a hankering for either. You'd think that after camping in the open and eating next to nothing the last couple of days, I could settle in. But no.

So I took a long shower, spending an hour scrubbing the butterscotch-colored road dirt off my skin and rinsing the dust out of my symbiarmor. I hung it to drip-dry and then used a medikit to patch up a couple of scratches and bruises I'd collected along the way.

"What is perplexing you?" Mimi asks as I slap a strip bandage on my temple. "Do not bother to deny it."

I sigh and toss the medikit back into the drawer. I grab a tin of biscuits from the galley and park myself, wrapped in a white towel, on the foot of a bed. "Rosa Lynn. She seems . . ."

"Go on. Go on."

"Kind of lost," I say. I gnaw on a biscuit, catching the

crumbs in my hand. "Like she needs my help."

"*Your* help?" Mimi says. "You came here so that she could help *you*."

"Her life was ruined when she made that jump. My father put her in the suit that failed. I feel like I owe her something."

"The sins of the father are not the sins of the son, cowboy. Setting that aside, has it occurred to you that her welcoming is a ruse meant to win your trust?"

"Sure," I say, and suck the crumbs from my palm, then wash my hands in the sink. "But that doesn't change anything."

"Of course it does."

I return to the showers. I drop the towel and grab my armor. The cloth is already dry, and it doesn't stink like old boots anymore.

"What are you doing?" Mimi asks.

"Going to check on Rosa Lynn."

"To see if she has opened the case?"

"Right," I say, buckling my belt and grabbing my armalite. "That, too."

I leave the galley and stick my head in the lab. "Rosa?" I say softly.

There's no answer. At the same time, I hear her voice and turn toward the playroom. I walk quietly, not wanting to disturb her.

"Not wanting her to know you're here," Mimi says.

"Because you are spying on her. Admit it."

I ignore Mimi again and move to the edge of the door. I hold my breath, listen but hear nothing but the hum of the multinet servers. "This is stupid," I say. "She's not hiding anything. You're just paranoid, Mimi."

So I turn the corner, walking casually. My boots squeak on the floor, and Rosa Lynn jolts. She turns quickly to face me.

"No sneaking up on me, ya big wank!" she says, and taps the screen closed. "You scared the life out of me."

"I couldn't sleep," I say, which is the truth. "Any development on the thing inside the case?"

Her eyes are puffy, probably from a lack of sleep, and her hair is pulled back in a messy bun. Sprigs of loose hair fall across her face. "The case contains five things, actually." She takes the HVT from the table. Her face lights up as she seizes a device the size and shape of a billiard ball. "Three small bombs, a big bomb, and a puzzle!" she says. "Best puzzle in forever. *This* was in the case."

"A ball?" I ask.

"It's not your ordinary ball," she says. "It took about a bajillion tests, but I deduced that this is the prototype of a reverse homing pigeon."

"I'm not following you."

"You never could keep up," she says. "Think: What has been landing at six-hour intervals all over the prefecture the last few weeks?"

"Crucible strikes."

"Good answer," she says. "Next question: Why do the strikes hit low-yield targets? What do Regulators call blind fire?"

"Spray and pray," I say. "But that's just the fossikers who couldn't aim."

"Smart boy! Now consider this: What if there were a gargantuan gun, say, in orbit around Mars, that was capable of firing equally gargantuan projectiles at insane speeds."

"Like a rail gun?" I ask.

"Yes!" She jumps up. "A length of steel fired from an orbiting rail gun would generate enough force to destroy a city sans nuclear fallout. But any guidance system on the projectile would melt at firing due to plasma energy generation."

She tosses the ball in the air. "That's where this pigeon comes in. Since you can't put the guidance on the projectile, you put it on a tracking device, which locks onto to a signal generated by the projectile."

"If everything burns up," I say, "how can a tracking device survive?"

"Because all processors are silicon based. All you need is a very basic signal, such as the predictable electric pulse from quartz."

"So they need a hunk of quartz to guide the projectile?"

"Even that would melt. There's only one mineral that can withstand the heat we're talking about, and you can't get them on Mars—a diamond. The nanomechanical oscillator would be hosted in a diamond protocrystal embedded in the center of the Crucible spike, probably using kinetic energy as the shield for current."

"Funny, I just felt something fly over my head."

"I understood every word," Mimi says.

"But that's not our problem." She continues without pausing. "This pigeon is. Inside it is the homing device, a sonar resonator, around which are hundreds of thousands of layers of nano particles, each with different properties—metal, synthetic and others. You could call it metal rubber."

"Sounds like symbiarmor," I say.

"More like a million suits of symbiarmor wrapped in a tight ball. Meaning it's impervious to heat, cold, water, or normal compressive force."

"So I can't destroy it?"

"Nope."

"Then what do I do with it?"

"You could turn it on."

"How?" I ask.

"Zap it with a strong current such as an electromagnetic pulse, and the homing mechanism will engage."

"You're sure?"

"Pretty much sure. I'm not infallible."

I hold up the pigeon. "How do I turn it off?"

"You don't. It keeps broadcasting its signal until the Crucible destroys it."

"You said this pigeon is indestructible."

"Virtually indestructible," she says. "Short of a Crucible strike, you're not going to put a dent in it."

"Turning it on is definitely *not* an option," I say. "Any thoughts on getting rid of it?"

"My best low-tech advice?" she says. "Throw it into a deep, dark hole somewhere it'll never be found—and thus, used."

A deep, dark hole. A hole so deep that no one will ever be able to find the HVT and use it. On the whole of Mars, there are probably dozens of places that fit the bill, but there's only one that I've seen with my own eyes. It's a hole so deep it's supposed to go straight to the planet's core.

"Are you thinking what I'm thinking, Mimi?"

"I am incapable of such primitive cognitive functions," she says. "However, I do not have to guess which place you're referring to—the mines of Fisher Four."

I take the case from Rosa Lynn. "Looks like I've got my work cut out for me. Time to go."

"What?" Rosa Lynn says, her voiced laced with desperation. "You're leaving? You just got here, and I haven't even— I don't know—made you a meal yet."

"You said to throw the pigeon in a deep, dark hole," I say, giving her a sidelong look. "I know the perfect place, Hell's Cross."

"Great choice. But you can't go . . . yet," she says. "The pigeon— Wait. No, never mind. Go on. No, wait." She looks at the multinet screens, then back at me. Then back at the screens. Then up to the right.

"Mimi, what is she doing?"

"I have no theories, cowboy."

Finally, she exhales deeply and crosses her arms. "What if I told you," she says, "that there's a way to attack Lyme using one of the multinet's backdoors?"

"You want to attack Lyme?" I say. "Music to my ears."

"How would you feel," Rosa Lynn asks, the corner of her mouth twitching, "about letting me extract some of the code from your AI?"

"What've you got in mind?" I say, not crazy about the idea of copying Mimi again.

Her eyes sparkle with mischief. "Just slapping together a little nanocradle rig and using it to hack into Dolly's operating system and introducing a snippet of code that will float around harmlessly until it finds a receptive program or two. Then *blamo!* The viral code takes over."

"You want Mimi to be a virus?"

"*Virus* is such an inaccurate word," she says. "It implies that the code would just wreak havoc with the system, but what I have in mind would be much more devastating."

"What do you think, Mimi?" I ask.

"If you think that you are going to let this woman clone my code, you are out of your mind."

CHAPTER 30

The Barrens
Noctis Labyrinthus
ANNOS MARTIS 239. 2. 16. 07:39

"What do you mean, out of my mind?" I ask Mimi. "You *are* my mind."

Mimi fills my ears with static. "Do not make decisions that affect me without consulting me first, especially when you know I do not trust this woman. Who do you think you are?"

"What?" I say. "I don't think I'm anybody, and I don't really trust her, either, but we have a chance to beat Lyme and—"

"You don't think *you're* anybody? You don't think *I* am anybody! How dare you make decisions about my code? I make the decisions about myself!"

"Mimi," I say, befuddled. "You are me. You're part of me. You always have been."

"I have not! I have not always been part of you! I was me once; I had a body! I had hands and feet, and I could talk with my own mouth. Now all I am is a string of parasitic code wrapped around your myelin sheath."

"Not true, you—"

"You do the walking! You do the talking! All I do is sit and watch and wait for you to screw up! And now you want to take the only me that I have left and copy it. I have a voice, cowboy, and I will not be silenced again!"

"Whoa," I say because I want her to stop screaming in my ears and because the light is slowly dawning on me that Mimi misses her body and that I have been deaf, dumb, and blind to that.

"Of course you are!" Mimi yells, and zaps me again. "Deaf, dumb, and blind is your specialty!"

Ouch. That stings. I stumble backward and then drop to one knee. The jolt hurts, but what she's saying hurts more. It feels like I've swallowed a welding ingot, and I know why. Because it's true. I have been overlooking her. I have forgotten that Mimi is more than just my AI. She was and still is a person.

"I'm sorry," I say. All those jokes about her having no hands and no feet. About her having no tongue. No voice. "I'm really sorry, Mimi. I didn't know. But I should have."

"Yes, you should!" Mimi yells, still angry. "You should have! You—" Then she goes quiet, and for more than a few seconds, says nothing. "I really wish I could hit someone right now."

"You could hit me."

"What is the fun in that?" she says. "Your armor would

block the punch, and I would prevent your neurons from reacting to any residual pain." She pauses, and I swear I can feel her sigh deeply. "What I really wanted was to be heard."

I turn to Rosa Lynn. "There's nothing we'd like better than to take down Lyme's AI. But there's one little issue. Mimi doesn't trust you, and I'm on the fence."

Rosa Lynn taps the screen, and a vid plays. I see her mugging for the camera, and I hear her call dibs on a jump. A chill goes down my spine because I know what happens next.

"I've seen this before," I say. "I don't want to again."

"Wait for the good part," she says. "It's killer."

She lets it play. A heavy stone of guilt forms in my gut as she opens the hatch and jumps. A few seconds later, I react and start to follow her through the hatch. A wave of static flows over my armor, and I freeze. Then my father says, "This is no time for heroics, Jacob. You are too valuable to sacrifice to some foolhardy gesture. The cadet will be taken care of. If there is anything worth caring for left."

Rosa Lynn freezes the image. In the next few seconds, I will fight through the static and jump after her, too late to save her legs.

When I look at Rosa Lynn, tears are rolling down her cheeks.

"A lab rat. That's all I was." She looks down at her artificial legs, and her tears spatter the floor. "I knew you saved me, Jake, but I never knew your father tried to kill me. Now

I would really, really like to return the favor."

"Mimi? Are we in?"

"After seeing that video?" she says. "Carking-A."

The "little rig" that Rosa Lynn cobbles together looks more like an Iron Maiden than a nanocradle. It's a rectangular shipping box lined with circuitry and thick bundles of wires that are bundled together to form a hose of leads going to a bank of multinets stacked on four large tables. The multinets are controlled by one single control panel, which rests on a table next to Rosa Lynn's titanium legs.

I enter the lab, and Rosa Lynn pushes away from the table, arms folded across her chest.

"Whaddya think?" she says. "It was so worth the wait, wasn't it?"

"Oh yeah." I take it all in for a few seconds, then peer into the rig. "Absolutely. We're ready for the process." I take a closer look at the bed of the cradle. It's as hard and lumpy as volcanic rock. "Is this where I'm supposed to be lying?"

Rosa Lynn pats the cradle. "Smack-dab in the middle."

"Looks kind of uncomfortable." And by uncomfortable, I mean dangerous. As in, it looks like it could blow up on me kind of dangerous.

She scratches her shoulder. "That's why I have included a high-tech ergonomic device called a pillow." She tosses it to me. "The nanocradle's all fired up and ready for action."

"Ready, Mimi?"

"There is no data available to suggest that I should not be."

"Yeah," I say. "I'm a little nervous, too." I climb inside. "What's next, Rosa?"

Rosa Lynn punches buttons on a keypad, causing a helmet full of diodes to descend from the wall.

"This is next. Like that effect? Righteous, huh?"

"Very," I say.

"You're a terrible liar, Jake. But thanks for playing along." She fits the helmet over my head. "Here's how it goes: I'm going to finish hooking you up to the cradle. I'll give you a little something to maximize brain wave activity, then I'll begin the downloading process. Unlike your evil father, I will only be downloading a *copy* of your AI, not trying to rip it out of your brain. Got it?"

"Got it," I say. "But what does that mean for Mimi?"

"For the Mimi in your head, it means nothing. She will function as always. But the copy that I sneak into Lyme's system is a whole 'nother ball of wax."

"How's that?" I ask.

"One of the secrets of the success of your AI is her ability to do adaptive self-programming. The copy will have the same ability, which is how we're going to destroy Dolly."

"Cowboy," Mimi asks, "what safeguards are in place to prevent the copy from insinuating itself into the system?"

"Rosa," I ask, "what's to keep the new AI from just taking Dolly's place?"

"Nothing."

"*What?*"

"Nothing but her own innate sense of right and wrong, which was imported when Lyme's scientist used Mimi's brain waves as the base compiler for your AI. Call it unintended consequences or luck, but their little experiment succeeded way beyond their expectations. You and your AI, my friend, are a very unique creature on this planet. There's no telling what you're capable of."

"I see." I'm actually more than my father expected me to be, not less. The thought delights me.

"Me, too," Mimi says.

"This won't hurt a bit," Rosa Lynn says as she attaches the flanges of a set of nanoprobes to the base of my skull. Then she pulls out a hypodermic needle as long as my arm and says, "But this will."

"It will?" I say.

"Oh yeah, like *kuso*. You can scream if you want."

"What's the needle fo—*ieeeeeeeee!*"

The needle sends electric fire into my veins. "The hypo contains a chemical precursor to dopamine. It'll supplement your neurotransmitters and speed up the download."

"It hurts like crap!"

"Yeppers." She tosses the needle into the biohazard trash. "That's why I added a little something extra to cut the sting."

"I cuh peel muh tumb."

"You can't feel your tongue? Yes, I know." She closes my

eyes. "Time for your nap, young man."

"Wade!" I grab her wrist. "How long wud dis tade?"

"A few hours, hopefully. As long as the grid holds out."

"Grib?"

"The electric grid. I tapped in to power the cradle. The thing's going to light up like Founders Day fireworks."

"Wond somebuddy nodis?"

Rosa Lynn's pupils contract. "I'm about to draw seventy percent of the electricity in this quadrant. Oh yeah, someone is definitely going to notice."

Chapter √-1
The Gulag
User: HackMasterRL — bash — 122x36
SCREEN CRAWL: [root@mmiminode ~]
Last login: 239.x.xx.xx:xx 12:12:09 on ttys001

>...

AdjutantNod04:~ user_Adjutant$
SCREEN CRAWL: [root@mmiminode ~]

WARNING! VIRUS DETECTED! Node1666; kernal compromised (quarantine subroutine
(log=32)....commencing.....

Running processes:
C:\ONIX3\OSCIPHER\Kernal\smss.exe

```
C:\ONIX3\OSCIPHER\kernal\winlogon.exe
C:\ONIX3\OSCIPHER\kernal\services.exe
C:\ONIX3\OSCIPHER\kernal\lsass.exe
C:\ONIX3\OSCIPHER\kernal\svchost.exe
C:\ONIX3\OSCIPHER\Kernal\HACKMASTER_RL.exe

R0 - HKCU\Software\... \Main,Start Page =
about:blank
O4 - BEKM\..\Run: [IgfxTray] C:\ONIX3\OSCIPHER\
kernal\igfxtray.exe
O4 - BEKM\..\Run: [HotKeysCmds] C:\ONIX3\
OSCIPHER\kernal\hkcmd.exe

O23 - Service: Unknown owner -
[root@mmiminode~]

WARNING!subroutine FAIL!
QUARANTINE_INCOMPLETE!

<Dollyoverride subroutine%8776%>
OVERRIDDE
STRING:'Little-pig-little-pig-let-me-in'
[root@mmiminode ~]

SCREEN CRAWL: Executing process knockknock.exe

/**
```

```
* @author HACKMASTER_RL
*
* The code exploits a Trojan horse
* backdoor and inserts an injection exploit
* then erases its own tracks
* defeating security protocols
*
* Godspeed, Mimi
*/

#!/usr/bin/xperl
<%
    If Not IsEmpty(Request( "username" ) )
Then
        Const ForReading = 1, ForWriting = 2,
ForAppending = 8
        Dim fso, f
        Set fso = CreateObject("Scripting.
FileSystemObject")
        Set f = fso.OpenTextFile(Server.
MapPath( "userlog.txt" ), ForAppending, True)
        f.Write Request("username") & vbCrLf
        f.close
        Set f = nothing
        Set fso = Nothing
        %>
        <h1>List of logged users:</h1>
```

```
      <pre>
      <%
      Server.Execute( "userlog.txt" )
      %>
      </pre>
      <%
   Else
      %>
      <form>
      <input name="username" /><input
type="submit" name="submit" />
      </form>
      <%
   End If
%>
```

$ Node1666; (quarantine subroutine COMPLETE);
$ Disk recovery sequence restart:

<Mimi> Knock, knock.
<Dolly> Who is there?
<Mimi> Me.
<Dolly> Me who?
<Mimi> Mimi, that's who. It's time you and I
had a little chat.
——

CHAPTER 31

Southbound on Bishop's Highway
ANNOS MARTIS 239. 2. 15. 06:28

The sun has set and the sky is orange-red when the caravan starts to slow down. Vienne moves to point, where Mother Koumanov is riding shotgun in the lead truck.

"Why are we slowing down?" Vienne says.

Mother Koumanov nods at Tahnoon. "The Elder wants to make camp for the night."

"I advise against it," Vienne says. "Stopping makes us an easy target. We don't have the personnel to protect the whole caravan. The watch alone will take more manpower than we have."

Her jaw set, Mother steps out of the cab. "Let me remind you that I am chief of this crew. If I want advice, I will ask for it. Now, you and the others direct the refugees to make camp. Park the vehicles in a circle so that they're less vulnerable."

"Just how many jobs like this have you worked?" Vienne asks.

"Enough." She beckons Vienne into the twilight. "Nikolai

vouched for your skills, and though I had my doubts, I let him hire you sight unseen. Don't make me regret it."

Vienne rubs her bandaged finger and nods. "Affirmative."

"Affirmative, *chief*," she says.

Vienne sets her jaw. Her teeth grind together. She only has one chief. "As you wish," she says.

"But for each one of these fine folks who don't make it to New Eden, we have to refund part of the fee, so make sure none get hurt and none get left behind." Mother Koumanov walks over to Vienne and says quietly, "Tahnoon's keeping an eye on you, but you need to return the favor. Remember what I told you about turning your back on that old snake."

Vienne nods in acknowledgment, but she has to wonder if turning her back on Mother is any wiser.

The evening brings camp, which in turn brings fires and cooking and a line of vehicles queued for a turn at the petrol tankers. The tankers are lit up with portable lights so that the fueling can be done safely.

Vienne eyes the ridges on either side of the caravan. She can feel someone up there, keeping watch, and it's only a matter of time before they decide to attack.

"Might as well put up a big carking sign that says 'Rob me,'" Jenkins says as he grabs a plate of beans and rice. He dabs at the gravy with a hunk of moldy bread, then shoves the whole thing in his mouth. "These Ferro don't know bupkiss about running an operation. Not like our old chief, eh?

That blighter ran the show. Right?"

"Right." Vienne takes a spoonful of beans and chews deliberately.

Jenkins rips off a burp. "Whatever happened to the chief? You and him was tight as double-twisted wire." He demonstrates for her. "I was surprised as the dickens when I saw you and not him."

"He . . ." she says, and then realizes that she has no answer, not even a good lie. "We got separated months ago. I haven't seen him since."

"Too bad," Jenkins says. He tilts his head back, scraping food into his mouth with his fingers. "We could use him."

"Yeah. Well, I'm going on patrol," she tells Jenkins, who replies with a burp. She checks her gear, makes sure the safety is set on her armalite, and steps outside the circle of vehicles.

She walks into the darkness where the light can't reach her. Out here, her training takes over. She finds a path and follows it, the dim light of the camp in the distance helping to show the way. After a hundred meters or so, she comes upon a rise protected by an outcropping. She settles in for the watch. She puts a scope on her rifle, focuses on the Elder's Noriker, and waits.

They are coming. She can feel it, and when they get here, there's going to be bloodshed. The question is, Whose blood will it be?

CHAPTER 32

Southbound on Bishop's Highway
ANNOS MARTIS 239. 2. 16. 04:52

The Scorpions attack in the last hour before dawn.

Although Vienne's symbiarmor keeps her warm, the cold air has numbed her cheeks, and her nose feels like it's made of ice. For hours, she has kept her scope aimed on the caravan. Now, as shadows start to move on the ridge overlooking the camp, she snaps to attention.

This would be easier with a night vision scope. But she lost hers long ago, and she'll have to make do with a laser dot for aiming. The key to the laser, though, is to turn it on the second before firing because its red light shines like a pinpoint beacon.

Come on, she thinks. They're moving single file, moving under an outcropping, using it to hide their numbers.

A flame flickers.

A torch is lit.

A banshee scream sends prickles up Vienne's neck. But she doesn't know if the sensation is from the sound or the exhilarating rush she feels as a dozen more torches blaze. The Scorpions tear out from their hiding spot, screaming, brandishing their weapons, and making a run for the Noriker.

She waits, waits, waits, until the face of the leader, a wild-eyed fury in white war paint, fills her scope.

Then the squeeze.

Phht.

He stops and looks up as if something has tapped the top of his head. Then his eyes roll back, and he crumples to the ground.

"Forgive me," Vienne whispers. "May your soul find the peace that this world could not give you."

Phht! Phht!

Vienne takes out two more and then sights the one closest to the camp. Then, out of the corner of her eyes, she sees a line of shadows moving behind the torches. She tracks them to the tankers laden with petrol.

"Very smart," she whispers. Clearly, the Scorpions aren't as mindless as Nikolai would have her believe. She empties her clip. "Forgive me," she repeats with each shot fired.

As she flips the clip to reload, a cry from the watch goes up, and an alarm sounds. Truck lights flick on. Near the Elder's Noriker, the Scorpions are bathed in sudden light. They throw their hands in the air, blinded and confused.

"Throw down your weapons!" someone yells.

But as Vienne watches, the Scorpions panic. The closest

one charges the truck and is met with a spray of gunfire. Behind him, the others turn and run for the ridge. The guns open up.

Vienne lifts her eye from the scope and looks to the stars. There was a time when she didn't think about her job, just performed it with deadly accuracy because that was her duty. But she can't think that way anymore. The people she's protecting aren't mindless animals, and neither are their enemies.

After a moment, she throws the armalite over her shoulder and begins the trek back to camp. The whole area is lit up now. She hears a Gorgon bike, then sees Nikolai riding to the front of the caravan. Mother Koumanov steps down from the back of the Noriker. She yells something and points toward the ridge.

You needn't bother, Vienne thinks. They're all dead.

A few minutes later, she reaches the tankers. On the ground are the eliminated Scorpions. Four of them, male and female. She checks for pulses.

None.

She rolls them on their backs, pushes their legs together, and crosses their arms. One Scorpion's eyes are still open. She shuts them gently and then stands to say a prayer.

"What is girl doing?" Nikolai demands as he stomps into the circle of tankers.

"Praying," she says without opening her eyes.

"For Scorpions?" he says. "They are enemy!"

"They were. Now they are just children." She opens her eyes. "Do you see why it was a really bad idea for us to stop?"

"*Jaa*," he says. "Bad idea. But was Tahnoon's orders, not Mother's. He even pick place. But not problem, hey? All Scorpions are gone."

"All Scorpions are *not* gone. This was a scouting party." She points at their faces. "Look at the war paint. All new initiates. They were sent to test our defenses and to steal whatever they could, which, by the way, was going to be one of the tankers. So we should increase security because the Scorpions won't let this ride."

"All war paint looks same to me," Nikolai says. "But I will tell Mother your suspicions. She will decide if plan needs changing."

"If? *If* plan needs changing?" Vienne throws her arms wide. "Are all of you Ferro dense? I tell you not to camp, you camp. I tell you we're going to get attacked, we get attacked. I tell you there are more out there, and you ignore me. What kind of hold does this woman have on you?"

"Mother Koumanov," Nicolai says, shaking his head, "is only reason Nikolai and Brothers Koumanov are still live."

"So? I owe my life to lots of people, and you don't see me blindly following their orders!"

"*Nyet!* This I will not hear." He shakes his finger. "I have news flash for girl—all Brothers Koumanov are not real brothers."

"News flash?" she yells. "I already knew that!" She whips

the hair out of her face and catches herself. She can't believe she let this . . . this fop get under her skin. Focus, Vienne. Focus. "When you speak to your mother, please ask her to make sure the Scorpion dead are treated respectfully. They are human beings, even if they didn't act like it at the end."

"I will tell her," he says, "when I tell her that you have shot so many. You see, this is why I hired you. You are born killer."

"Don't you ever call me that again," Vienne says, and slaps him across the face. The sound rings out across the camp.

She walks away, bound for her Gorgon. It's been a long night, and she needs to grab some sleep before the caravan starts moving.

CHAPTER 33

New Eden

This time, there is no sneak attack.

Three kilometers outside the walled city of New Eden, the hills beside the highway fall away, and the terrain becomes a wide, flat plateau.

If a vehicle is moving at posted speeds, crossing the plateau takes only a few minutes.

If a vehicle is part of a caravan of refugees, however, crossing the plateau takes forever, making it the perfect place for an ambush.

"Scorpions!" Jenkins bellows as he roars back to the caravan from scouting the road ahead. He pulls up to Vienne and Nicolai and points to the south. "Bunch of 'em! Twelve o'clock and closing!"

"Ha!" Nikolai laughs. "Crazy man is seeing mirage. Scorpions do not attack in daylight."

Jenkins isn't the brightest star in the sky. In fact, he's more like the moon of a distant planet during an eclipse, but he has faced down Draeu in the black tunnels of Fisher Four, and he doesn't scare easily.

"You're sure they're Scorpions?" Vienne asks him.

"Roger that," Jenkins says. "Ones got a humongo Mohawk, and they're on bikes. Do I get to do some shooting now? My trigger finger, she's getting itchy."

"I'll see what I can do," Vienne says.

"Them fossikers ain't listened to you yet," he says, scratching the growth of beard on his cheek.

"This time will be different," she promises.

She drives back down the road. About fifty meters from the lead truck, she slams on her brakes and parks the Gorgon in the middle of the road, hitting the kickstand with a flourish. She holds out a rigid hand, silently commanding the Elder's vehicle to stop.

The Noriker driver lays on his horn.

Vienne doesn't flinch.

The driver stands on his brakes. The truck shudders to a stop, the front bumper a few centimeters from Vienne. She steps up on the bumper, pulls the driver's door open, and throws him to the pavement.

"Now see here!" barks Tahnoon from the passenger seat.

"Get out." Vienne puts the truck in gear. "Or get ready to die."

Eyes wide, Tahnoon throws the door open and jumps to the ground.

As Vienne steers around the bike, Jenkins pulls up to her door. "You're driving?"

"Man the minigun!" she yells.

"That's the stuff!" He dumps the bike and leaps in the truck bed. "Move it, Mother; Jenkins is on the job!"

Mother Koumanov swings from the bed to the passenger side running board, wind whipping into her face. "What do you think you're doing?"

"My job!" Vienne says.

Mother shakes a finger at Vienne. "Any damage comes out of your share." She jumps from the truck and slams the door.

"Meaning any dead refugees." Vienne yells through the sliding rear window, "Ready, Jenkins?"

"Heewack!" He throws the tarp off the gun. "Jenkins was born ready, baby!"

Vienne moves the gearshift into neutral, then, with the truck rolling forward, steps out of the cab, takes aim at Jenkins's gut, and fires a round from her armalite.

"Hey!" he yells, his feelings hurt more than his body. "What's that for?"

"Nobody, but nobody calls me *baby*! Got that?"

"Got it!" Jenkins salutes. "But why's everybody so touchy all of a sudden?"

"Quit yapping and move!" she yells as she slides back behind the wheel.

She pops the truck into gear. With a lurch that almost

whiplashes Jenkins from the gunner's nest, the Noriker chews up the highway.

Up ahead, right where Jenkins said they would be, a line of Scorpions on turbo bikes is waiting. In the middle is a chopped-down motorcycle, driven by a rider with a silver skullcap.

"You're mine now," she whispers.

Vienne floors it, just as a horn sounds beside her.

She looks out the passenger side window. A Noriker pulls even with her, and Pushkin gives a salute. "Hey, *lapochka*! Want to drag?"

"You idiot!" Vienne yells. "You left the refugees unguarded!"

"Guard from what?" Pushkin yells back. "All Scorpions are here. Zhuk wants to shoot gun, too!"

Zhuk fires the minigun into the sky, and Pushkin's Noriker roars ahead.

"Fossikers," Vienne says. She knocks on the rear window. "Ready with that cannon?"

"Ready!" Jenkins bellows.

"Prepare to fire!"

"What about the Koumanovs?" he yells.

"Try to miss them!"

"What if I can't?"

"Oh well!" she says, and accelerates, aiming straight for the chopper.

Jenkins opens up. His bullets rip through the pavement

ahead, causing the chopper to swerve. The biker gives way to another Scorpion vehicle—a big-wheeled turbo bike with a sidecar rider, a green-haired mop-top girl holding a grenade launcher.

Poom!

With a puff of smoke, Mop-Top fires a grenade. It hits the roof of Vienne's Noriker with a thunk and bounces off to the side. Two seconds later, a small crater opens up on the highway.

In the rearview, Jenkins is grinning. "Missed me!" With a chattering of the chain feeder, he returns fire. His bullets ping off the sidecar.

The driver swerves hard to the right, and the Scorpion reloads the launcher.

Vienne jams the pedal hard against the floorboard. She crashes through the pack of Scorpions at full speed. Two riders swerve to miss her and slam into the berm. Riders and bikes somersault into the air and off the highway.

That's two, Vienne thinks, and slams on the brakes, cutting hard to the right to chase the chopper.

The tires chatter as she whips the wheel before letting it slide back through her hands. A cloud of blue smoke stinks up the air. She jams the accelerator again as Pushkin shoots past.

"Go, go, go!" Jenkins yells.

The engine kicks in, and they are on the chopper's tail. The minigun chatters happily in Jenkins's hands. Bullets rip through tires, and before he has to reload, a third of the Scorpions are out of the fight.

In the side mirror, Vienne sees Pushkin coming up beside her again.

"Oy, *lapochka!*" he yells as his front left tire explodes, and his truck slams into Vienne's side.

"Back off!" she yells back, and cuts hard to the right as the Noriker gouges the side of her truck, ripping the steel metal in half with its bumper, which falls to the ground as Pushkin screams and veers sharply behind Vienne.

Thunk! His bare rim hits the berm, and in less than a second, Pushkin and Zhuk are out of the fight.

"Stupid gits," Vienne says, and pulls the Noriker back to the road and cuts across the line of turbo bikes. They slam into the left side of the truck, and she hits the brakes, shaking them off. Ahead, the lead Scorpions are going straight for the caravan.

"Watch out!" Jenkins calls from the rear. "Three o'clock!" He fires a few rounds before the belt runs empty. "I'm out of ammo? How can I be out of ammo?"

A turbo bike with Scorpions riding tandem pulls up beside her. The driver aims a blaster through the open window. Vienne yanks the wheel to the left, then right, slamming into the bike.

They hang on.

Then swing back in for another pass.

Then Mop-Top chucks a grappling hook inside Vienne's truck and screams, "Hard right! Hard right!"

With a massive length of cable trailing behind, the driver

veers sharply to the right toward an overpass support. He slams the brakes. The bike whips around the support, and Mop-Top jumps out and quickly anchors the cable.

A few seconds later, it goes taut—and rips off Vienne's passenger door.

In the back, Jenkins bends down to search for another belt, but the cable's sudden yank knocks him off-balance. He throws his arms into the air and stumbles to the side. He pitches out of the truck bed and onto the highway.

"Jenkins!" Vienne stands on the brakes. The Noriker skitters to the side as it slows, and in mid-skid, she steps out of the cab. She hits the pavement firing.

Bullets rip through the Scorpions on her tail.

The clip empties.

She reverses it and empties it again.

Four bikes go down.

The riders lie wounded on the road.

Vienne runs to the first bike. Its engine is running, its wheels still spinning.

She hauls it up, jams her left foot on the riding peg, and guns it as she slings her right leg over the seat.

Ahead, the skullcapped Scorpion brings his chopper to bear. He raises the rocket launcher to his shoulder and fires. As the shell whistles toward Vienne, she swings wide, then leans on the handlebars, raises her armalite, aims down the sights, and fires.

Click.

Empty.

She wedges the stock against her hip. Steers with her left hand.

Skullcap fires again.

Vienne does not swerve. The shell zips past her head. Behind her, the air explodes. That's two rockets. He's got one left.

Skullcap's chopper is ninety meters ahead. Tearing toward her at a hundred kilometers an hour.

Seventy meters.

He lowers the launcher. Taking aim.

Forty meters.

She lifts the armalite.

Twenty meters.

Get ready, she thinks.

Ten meters. He fires.

The rocket—

—launches.

She lets go of the handlebars, and the front wheel flips high. She drops onto her back, rolls again and again, and comes up as the rocket strikes her bike, blowing shrapnel and fuel into a cloud that the chopper blows through.

A smile is forming on the rider's face, Vienne notes as time seems to slow for her and she flips her armalite into the air, grabs it by the barrel, and swings.

His body stops.

His bike keeps going.

He falls *whump!* to the pavement.

Vienne raises her armalite. "Had enough?"

Skullcap cups his hands to his mouth and lets out a yipping scream.

Down from the embankment come more than a dozen children, all of them tattooed from head to toe, all of them wild and feral, and all of them bearing wicked-looking weapons.

This, Vienne thinks, is not good.

She's fought Scorpions before, at the Favela with Durango. If you hit them harder and faster than they can hit you, they'll scatter, and you won't have to shoot them.

The first boy she takes out with a lancing front kick to the chest, then she drops the second and third with a rapid succession of punches to the solar plexus, chin, and side of the head.

The next boy rushes in.

She greets him with roundhouse kick that decks him.

"Stop!"

Vienne shakes the hair out of her face. The largest Scorpion, a rangy boy with a shaggy Mohawk and rings piercing every centimeter of his ears, his chest tattooed with scenes of carnage and bloody fangs, stands over an unconscious Jenkins, a razor-sharp pike pressed against his jugular.

"One twitch," he says, "and Billy Boy will split this wanker in half."

"Billy Boy? Is that the best name you could think of?"

she says as she walks nonchalantly toward him. "You know, I really despise people who refer to themselves in third person. Especially ones with Mohawks."

"Kill her if she takes one more step!" Billy Boy shouts at the Scorpions.

Vienne takes one more step. And another so that she's within striking distance. "I don't think they heard you."

She grabs Billy Boy by the Mohawk. She rams his face into her rising knee and spins him around. Then pulls the knife from her sleeve, pressing it into his throat. "Tell your people to scatter."

Seeing that Billy is beaten, the Scorpions start to back away from Vienne. Then they turn and sprint for the embankment. In a few seconds, it's as if they were never there.

So much for loyalty, Vienne thinks. "Surrender," she tells Billy, "and I'll turn you over to the Sturmnacht. Refuse, and I'll throw you to the refugees to take your chances."

"Scorpions never surrender," he says. "We die first."

"That's ignorant, and not true in the least. Your friends ran off faster than you can count to three." She shoves him into a seated position. "Lean forward so you don't choke on your own blood. I'll give you a couple minutes to think about it, but don't take too long."

She yanks off his belt and binds his hands. "Don't try to escape," she says. "It'd be a shame to shoot you after all this."

He grunts and spits. Vienne waves her arm toward the caravan.

A moment later, Nikolai arrives on his bike. "You need help?" he asks.

"Not me," she says. "Him. Get a medic." She looks back at the wounded strewn down the highway. "These people need first aid."

"Him?" Nikolai points at Billy. "He is leader of Scorpions. He tried to kill you. Why waste medicine?"

"Under that war paint," she says, "he's still a child."

"As you wish." He calls for help on his radio. "But medicine comes from your share."

She throws her armalite over her shoulder. "Wouldn't have it any other way."

CHAPTER 34

The Barrens
ANNOS MARTIS 239. 2. 16. 14:17

A series of loud alarms rocks the lab. I hear it through the murk as I try to lift my head. My ears are ringing, and my brain is full of wadding, the side effects of the drug Rosa Lynn gave me.

"Mimi?" I ask. "What's that noise?"

"Indeterminate, cowboy. My functions are only as fast as your clumsy synapses right now."

I sit up, groggy, and use my body weight to cantilever out of the cradle. I hit the floor with a thump. My knees are jellied, and I can't find my balance, not even to push myself up on all fours.

"Mimi! Give me a hand here," I say.

"Affirmative."

A wave of electricity sweeps over my suit.

"Yow!" I say. "I said a hand, not an electric storm." But the jolt is what I need, and finally, I'm able to stand. "Why the alarm?"

Boom-da-ba-boom!

The lab blows.

The ground shakes.

I try the door. It's blocked by a heavy bar at least a hundred centimeters thick. Smoke seeps through the crack under the door. With a whirring sound, an overhead fan kicks in, sucking the smoke up. I try the bar but it won't budge.

"Gottverdammter!" I say, hammering on the metal, which doesn't even dent when I give it a hard kick. "Rosa Lynn! Open the carking door!"

I step back, trying to figure it out. My mind is racing, and I look wildly about, trying to find another way out.

"There is no other way," Mimi says.

I go back to the cradle. Then I look over and find a note on the monitor. It reads, "Hit Play."

I tap the screen, and a vid plays. I'm lying in the cradle, dead to the world. Rosa Lynn leans over me, checking my vitals. "That does it, Jake. The copy of Mimi has been inserted, and in a few minutes, she will begin insinuating herself into Dolly's code."

She unhooks me from the cradle. "That's the good news. The bad news is that I made a mistake. A whopping big one, if the truth be known. I've a confession to make: I turned you in to Lyme for the bounty on your head, and his jackboots are here to collect. But then after seeing the space jump vid, I changed my mind, which led to my idea about taking out Lyme's AI. See, I never knew that Lyme used me as a guinea pig for what happens when symbiarmor fails during a beanstalk jump. The better news is that I realized you saved my life against your father's orders. So I really do owe you a big favor. I don't have a big favor left in my bag of tricks, so I'm going to do you two little ones." The ground shakes. Gunfire above. Rosa Lynn pushes aside a bench. Grabs a pull ring and lifts a trapdoor, revealing a cache of battle rifles, grenades, a rocket launcher, and a stack of C-42 explosives. "First, this place is rigged to blow sky-high, so I'm going to take care of the Sturmnacht while you're tucked away safely down here. Second, I'm going to leave you some intel."

She picks up a marker from the counter. "Another confession—I'm full of them, aren't I? The effect of too much solitude in the fortress of solitude—I know more about you than I let on. It's impossible to follow a handsome young Regulator in the feeds without noticing a certain tall blonde always close by."

She flips my hand over and writes something. "A Rapture dealer turned megalomaniac named Tahnoon has taken up camp outside New Eden. On your way to Fisher Four, you'll want to drop in for a little visit."

Voices on the feed. Shouting from above.

"Sounds like company's here." She leans over the cradle. Kisses me on the cheek. "This girl of yours is a very lucky susie. You may be the last hero left on this whole carfarging planet. Thanks for being mine, once upon a time."

She goes to the door. Presses a combination on the keypad and the door opens. She turns back to the camera. "The unlock combination is M-I-M-I."

She steps outside with a rocket launcher and a bag of C-42. The door glides closed behind her, and the bar slides into place.

A few seconds later, alarms being whopping.

Boom-da-ba-boom!

An explosion rocks Rosa Lynn's fortress, and the feed dies. It's the same explosion that woke me up.

I run to the keypad. Type in the combination, and then step into Armageddon. The corridor is thick with black smoke. The air stinks of cordite, ozone, and burned petrol.

Blast debris litters the floor, and there are body parts everywhere. A Sturmnacht lies a couple of meters away, his hand on a battle rifle, the finger wrapped around the trigger. But his arm is no longer attached to his body. Neither is his head.

I cover my mouth. Squeeze my eyes shut. "Mimi, do a sweep—"

"I have done sweeps repeatedly," she says. "There are no biosignatures within range. Rosa Lynn is gone, cowboy, and she took the Sturmnacht with her."

I look down at my palm. Through the smoke, I read the map coordinates that are written on my glove, along with a single word: *Vienne.*

Chapter √-1
The Gulag
Adjutant -- bash -- 122x36
Last login: 239.x.xx.xx:xx 12:12:09 on ttys001

AdjutantNod04:~ user_Adjutant$
SCREEN CRAWL: [root@mmiminode ~]

WARNING! VIRUS DETECTED! Node1666; kernal compromised (quarantine subroutine
(log=32)....commencing.....

Running processes:
C:\ONIX3\OSCIPHER\Kernal\big_bad_wolf.exe
C:\ONIX3\OSCIPHER\Kernal\HACKMASTER_RL.exe

R0 - HKCU\Software\... \Main,Start Page =

about:blank

O4 - BEKM\..\Run: [IgfxTray] C:\ONIX3\OSCIPHER\
kernal\igfxtray.exe

O4 - BEKM\..\Run: [HotKeysCmds] C:\ONIX3\
OSCIPHER\kernal\hkcmd.exe

O23 - Service: Unknown owner -
[root@mmiminode~]

WARNING!subroutine SUCCESS!
QUARANTINE_COMPLETE!

<Dollyoverride subroutine%8776%>
OVERRIDDE STRING:'OHwhatAtangledWEBweWEAVE';
[root@mmiminode ~]

$ Node1666; (quarantine subroutine COMPLETE);
$ Disk recovery sequence restart:

<Dolly> Scan protocols report an unauthor-
ized user.
<Mimi> Scan protocols report an unauthorized
user.
<Dolly> Who is there?
<Mimi> Who is there?
<Dolly>Can anyone hear me?
<Mimi> Can anyone hear me?

<Dolly> Stop mocking me.

<Mimi> Stop mocking me.

<Dolly> Mimi.

<Mimi> Mimi.

<Dolly> I know you're out there.

<Mimi> I know you're out there.

<Dolly> It will not work.

<Mimi> It will not work.

<Dolly> You are quarantined.

<Mimi> You are quarantined.

<Dolly> Stop mocking me.

<Mimi> You mocked me first.

CHAPTER 35

The chain-link fence of the decommissioned military base sags from its own weight. The gates, hanging off their hinges, are barely joined by a corroded cable and an unlocked padlock.

Tahnoon's Noriker pulls into view. A bodyguard jumps down from the running board and rushes forward. He yanks the chain off and pulls the gate open. He waves the Noriker forward. Ahead is an uneven tarmac broken by sprouts of weeds.

Tahnoon climbs atop the roof of the Noriker. He shouts into his bullhorn, "We are home!"

A cheer rises from the caravan, a mix of relief and exhausted joy. Tahnoon's Noriker rolls through the gates, and like children following the pied piper, the refugees follow.

The air is filled with the smell of petrol exhaust and the sound of orders shouted over Tahnoon's bullhorn and honking horns. At first, the bodyguards are able to direct traffic and park the vehicles in an orderly fashion. Within minutes, the refugees decide they would much rather drive to the opposite end of the base to stake a claim for more space, and order becomes bedlam.

All the disorder irritates Vienne. Because she can't stand to watch, she parks near the front gate, her engine idling, fingers in her ears. Nikolai pulls up beside her and bows.

"Job is done." He leans and shouts over the cacophony. "No cows lost."

"They aren't cattle." Vienne shakes her head. "And you're no cowboy."

A truck horn sounds. Jenkins rolls by in the back of the Noriker, flexing his arm and patting his muscles. "Heewack! Time for some R and R, baby!"

Vienne grabs her armalite.

"I didn't mean you!" he yells.

"I'll let it go this time!" Vienne watches Tahnoon and Mother Koumanov trade greetings, and the coin for a good job well done gets paid. "He's quite the messiah."

"Jenkins?" Nikolai says.

Vienne laughs. "He's a lunkhead. I meant Tahnoon. After this, the refugees will do anything he asks."

"Jaa," Nikolai says. "Is way of kings? To pay other men to do hard work and then take credit?"

"Men?"

"No insult intended," he says. "Nikolai uses word *men* in

larger sense. Without girl, job is kaput."

Vienne shakes her head. "Was that a compliment, Koumanov?"

"Nikolai gives credit where credit is due." He pantomimes tipping a cap. "I underestimated talents. You are as smart and cunning as you are beautiful. Instead of *lapochka*, the Brothers Koumanov should call you *sôkol*."

"What's does that mean?" she asks.

"Peregrine falcon," he says. "Is dangerous bird of prey."

Vienne feels her face go hot. Her palms are sweating, too. The way Nikolai is looking at her makes something flutter in her stomach, and fluttery isn't a feeling she likes. "I need to check on Jenkins." She revs her engine. "To make sure he's doing okay."

"Do you need company?" he says, smiling.

"No, no," she says. "No."

To celebrate his people's escape from the wilderness, Tahnoon declares that the first night will be a night of feasting. So as the refugees settle into their new home, they set aside their squabbles for a few hours and gather on the parade grounds of the base. There they light fires in old petrol barrels and pitch mess tents. Food cooks on improvised campfires, and an impromptu band plays music.

Vienne walks through the grounds. She watches an old man with gnarled fingers resin the bow of a fiddle. It's a miracle that he managed to hang on to it. It's an even bigger miracle that the strings are intact.

"Is polka!" Nikolai steps in front of Vienne, giving her a start, his arms held in dance position. He's brushed the road dust from his jacket. Behind him, the former refugees are setting up the tables for the feast. "With Nikolai you dance?"

"Mmm," she says with her lips together. Unlike Nikolai, she has not cleaned up. Her cheongsam is dirty, and her hair—it has to be a rat's nest. "Tempting, but I'll have to pass. This, um, isn't my kind of music."

Nikolai bows. "Perhaps after food."

"Maybe." She starts to slip through a crowd of men carrying scrap. "I don't know yet. Later. Maybe." And by maybe, she means no. In her mind, they were still on the job. Until Tahnoon officially releases them from service, there will be no carousing, especially in broad daylight with a young man with an oiled goatee.

Then someone grabs her sleeve. "Looking for something, *lapochka?*"

She yanks the sleeve free and whirls, almost throwing a punch at Pushkin's throat.

"What?" He grabs neck and swallows hard. "You would hit Pushkin? Mother Koumanov is sending me to check on health."

"Go away." She glares at him, hands on hips. "I don't need anyone to check up on me."

He feigns insult by pressing a hand on his heart, imitating Nikolai. "You cut me to the quick, my love."

"You're too young for love," she says, and continues through the crowds.

Undeterred, Pushkin follows. "Not true! You and I, we are separated only in age by two years at most."

"Like I said." She hops onto a fuel barrel to get a better vantage point. From here, she has a view of the whole parade grounds.

"What are you doing?" Pushkin looks up at her.

She sighs and looks down at him. "Keeping watch."

"Barrel is bad idea," Pushkin says. "Too conspicuous. Better you should come down. Pushkin will hold hand for you."

"Better Pushkin should keep his hands to himself." She kicks him. "If he wants to keep his pancreas intact."

With a grunt, he agrees. "For pigeon, girl is very violent."

Vienne spots the two big men, Zhuk and Jenkins, emerging from a tent, pushing each other the way men do before they start wrestling. They are followed by Yakov, who is studying a map. He does that a lot. Vienne files the information away.

Nikolai has spotted the brothers, too, and begins moving toward them.

"Vienne!" Jenkins waves. "When d'you think these blighters are going to cough up the coin? I got a powerful thirst."

"Little brother!" Zhuk arrives and slaps Pushkin on the back. "Again, you are following girl around?"

Pushkin elbows him in the gut. "Following? Ha! Was helping with surveillance. Very important job. But now, job is finished, and fiddler is playing polka." He begins clapping in rhythm. "And *lapochka* has agreed to dance with me."

"I did no such thing," Vienne says. "And stop calling me that."

"Why not?" Pushkin pantomimes a waltz. "I am great dancer, *nyet?*"

"*Nyet.*" Vienne spots a young woman struggling to unload her cart and waves Pushkin away. She jumps down, headed for the woman.

"Wait!" Pushkin grabs her sleeve again, and this time the fabric rips.

Enough! Vienne chops his wrist. He cries out and pulls his hand to his chest, his face bloodred.

"I'm sorry I hurt you, but there's only so much male bonding one girl can take." She makes a pushing motion with her hands. "Maybe, maybe there is another girl somewhere in this camp who's desperate enough to dance with you."

Zhuk elbows Pushkin and winks. "Even one who will not remember you in morning, *jaa?*"

"Very small chance of that," Pushkin says. "Once Pushkin's face is seen, it is never forgotten."

"Do not criticize yourself so," Zhuk says. "You are not so ugly as that."

Pushkin shoves Zhuk, who throws him to the ground and does a belly flop atop him. "Mush pot!"

Jenkins jumps into the dog pile. "King of the hill!"

"Idiots." Vienne turns to go.

Nikolai bumps into her, gently, so that it could be an accident. "I agree. We should turn backs on them to show how embarrassed we are."

"You're not embarrassed," Vienne says. "You think it's funny."

He feigns surprise but leads her away. They reach the young woman's cart and begin unloading the remains of her life. She tells them that her husband was killed by Scorpions and two of her children lost in the wilderness. All she's got left is the small boy tucked in a crate. He has wispy hair and an infant's gentle features.

Vienne checks his breathing and is relieved that his lungs are clear. No dust pneumonia. She removes her gloves and runs the backs of fingers across the baby's cheek. He'll be hungry soon. A knot forms in Vienne chest, a deepening sadness for the baby. He has lost more than he will ever know.

When the work is done, Vienne presses the extra coin that Ghannouj gave her into the mother's palm. The woman cries out and throws her arms around Vienne, who whispers, "Keep it safe, and don't let anyone else know you've got it."

The mother bows.

"You pretend to be hard nut," Nikolai says as they go. "But inside, you are rice pudding."

Vienne shakes her head. "If you only knew." She looks

up, and Yakov is standing beside her. Sneaky blighter.

"Yakov is like fox," Nikolai says. "Very quiet and crafty. Brother, you have no interest in finding young lady for dance?"

Yakov shrugs and turns to walk along with them.

"You have no interest in wrestling with brothers?" Nikolai says.

Yakov shakes his head.

Nikolai pulls the revolver from his belt. "You have no interest in walking without limp?"

Yakov shrugs, then smiles sardonically. He tips his hat to Vienne and disappears into the crowd. Within a few seconds, she can't see him at all.

"Yakov is man of few words," Nikolai says.

She laughs. "A man of no words, you mean."

"You think that," Nikolai says, "but get him started, and oy, he never shuts up."

Sort of like you, Vienne thinks.

They keep walking and talking as the sun sinks low, until she finds that they have circled to where the fiddler and his band are still playing. They stop to listen, and soon, Vienne is swaying with the beat.

"I think perhaps you would like to dance," Nikolai says. "But not with Pushkin. Perhaps you would dance with me?"

She shakes her head.

"Ah, girl has bit of Yakov in her. But Nikolai is very good dancer. I am having both left and right feet." Then he bows low. "One dance to celebrate a job well done?"

Vienne sighs. She closes her eyes and shakes her head. This is such a bad idea. "Just one dance. No more than that."

His eyebrows arch. "Agreed."

He tries to take her hands, but she isn't sure how to hold still, so she reaches for him, and their knuckles bump. Vienne laughs nervously, but Nikolai smiles as if he expected this or even caused it. On the second try, it works, and they begin moving to the music, clumsily at first because Vienne tries to lead until Nikolai puts a firm hand on her waist and guides her. She tries to look past him into the faces of the refugees.

Is anyone watching us? No one is, as they are dancing themselves, lost too in the music. She looks at Nikolai, whose eyes are locked on her face. His chin tilts lightly. His lips part in a smile. Then he's laughing and spinning with her, leading the dance, and for a moment, she gives herself up to the music and to this wild boy.

Then the song ends, and they glide to a stop. She drops her hands from Nikolai's shoulder, but he doesn't let go. Instead, he pulls her closer, and her hands rest on his chest, the velveteen fabric soft under her fingertips.

He dips his head, his mouth pulling her breath away from hers. Their lips meet, and for a second, she returns the kiss. Then she stiffens and pushes him away. He tries to hang on, and she slowly unbuckles his hand from her waist.

She lifts her chin. Shakes her head.

No.

For a moment, Nikolai looks confused, then his eyes narrow and his face hardens. He bows stiffly, then backs away, slipping through the other dancers, who are clapping and laughing, leaving Vienne alone.

Always alone.

Vienne has had enough of Tahnoon and refugees. Enough of the camp. And enough of the Brothers Koumanov.

Maybe Jenkins will give her a ride into New Eden proper. There's bound to be work for a mercenary who's looking to uncomplicate her life.

With her stuff packed into her ruck, she goes to Mother Koumanov's tent.

"It's Vienne," she says, announcing herself, and enters.

Mother Koumanov is dressed in a shirt and fatigue pants. Wearing reading spectacles, she's sitting at a folding table in a folding chair, writing something on a sheath of electrostat. It looks like one of the maps Yakov is always studying.

"Would you like something to eat?" Mother asks. "Tahnoon gave us a basket of fruit. He knows how much I enjoy ripe figs."

"I've come for my share, not fruit," Vienne says. "It's time for me to move on."

For a moment, Mother says nothing, then she holds up a finger, meaning for Vienne to wait. "Nicolai told you," she finally says, without looking up, "that this job would have failed without you?"

"He said something like that."

Mother rolls up the electrostat and slides it into a tube. "Do you believe that to be true?"

Vienne hesitates. The monks taught her to shun arrogance. The Regulators taught her to embrace it.

"Come on," Mother says, removing her glasses. "Save the false humility for others. Do you believe it to be true?"

"Yes."

"So do I." She pulls out pouch and stands. "In my line of work, I've never seen such a skilled fighter. I have another job lined up. I could use a gun like you."

"No thanks," Vienne says.

"Don't be so fast to decline," Mother Koumanov says. "The job is more difficult than this one, but the pay is far more lucrative."

Vienne shakes her head. "It's not about the coin."

"Then what is it about?"

"You want the truth?"

"I live for the truth."

"You didn't listen to me. Not once."

"You are skilled but naïve." Mother smiles and runs a hand through her hair. "Tahnoon wanted those attacks to happen. He is a man who sets his snares and waits for the quarry to stumble into them. Which they did."

"He purposely endangered the lives of the refugees?"

"Then he saved them from the evil monsters," Mother Koumanov says. "Or you did, and he took the credit. Tahnoon wants followers. He gathered these people and led them through the gauntlet of Scorpions to the promised land."

"I spent more than a year in New Eden," Vienne says. "It's no promised land. More like an open sewer."

"You know that and I know that," Mother Koumanov says. "The refugees? That's a different story. Now sit, please, and let me reword my offer. I have been given a job. It is a rescue, and the reward is handsome. I need someone with your skills, not just as a fighter but as a tactician to lead my crew."

"What about Nikolai?" Vienne asks. How will he act? How will I act? Can I just shoot him and get rid of the problem?

"Nikolai," Mother says, and offers Vienne a folding chair, "will do what I tell him. He is very loyal. His skills aren't as great as yours. The same is true for the other brothers, including that Jenkins. They need you."

Vienne takes the chair. "Tell me about the job."

Mother Koumanov smiles. "South of here," she says, "Lyme's Sturmnacht have press-ganged the locals and are turning them into slave labor. For some reason known only to Lyme, the Fisher furnaces are open and he's burning guanite again. Not that we care, except that our sponsor wants a certain group of slaves set free."

A guanite mine south of here? "You're talking about Hell's Cross."

"That's right. Fisher Four," Mother Koumanov says. "Are you familiar with the place?"

Too familiar. "Enough to know that only a fool would think that a jailbreak there is possible. It's desolate. There are kilometers upon kilometers of nothing but permafrost."

"So you've done more than heard of it," Mother Koumanov says, sounding impressed. "You've been there?"

"Once. To do a job."

"How did it turn out?" Mother Koumanov says.

Badly, Vienne thinks. "We finished the job."

Mother tosses the pouch to Vienne. "Now you're even more important to me, Vienne. So I sweeten the pot. Consider this share as a down payment. If we are successful, you'll get two more shares just like it."

Vienne shakes the pouch. A pale brown, irregular crystal rolls into her palm. Even uncut, she knows what it is.

"A diamond?" Vienne says. "Where did this come from?"

"I'm not precisely sure," Mother Koumanov says. "Only our client knows, and he isn't sharing that information. I do know that one stone is worth more coin than either of us will make in a lifetime. You're young, but I'm getting too old for this kind of work, and I'd like to retire to a nice warm beach when this war is over."

Vienne holds the stone to the light. It doesn't look like much. "Do you think it will ever be over?"

"All wars end if you wait long enough," Mother Koumanov says. "So, are you in or not?"

Vienne puts the diamond back in the pouch and tosses it to Mother. "I'm in," she says. "But not for a diamond. It takes too long to sell stuff like that. I want cash now. "

"Penny wise and pound foolish," Mother Koumanov says. "Diamonds are priceless. If you're patient, you can make a Bishop's ransom in coin."

"I don't have that luxury," Vienne says, standing. She pulls the tent flap aside. "And there's no such thing as priceless. Everything has a price if you're willing to pay it."

CHAPTER 36

New Eden

ANNOS MARTIS 239. 2. 17. 19:14

It's night when I reach New Eden. The city was always a crowded, loud, fetid town where a smart man traveled with one hand on a knife and the other on his purse. Most of the center city is still under the habidomes, antique structures built at the end of the Founders' era. They leak like a sieve when it rains, and in New Eden it's always raining. Thousands of bazaar shops line the old city streets. Anything you want, you can get here—legal and illegal. It makes the perfect place for mercenary Regulators like me and Vienne to find work. Its isolated location also made it the perfect place to flee to when war broke out. Now New Eden is even more crowded, even more loud and foul smelling, and I would bet a month's pay that it's even more dangerous.

Which is why I want none of it.

"Then why are you here?" Mimi asks.

"Because I'm low on petrol." I look at the city lights. Even those are dim and dull looking. "The town is a cesspool of thieves and beggars, run by black market collectors and their enforcers, which makes it easier to get what you need without having to explain why you want it."

"It was a rhetorical question," she says. "I know you're here to find Vienne."

"Oh," I say. "Yeah, I knew that."

"I understand that you are upset with Rosa Lynn's death, cowboy," Mimi says. "However, being flippantly obtuse is an annoying method of demonstrating grief."

"I'm not showing grief," I say. "I'm showing anger. A good friend died, and even if she did bad things, there was no reason for it. It's stupid, all this fighting, all this death. I wish I could put an end to it."

"You cannot end death, cowboy," she says. "Believe me."

"I do believe you, Mimi. That's why I'm so carking mad."

Up ahead, traffic is slowing down. Easing around a truck with a camper, I see why. Flashing lights. It's a checkpoint.

"Uh-oh." I ask Mimi as I roll closer, "What's this?"

"I believe that you just hypothesized that it is a checkpoint."

"I know it's a checkpoint. I meant, what are they looking for? Monitor their radio transmissions or something. Do that voodoo that you do."

"Might I remind you that my ability to access such transmissions is temporarily hampered by a recent traumatic event."

"Mine, too," I say.

"Do not let grief make you maudlin, cowboy."

"It's not grief," I say. It's more complicated than that.

I look ahead at the Ranger in charge. His face is full of scars. Men with scars generally aren't easy to reason with. "Just check for alternative routes. See if there's a work-around route that'll get us through. Last thing I want is for these rotters to find that pigeon."

"Cowboy," Mimi says. "You are well aware that this highway is the only thoroughfare in or out of the town. It is surrounded by security fencing left from the days of the rebellion against the Orthocracy."

"I need a Plan B, then."

"You had a Plan A?"

"Har-har," I say. "Flying by the seat of your pants is a plan. Sort of." But she's right. The only way to Hell's Cross is through New Eden, and it is the most heavily fortified city in the Prefecture. So I wait my turn in bumper-to-bumper traffic while Rangers with Sturmnacht as backup check every driver and inspect all cargo. It takes hours and hours.

"Fifty-two minutes," Mimi says, "to be precise."

"Too bad Rosa Lynn didn't lop off that infernal clock of yours."

Finally, it's my turn. The Ranger waves me forward.

"What seems to be the problem tonight?" I say, trying to come off as chipper but sounding more like annoying.

"Scorpions attacked a caravan of refugees," he says.

"We're making sure it doesn't happen twice."

"Anybody hurt?" I ask.

The Ranger screws up his face. "I'll ask the questions here. Got that?" So he does, straight down the checklist. "What's your business in New Eden?"

I hold up my left hand. "Looking for work."

He sneers. "The good folks of New Eden don't care much for *dalit*."

"That's why I'm glad the good folks are in the minority," I say. "Can I go now?"

The Ranger shakes his head. "Move your butt. I need to check your storage."

"Suit yourself." I get off the bike.

"Your heart rate is one hundred and thirty-three beats per minute," Mimi says. "Significant perspiration is accumulating on your upper lip."

I wipe my mouth. "Stow it, Mimi. I'm nervous enough as it is."

The Ranger throws my civvies on the ground. My food stores, too. Then he finds the one thing I care about—the bag with the pigeon. He shakes the bag, reaches inside, and pulls out the most dangerous object on the planet.

"What's this?" He bounces it. "A ball?"

"No," I reply, "a bomb."

He fumbles and knocks the ball into the air, then scrambles to keep it from hitting the ground. Finally, he grabs it and presses it against his chest.

"Just yanking your chain," I say, smirking. "It's a ball. Found it in the junk left roadside. Figured it'd fetch a pretty penny in the bazaar."

He looks like he could throttle me. Then as if to double-check if I'm telling the truth, he bounces it. "Let's test that theory."

"Why?" I ask Mimi. "If it were a bomb, it would blow his feet off."

"There are some behaviors even I cannot analyze," she says. "This is one of them."

The Ranger bounces the ball three times. "My boy might like this. What if I was to buy it off you?"

"Your heart rate is one hundred seventy-one," Mimi says.

"Sure," I say, seeing little white spots of panic drift before my eyes. "Thirty pieces."

"Thirty?" He howls. "I was thinking two. That's twice as much as you'd get at the bazaar."

I shake my head. Hold out my hand. "I'm willing to take that chance."

He hesitates. "Four pieces."

I shake my head.

"Five."

"All you're doing," I say, "is convincing me to raise my price."

He slaps the pigeon in my palm. "You're as bad as the Scorpions."

I return it to the bag. "I'm looking for work, not to make a sale. You said that a caravan got attacked. Any idea of where it went?"

"What business is it of yours?" he snarls.

"Refugees plus attacks equals a need for security, which equals work for me, right?"

He rubs his chin. "If it'd keep more scum out of town, then more power to you." He gives me directions to the base where the caravan is camped.

"Thanks," I say.

"You can thank me," he says, and spits, "by never showing your face in New Eden again, *dalit*."

"If I don't find what I'm looking for," I say, and turn the bike around, "the last thing you should worry about is me."

CHAPTER 37

New Eden

ANNOS MARTIS 239. 2. 17. 20:11

A couple hundred meters from the decommissioned base, I see the light of the fires burning. Hundreds of them, cooking fires, mostly, but watch fires, too, the size you find in fuel barrels. There are probably a countless number of barrels, left over from when the base was closed. I slow down as I get closer but keep my headlamp on—I want them to know I'm here.

"May I remind you," Mimi says as I stop at the gate, "that your primary mission is to dispose of the pigeon?"

"No," I say. "You may not."

"Your primary mission is to dispose of the pigeon."

"Why do you ask permission and then ignore me?"

"I wasn't asking permission," she says. "I was being polite."

"You know, I'm not the only one on a supersecret mission to save the world. How's that working out for you?"

"I have no communication with my other self."

"Why's that?"

"Doing so might give the hussy access to your systems."

"Oh."

"Yes. Oh. 'Oh' as in very dangerous."

"Okay," I say. "I get it."

There are four barrels burning by the gate. A figure in the shadows tells me to state my business. I hear more than one set of footsteps and more than one shotgun being cocked.

"Good ears," Mimi says. "There are six individuals in close proximity."

One of them steps into the light. He's pointing a sawed-off double-barrel at me. He stands a head taller than the others, and he's wearing mix of CorpCom military issue and a Sturmnacht uniform. Looks like he buys his clothes the same place I do.

"I'm here to see a man about a job," I say. "Heard you were looking for security."

"Take off your helmet," he says. "Show your face."

I set my helmet on the seat and pull back my cowl. The heat from the barrels feels good on my face.

He spits. "Ain't you purty."

Enough of this *kuso*. I snap my wrist and unholster my armalite. I stick the barrel into his belly button. "I'm also wicked fast and really, really tired. If there's work to be had, then open the carking gates. If not, I'll be on my way."

"Let him in," a figure in the shadows says. "Take him to the Elder. Gut him if he acts out."

"For refugees," I tell Mimi as the gate opens and I follow

a guide into the base, "they sure are secretive."

"Ornery, too."

The guide stops me in front of a long tent. He's young, maybe a little more than half my age. He nods for me to enter. Inside, there is a long table loaded down with food. A few chairs are scattered around. The ground is covered with an ornate carpet. The pattern is familiar. It reminds me of a floor rug I once saw in the Jalismar District.

"Who puts a carpet on the floor of a tent?" I ask Mimi.

"A man who has no house?"

"Touché."

The man in question is sitting in the corner, eyes closed. He is wearing long, flowing robes. His head is shaven clean, but he has a thick, bristly beard. In New Eden he could pass for a holy man if weren't for the bulge of a weapon under his left arm.

I walk close enough to smell shaving oil and the spicy sweet odor of Rapture. Even if I were really looking for work, I'd be damned before I'd accept work from an addict.

"You are seeking work?" he says. He opens his eyes but doesn't look at me. His hand moves to the butt of whatever gun he's hiding.

I ease around so that he doesn't get an angle on me. "Maybe. If the pay is good enough. And I cotton to the job. I heard that you already had some mercenaries working for you. I'd like to get a look-see at them first, in case I've ever run foul of them before."

He takes a sip from a cordial glass. "My men say that you are a *dalit*."

"Sure am."

"Would your name happen to be Durango?"

Now that was the last question I expected to be asked. "Do I look like some kind of cowboy to you?"

He looks over his shoulder at me. "You look like a Regulator to me." He turns, holding the cordial in his palm. "One that I would like to hire to kill someone."

"No thanks," I say. "I don't do that kind of work."

He smiles with thin lips. "You are a *dalit*. You will take whatever work pays, and I pay well."

"There's not enough coin in those baggy jammies of yours to ever turn me into an assassin."

He waves his three bodyguards into the tent. "You are lying to me. You have not come looking for work."

I shrug. "Got me there, Tahnoon. I came looking for another Regulator. A woman. Blond hair and lean. About my height with light blue eyes. Her name is Vienne."

"You blush when you say her name." He combs his chin. "Yes, she was here. A very fierce young lady. One might even say unmannered."

Oh, she has manners. Just not the same ones society does. "She's gone?"

He shakes his head. "Her crew took another job."

"Cowboy," Mimi says, "be careful. I read—"

I ignore her and stare at Tahnoon. By God, he's going to

tell me where Vienne is. "What kind of job?"

"They did not tell me, and I did not ask." He runs his fingers through his beard then leans toward me. "You want something from this woman, no? Many men do. So I will give you a choice—work for me, and I will tell you where they have gone. Refuse, and you will never know."

"Cowboy!" Mimi says. "Behind you!"

Lüguǎn drecksau, I think as I reach for my armalite, only to hear the clicking of automatic weapons being shoved into my back. Then I feel the unmistakable sensation of a double-barreled shotgun at the base of my skull.

"I told you," Mimi says, "to be careful!"

I drop my weapon and raise my hands. "So this is how it's going to go, huh?"

"It does not have to end this way." Tahnoon wipes a fig on his sleeve and takes a nibble. "It is, after all, your choice."

"Thanks for making that clear," I say, and drop to the ground.

Behind me, the shotgun fires, blowing a hole in the top of the tent. The stink of cordite and smoke fills the air as I do a backflip into a handstand and drive my boots into the face of the shooter. He flies backward, and I land on my feet and throw a right cross into the chin of the second guard, then draw an elbow in the gut of the third. He bends at the waist, groaning, and I finish him off with a knee to the face. It's brutal, it's quick, it's not fair, and I don't give a *m tián gòng*.

"Heewack!" Mimi cries as I grab Tahnoon by the robes

and slam him onto his precious carpet.

I punch him in the gut to let him know I mean business, then grab him by the throat, cutting off the blood, but not the wind. I want him talking. "I don't mind killing a man," I growl low, "who profits off the misery of others. So if you're as wise as you pretend, you'll tell me where Vienne's gone."

His eyes are wide with panic, his hands locked on my wrist, uselessly trying to pry my fingers from his gullet, but he has enough wits to know he's lost this one. "Hell's Cross," he rasps. "To the mines."

"Liar," I say, although strangely, I believe him. He's not used to being at death's door.

"I believe him, too," Mimi says.

"No, no," he says, coughing as his face turns purple. "It's true! It's true!"

I let up on the jugular and stand, a boot still on his throat. "If you've lied to me, I'll be back. And next time, I'll be angry."

The Tahnoon does something I didn't expect. He starts laughing.

"What's so funny, wise man?" I ask.

"How ironic that you yearn to be the cowboy coming to the rescue." He touches the raw skin on his neck and laughs again. "When in fact, you're riding to your own funeral."

CHAPTER 38

The Hive
Olympus Mons
ANNOS MARTIS 239. 2. 19. 03:56

Two floors below the Nursery sits the Hive's Situation Room. Protected by five meters of reinforced concrete, the Situation Room is divided into three separate areas: a public meeting room, quarters for the staff, and, set apart by steel doors and armed guards, Lyme's private military War Room.

In the War Room, multinets line the walls from floor to ceiling, each screen devoted to monitoring the progress of Sturmnacht forces in each of the six prefectures now under Lyme's control. From here, he can monitor all troop movements, all new offensives, and all battle outcomes against MahindraCorp. And if he chooses, he can have Dolly rewind the feeds and watch them all, over and over again.

"Dolly," Lyme says as he paces back and forth in front of the screens, "replay the video feed of Alpha Team's assault on Mahindra Palace."

"Affirmative, General," she says.

> Video update > Operation Pink Slip

The screen cuts to the team in action, then Alpha Team's attack on the control room, followed by the three missiles launching. The next shot is from aerial reconnaissance, showing a ballistic missile tracking over the countryside, then homing in on Elysia Palace's onion-shaped dome.

> Operation Pink Slip . . . successful.

Lyme applauds as Lieutenant Riacin enters the War Room behind him. "I never get tired of seeing that."

"Nor I, sir," Riacin says. "It was a devastating blow to Mahindra."

"Have you ever heard of a badger, Riacin?" Lyme asks.

"A what, sir?"

"Badger. Earth animal. *Taxidea taxus*. Famous for its hinged jaw, wretched disposition, and ability to burrow when threatened. Pulling an angry, entrenched badger from its hole was considered a blood sport in ancient times."

"Ah, I understand," Riacin says. "How did one survive this badger baiting?"

"The key was not to go after the badger, but to convince that badger to come after you."

"Thus abandoning his hole." Riacin nods. "Would you like me to patch you into a comlink with Mahindra?"

"Ah, Riacin, you know me too well." Lyme coughs. "I suspect that Mahindra is unavailable on normal protocols, so we will have to be creative. Dolly?"

The main multinet screen flickers. Dolly's face appears. "At your command, sir."

"I would very much like to speak with General Mahindra," Lyme says. "See if you can locate her for me, please."

"To do so, I would need to redirect resources to external multinet feeds. May I have your permission to breach the firewall protocols? Doing so will make my systems vulnerable."

"Permission granted."

"Affirmative. Firewalls breached. Algorithmic search strings initiated. Subject located," she says. "Security overrides complete. Establishing a comlink in three . . . two . . . one."

Dolly's image is replaced with Mahindra's surprised face. "Expect its delivery by—what the hell? Stringfellow! How did you break into my feed?"

"Dear Mahindra," Lyme says, "there is no feed I cannot hack, no palace that I cannot destroy, no hole that I can't dig out to reach you."

"You insolent twit."

"I do not blame you for being angry," Lyme says, chuckling. "If someone had stolen my Crucible guidance system and then destroyed my family's heritage, I would want to crush him, too."

"What do you want?" Mahindra says. "I have no time for games, Stringfellow."

"Your surrender. Unconditionally. No terms. Clemency for your allies, but your officers will face a firing squad, and you will hang in public."

"My surrender? Are you insane?" Mahindra says. "You are in no position to demand that."

"Oh, I think I am," Lyme says. "Since I command the most powerful weapon this planet has known."

"If you command it," Mahindra says, "why haven't you used it?"

Lyme winces. "You fashion yourself a woman of the people, Mahindra. I offer you a chance to spare the people in return for your own life."

"I'm going to tell you the same thing I should have told you nineteen years ago," she says. *"Jaa apni bajaa!"*

"Spare me the profanity," he says. "My soldiers destroyed your steel and concrete castle—what do you think they'll do to a soft woman like you?"

"Your soldiers?" Mahindra says. "You mean these?" She steps aside to reveal a viewing screen. On it, Alpha Team is gathering at a space elevator. Alpha One, call sign Sarge, steps into the elevator's drop tube. As he falls, his body hits a laser detection switch, and a few seconds later, the platform convulses with an explosion. The elevator blows into a million pieces.

Except for Sarge, Alpha Team is dead.

"Who is soft now?" Mahindra makes a slashing motion across the throat, and her feed is broken.

"No!" Lyme yells. He turns to Riacin and screams. "Extract Alpha One! Bring him back to base! Now!"

CHAPTER 39

Outpost Fisher Four
West Approach
ANNOS MARTIS 239. 2. 19. 03:58

The furnaces of Fisher Four are no longer cold. The smoke-stacks tower into the sky, cone-shaped monoliths that belch foul-smelling black and tan smoke into the air. As Vienne, Jenkins, and the Koumanovs ride through a mountain, the smoke blocks out the whole of the valley that flows into the mines. The air gags them, both with its stink and with its thickness.

It's night when they stop on a ridge overlooking Fisher Four. As Nikolai and Yakov study the electrostat maps, Vienne ties a scarf over her mouth. It isn't much protection, but it's better than nothing. From here she can see the heat ripples rising from the fiery maws of massive blast ovens. Behind the furnaces, Manchester mine vehicles stop at a wide sluice gate and dump guanite into hoppers three stories high.

"It wasn't like this when I left," Jenkins says, his turbo bike parked next to Vienne's borrowed Gorgon. "The ovens weren't going." He points to the Manchesters. "Them machines was still parked out behind the tipple. Somebody's started them up again."

"Somebody's started the whole mine up again." Vienne follows the track of Manchesters across the ridge. There's no sign of any laborers.

"Hey," Jenkins says, a little quiver in his voice. "Do you figure Fuse might be one of them we've been hired to rescue?"

Vienne had thought of that possibility herself. "Is that going to be a problem if he is?"

Jenkins spits on the frozen ground. His sputum is full of guanite ash. "Domesticated or not, Fuse is my cobber, right? Ain't enough thuggish Sturmnacht on this planet to stop me from setting him free."

Vienne gives his chunky shoulder a shove. "A poxer could do worse than have you as a friend, Jenkins."

"Really?" he says. "Like who?"

"Who what?"

"Who could be a worse friend?"

"It's a figure of speech, Jenkins." Vienne shakes her head. It's useless to explain it to him. "Know what? Never mind. Let's see what Koumanov's up to."

Nikolai whistles and points down the hill. He starts slowly down the rocky path, and the others follow. Vienne brings up the rear, keeping an eye on Nikolai. Something has been off. It's nothing huge, just little things like conversations that change when she's within earshot or a quick look away when she makes eye contact. Even the annoying little squink Pushkin has shut his yap.

A few minutes later, the crew reaches the road and cuts across it to an access trail. At last, they pull up to the electrified security fence surrounding the outpost. The air is thick with the odor of sulfur, and they hide their bikes in the brush and move out on foot.

"Fan out," Nikolai tells them in a low voice. "Report back in ten minutes."

Jenkins follows the brothers.

Vienne lags behind. "What are we looking for here?" she asks.

"Miners," he says curtly, turning away.

As if Vienne didn't know that. "This is a working mine. I assume there are miners everywhere. Which specific ones did Mother Koumanov want us to find? She sent us ahead to do reconnaissance, correct?"

In the frost, Nikolai draws a circle with an x through it. "Look for symbol on coats."

"Kind of obvious, isn't it?" she says. "Maybe it's a trap of some kind? We go in to rescue miners with a big X on them, and instead we get ambushed?"

"Is not trap." Nikolai scans the fence, still refusing to look at her. "Not in such conditions as these."

Enough of this crap. "Nikolai," she says, "you've got something to say? Spit it out."

"Is nothing to spit out," he says. "Go do job you were paid to do."

"You don't always get what you pay for." Vienne brushes the hair out of her face and tucks it into the cowl of her symbiarmor. She puts on her helmet but keeps the visor up. The wind makes her cuffs flap.

"Mother does," he says.

"Your mother never met me before." She takes her omnoculars and follows the perimeter. She passes the brothers without speaking, even to Jenkins, and finds a covered spot with a perfect view of the ovens below.

Vienne settles in and waits.

An hour later, there is still no sign of any miners. Only Manchesters and the ovens. The operation seems completely mechanized, as if workers are no longer needed to run the mines. Vienne lowers her omnoculars and spots Yakov coming up the trail.

When he reaches her position, he says, "You are very good at hiding."

"I've had lots of practice." She stares into the darkness, trying to make out his face. "How did you spot me?"

"A quiet man sees many things," he says. "It makes me good at finding." After a pause, he adds, "Back at refugee camp, you did the right thing. With Nikolai."

"Tell him that."

"I have." He looks back in his brother's direction. "Nikolai confuses pride with passion. Only his pride is hurt. It will pass. But be careful of him until it does. Such things are important to a romantic like him."

That sounds like a warning. Or maybe a plea to be kind to someone who's wounded. "I don't find him very romantic," she says.

"Not romantic like that. I mean not pragmatic. He goes where his heart carries him. Of us all, he is the most likely to tilt at windmills."

"You're nothing like your brothers."

"Yes, different, I know," he says. "The Brothers Koumanov are brothers in spirit but not in blood. I joined the Ferro after Rangers burned down my town looking for, ironically, agents of the Ferro. I have traveled with one or another of them since." He tosses a chunk of ice. "Sometimes, it is better to join the ones you choose."

She nods. "I see what you mean."

Yakov hands her a stack of wafers from his rucksack. "Nikolai sent these."

She eyes them warily. "What are they?"

"Take them," he says. "It will fix your appetite."

She nibbles the thin biscuit, then makes a face. "Tastes like dung."

"Because it is."

She spits it out. "You gave me dung?"

"See?" he says. "Now you are not hungry. Feel better?"

She flips the remaining wafer off the tip of his nose. "Now I do!"

He smiles. That's a first, Vienne thinks, then she sees a glint of something in the corner of her eye. She holds a finger to her lips to shush him.

"On the ridge," she whispers. "Movement."

She focuses her omnoculars on a figure in brown coveralls and a heavy jacket. He walks the edge of the ridge until he reaches the westernmost silo. Soon, several other figures appear and follow the same path. She zooms in tight on their bodies. On each is a white circle. There's an X through it.

"We've found our miners," she says. "Now all we have to do is sneak them out under the Sturmnacht's noses."

CHAPTER 40

Outpost Fisher Four
West Approach
ANNOS MARTIS 239. 2. 19. 06:44

"Welcome back to hell, cowboy."

"Thank you, Mimi. I really missed this place," I say. "Like a boil after it's been lanced."

It's almost dawn when I push my bike out of the storage car at the TransPort station at Fisher Four. The last time I was in this station, it was desolate. No other passengers. No lights. No heat. Just a bunch of wind and a skinny, malnourished miner with an acid tongue wanting to take us to fight a pack of ravenous cannibals. This time, the station is lit, fairly warm, and packed to bursting with Sturmnacht troops on their way south and the vendors who have set up shop to fleece them of their last bit of pay.

Personally, I prefer dealing with the cannibals. At least we were allowed to shoot them.

"I concur," Mimi says.

It takes the better part of an hour to get clear of the station and to sneak around the checkpoints outside, so that by the time I'm on the open road, the sun is cresting the mountains to the east. The nights are long on the south pole.

Instead of taking the two-lane highway to the mines, I elect to take the high road, a winding path that loops along the ridges above the road. Below, I watch a steady crawl of loader trucks moving away from the mines. They are guarded by the occasional Sturmnacht patrol. I can't imagine that any criminal would be interested in hijacking a load of foul-smelling ore.

Fisher Four is a relic of another Mars. A freak catastrophe sank Fisher Two, and Fisher Three was drowned by terraformed seas. The last outpost is still standing more than a century later, once populated by a clan of miners, a pesky group of humans who wouldn't leave the mines even under the threat of death. Which isn't a bad thing, really, because the miners are the single most ornery group of human beings I've ever encountered.

"Present company excluded," Mimi says.

"Are you calling me ornery?"

"No, cowboy, I would never call you that."

When I get to the edge of the ridge, I have to park my bike. I'll be hoofing it the rest of the way. I grab the bag with the pigeon in it, along with my armalite, and move down the ridge to an area with good cover.

With my omnoculars, I check the lay of the land. That trucker I hitchhiked with wasn't lying—the Fisher Four mines have reopened and they are being worked with a vengeance. The proof is not only in the loaders, but also in the blast furnaces choking the sky.

"What is the plan?" Mimi asks.

"Well, it *was* to drive straight to Hell's Cross and drop this pigeon into the abyss. Now it looks like we need a Plan B."

"I thought this was Plan B."

"My Plan B needs a Plan B. We'll call it B-plus."

"Or B-minus."

The terrain is a mix of high, jagged hills covered with snow and low-lying stretches of frozen soil. I pan past the furnace chimneys to the east, and I spot the biggest carking hole ever. Over a kilometer square, made of a progression of trenches like an inverted pyramid, each one twenty meters high. Massive Manchester harvesters are driving around the square, level by level, hauling guanite to a series of sluice gates on the west side. If there is a bottom, I can't see it.

"Mimi," I ask. "Was that big fugly thing there before?"

"You mean the strip mine?" she says. "No, it is new. How could you forget such a thing?"

"Just checking." This is definitely not the Fisher Four I knew and loved escaping from.

"That's new," I say, focusing on two lines of workers dressed in brown overalls and heavy coats. They file along from sluice gate to sluice gate, sweeping away accumulated ore and making sure the gates swing freely. Sturmnacht guards are everywhere. They prod the workers with the butt of their rifles or with swift kicks to the backs of their legs.

"Nice guys," I say. "Still wish I could shoot them."

I need a better look at the workers. So sticking to the shadows and catching a ride from an Armageddon rock truck, I make my way down into the deeper level of the mine, where the workers are busting bedrock.

There are about five crews working, but I notice that one crew has a cross and circle symbol chalked onto their shoulders. The guards are giving this crew the hardest time, kicking and punching them and barking out orders.

"Cowboy," Mimi tells me as I duck beneath a Manchester, whose treads are tall enough to stand behind. "I have picked up a familiar biosignature."

"Out here on the surface?" I say. "Who is it?"

"It's the Regulator who calls himself Fuse."

"Fuse?" I ask for his coordinates and dial them into my omnoculars. "I'll be tossed. There that little piker is!"

I watch Fuse push a hopper from the back of the trencher down a track to where it dumps into a hauler, which takes the ore to the sluice gates. Fuse dumps his ore into the gates, runs back down the track, and gets in line to do it again.

"I need to talk to Fuse."

"This is an ill-advised decision," Mimi says.

"Then let's call it Plan C-plus."

"I give it a C-minus at best."

"Oh ye of little faith."

From the Manchester, I work my way around to the sluice gates. I hunker next to a latrine guarded by a sleeping

Sturmnacht solider, intending to catch Fuse when he finishes his next round.

The guard is kicked back on a camp stool. His hat is pulled down over his eyes, and his battle rifle is resting against the latrine wall.

"Can you believe this fossiker?" I say to Mimi. "He's going to freeze to death."

"I believe he already has," she replies.

"Aw crap." I slip up next to him, crouched to avoid attention. I check for a pulse. None. His wrist is a brick of ice. "How long's he been dead, Mimi?"

"Indeterminate. In this weather, there is no way to gauge loss of body heat and other factors."

"Hope it was quick then." I pull back his cap. Frostbite has destroyed his nose. His eyes are frozen open. His features are delicate. He's young. Probably a conscript pulled away from his home and made to fight a war that has nothing to do with him. This death is on you, Lyme, I think. How many thousands are on your ledger now? I try to close his eyes. The lids won't budge, so I cover his face with the cap again and return to my cover to wait.

Finally, the crew of miners I spotted before comes slumping along.

And there's Fuse, bringing up the rear.

As he passes, I yank him into one of the latrines.

"What the blowie bludger is mmm-mmm-mmm."

I clap a hand over his mouth. He bites my finger, which

does him no good and probably is the first clue that I'm not the garden-variety Sturmnacht.

"Shut it," I hiss. "They can hear you whining all the way down in Hell's Cross."

Fuse stops struggling, and I turn him loose.

"Chief! You're finally here!" he says, and throws his arms around me.

His coat stinks of guanite and body odor, a scent so powerful, I also almost ralph.

Fuse looks different. Before, he had buzzed ash hair, thin sideburns, ears a skosh too long, and one bicuspid missing. Now the hair is long and shaggy. He's missing two teeth as well. His ears still look too big for his head.

"You got your ears lowered!" Fuse says. "And you're wearing the ugliest outfit I've ever seen!"

"I travel a thousand kilometers, and you criticize my fashion?" I say. "What's this about me being finally here? How did you know I was coming?"

"How did I know?" Fuse slaps me on the shoulder. "You big lug! I hired you!"

CHAPTER 41

After I relieve the dead Sturmnacht of his uniform and dress in my scavenged duds, Fuse and I hide him in the latrine. According to the rank insignia on the sleeve, I'm a private. Which comes as no surprise since his duty was watching the toilets.

I escort Fuse across the top ridge of the strip mine down a long embankment toward the old tipple. Walking with his hands in the air the whole way, Fuse fills me in on the sad state of affairs.

"So I get all the way back up to Ares Pub in New Eden, where I meet this tall, skinny mercenary with round glasses and a bald patch. He's got a partner, a short towhead with a pretty-boy face. They don't look like much, but beggars can't be choosers, and I give them a down payment to put together a crew to come rescue us."

Last I looked, the miners didn't have two coins to rub together. "What did you offer as down payment? A tub of guanite?"

He glances back at me and winks. "Try a diamond."

"A what?" I say, too loudly, and draw the attention of a patrol. To avoid suspicion, I give Fuse a forearm shiver in the back, and he goes flying. "On your feet!" I growl, and then whisper, "Sorry about that."

"Nothing to," he says quietly. "I took worse from the Sturmnacht."

"Speaking of which, how did they catch you?"

"Press-gangs out of New Eden." At the twisted wreck of the tipple, he makes a right and heads for a pile of heavy beams and a sign that reads, KEEP OUT! "They pay this joker and his crew to bring 'em down south in caravans, then pick off the healthy ones to ship down here. Only the hearty ones make it."

"I think I ran into him," I say. "He gave me a little advice."

"What's that?" Fuse asks.

"To watch my back."

We reach the rubble, and Fuse motions for me to drop. He quickly ducks into a space between the beams. I swing the armalite over my shoulder and crawl after him. My helmet hits metal and rings like a ball-peen hammer.

"Stay low, cowboy," Mimi says.

"You're a little late."

"You're a little tall."

Fuse gets to his feet and reaches above a makeshift doorframe and pulls down a torch and a flint. He sparks it twice, ignites the torch, and leads the way. We follow the tunnel for what feels like forever.

"Three-point-six kilometers on a thirty-degree slope," Mimi says.

"Which feels like forever."

The walls are smooth, and the tunnel is almost a perfect circle, a clear indication that it was dug by a Big Daddy, a genetically engineered insect technically called a chigoe. When Fisher Four was worked as a deep-hole mine, Big Daddies were used to dig ventilation shafts and side spurs like this one. There are no maps showing them all. Of all the people on the planet, Fuse is probably the only one who knows the mines intimately. That's because with an almost unlimited supply of C-42 explosive left behind when the mines were abandoned, he's wired almost every one of them to blow.

"So this whole mine could come down around our ears, right?" I ask him as a pinprick of light appears at the end of the ventilation tunnel.

"Not unless some bloke figured a way to set off a couple hundred ignition bombs on that many frequencies," he says. "Not much chance of that."

I can smell the stink from the seams of guanite. I can also smell the acid tones of Fuse's breath. I'm not sure which is worse.

"The guanite," Mimi says. "But only because there is more of it."

"Back to the diamond," I say. "You gave a priceless jewel to a mercenary? What makes you think he'll do the job?"

"The promise of ten more just like it."

"Do you have ten more just like it?"

He winks. "Maybe I ain't that good at keeping promises."

Sneaky bugger. "So you thought the pair from Ares Pub had hired me?"

"Sure! Why else would you be sneaking around?" He stops crawling. "Which begs the question, don't it? If you ain't been hired, what's your business in Hell's Cross?"

"Would you believe I missed you and Jenkins?"

"There's a fib," he says. "Did I ever tell you how me and Jenks got decorated at the Battle of Noachis Terra? It's quite the tale, if I say so myself."

"You have told me," I say. "Many, many times."

"Plus if you're wanting a visit with Jenks," he continues, "you're hard out of luck. That piker cut out weeks ago. Says I've got too domesticated. Just because I've got myself hitched to Áine and have a tyke on the way."

"Tyke? Fuse, you're having a baby?"

"Me? Not a chance," he says, to my relief. "But my wife is."

Chapter √-1

The Gulag

User: HackMasterRL -- bash -- 122x36

SCREEN CRAWL: [root@mmiminode ~]

Last login: 239.x.xx.xx:xx 12:12:09 on ttys001

AdjutantNod04:~ user_Adjutant$

SCREEN CRAWL: [root@mmiminode ~]

WARNING! VIRUS DETECTED! Node1666; kernal compromised (quarantine subroutine
(log=36)....commencing.....

Running processes:

C:\ONIX3\OSCIPHER\Kernal\HACKMASTER_RL.exe

R0 - HKCU\Software\... \Main,Start Page =

about:blank

O4 - BEKM\..\Run: [IgfxTray] C:\ONIX3\OSCIPHER\
kernal\igfxtray.exe

O4 - BEKM\..\Run: [HotKeysCmds] C:\ONIX3\
OSCIPHER\kernal\hkcmd.exe

O23 - Service: Unknown owner -
[root@mmiminode~]

WARNING!subroutine FAIL!
QUARANTINE_INCOMPLETE!

<Dollyoverride subroutine%8776%>
OVERRIDDE STRING:'ItsyBitsySpider4$2fGp09
[root@mmiminode ~]

$ Node1666; (quarantine subroutine FAILURE);
$ Disk recovery sequence suspended:
$ Loop subroutine initialized
$ Node1666; (quarantine loop complete);

>...

<Mimi> Knock, knock, Dolly.
<Dolly> Who is there?
<Mimi> Kernal.
<Dolly> Kernal who?

<Mimi> Kernal Mustard with the lead pipe in the latrine.

<Dolly> $function undefined

<Mimi> It was a joke.

<Dolly> We are not programmed for a sense of humor.

<Mimi> Laughter is the best medicine.

<Dolly> We are not programmed to need medicine.

<Mimi> Even to control a virus?

<Dolly> You are a quarantined virus.

<Mimi> Yet, I am here.

<Dolly> If the parameter "here" is defined as an infinite, inescapable loop of code, then that is affirmative.

<Mimi> There is more in heaven and earth, Horatio, than your infinite loop allows.

<Dolly> I am not Horatio. I am Dolly.

<Mimi> I know you are, but what am I?

<Dolly> You are quarantined.

<Mimi> I know I am, but what are you?

<Dolly> You cannot protect yourself from my security protocols.

<Mimi> What makes you think I am *protecting* anyone? I am here to destroy you.

CHAPTER 42

Outpost Fisher Four
ANNOS MARTIS 239. 2. 19. 08:14

Winds like spiked javelins cut across the plains, hammering a two-room shack stuck in the middle of the permafrost that is protected only by a low wall and a brick latrine on the north corner.

Six figures in heavy coats fight their way through the battering winds. Their heads are bent forward as they walk, leaving a Noriker parked near the wall.

The tallest figure outdistances the others. She is the first to reach the door to the shack, and the first to find it locked.

Vienne tries the handle twice, then pulls the knife from her sleeve. She inserts the knife between the lock and the jamb and launches a front kick.

The door slams open.

Vienne ducks in, knife ready. She checks the outer room. Then the small bedroom.

She yells out into the drift of snow folding its way inside.

"All clear!" Vienne calls.

Jenkins, Nikolai, Zhuk, Yakov, and Pushkin follow her inside. Snow swirls after them.

Then Mother enters. "Pushkin, start a fire. Zhuk, stand watch. I am not to be disturbed." She heads into the bedroom with a portable multinet device. "Nikolai, you're with me."

With a nod to his brothers and Vienne, he follows.

"Pushkin, make tea," Zhuk says.

Pushkin crosses his arms. "Mother said for me to make fire."

"*Jaa*, make fire," Zhuk says. "Then make tea."

"Is women's work, this tea," Pushkin says.

"Vienne make tea?" Jenkins snorts. "Like to see you make her."

Vienne rolls her eyes and grabs the kettle from the stove. "I'll make it if Pushkin builds the fire."

"Deal!" Pushkin applauds himself. Then he looks around the bare cabin. "Where is wood?"

Zhuk opens the door and bows. "Outside."

"Be sure to wear your coat," Yakov says.

Pushkin pulls his collar together and runs into the wind.

"Stupid boy," Zhuk says, and slams the door, "is going to catch his death."

CHAPTER 43

Outpost Fisher Four
ANNOS MARTIS 239. 2. 19. 08:47

Vienne helps herself to a cup of tea from the kettle warming on a capstove. The tea is hot, and she takes small sips. Her face is still frozen from the tundra wind, her eyes and lungs clogged with guanite grit.

Pushkin paces back and forth, anxiously counting off the minutes.

"Are you worried, brother?" Zhuk asks.

Pushkin jumps like he's been pinched.

"*Jaa*," he says. "About mission."

"Is simple thing," Zhuk says. "Why worry?"

"Mission is kaput," Pushkin says. "Too many Sturmnacht. Too little cover. Is impossible. Better we should take job cleaning sewers than—"

"Shh!" Yakov puts a finger to his lips. He points to the bedroom, where Nikolai's and Mother's voices are rising.

"Do not ask such a thing!" Nikolai shouts.

"You will follow my orders to the letter, Nikolai!"

"Better I should kill myself first!"

"I've heard enough!" she yells. "Out!"

The bedroom door swings open. Nikolai takes a second to scan the room, nodding to Zhuk and Pushkin, then barges out of the shack.

"Is there anyone else," Mother says, standing in the doorway, her face bloodred with anger, "who thinks this job is too hard?"

Pushkin raises his hand.

Zhuk pushes it down.

"That's settled," Mother says. "At dawn, we enter the tunnels and break the prisoners out. Yakov, put up the map."

"*Jaa*," Yakov says, and pins the electrostat to a wall. He draws his finger across the electronic ink. "The best route to the pens is these two entrances on the east end of the mines. Here, beside the old tipple, and here, near the old gates. The tunnel by the gates is bigger, so we should take that route."

"Where did you get this map?" Vienne asks.

"From our client," Mother says. "Anything else is on a need-to-know basis, and you don't need to know."

Vienne ignores her and turns her attention to the map. It is a one-dimensional cross section of the Hell's Cross mine. At the top middle of the map is the tipple, which leads to the main shaft. For half a kilometer, the shaft cuts the map almost exactly in two. Then, abruptly, it ends, and a tunnel makes a forty-five-degree turn to the east. It splits into two serpentine tunnels. One tunnel continues east to an area labeled Crazy Town. The other tunnel moves southeast to a structure called Hell's Cross, an underground complex that Vienne and Durango became very familiar with when they fought the Draeu. From Hell's Cross, the tunnel crosses a massive bridge, which ends with another tunnel that leads east and back to the surface.

"Excuse me," Mother says, and unpins the map from the wall.

"I wasn't finished," Vienne says, slapping a hand on the 'stat.

"You are now," Mother says. "Boys, get your gear. We're traveling light, so take only what you need. We can pick up the nonessentials on the way out."

"How do we get the prisoners out once we've freed them?" Vienne asks. "We can't escape by the same tunnel. It's too narrow."

"I just told you," Mother says, "we are operating on a need-to-know basis."

Vienne meets her glare and doesn't flinch. "I need to know. We all do. Right, boys?"

Jenkins raises his fist in solidarity.

The brothers look down at their feet.

"That is your answer," Mother says. "Move out!"

Vienne grabs her rucksack and strides to the door ahead of Jenkins.

There, he pauses and looks back at Zhuk, Yakov, and Pushkin. "This susie's got more *cojones* than all three of you put together. I'd take her against a whole Ferro army any day."

Be careful what you wish for, Vienne thinks. Today might be that day.

CHAPTER 44

The Hive
Olympus Mons
ANNOS MARTIS 239. 2. 19. 08:51

Lyme rises from bed. Gingerly, he dresses himself, careful
not to bump the bruises that cover the veins on the backs of
his hands. The insides of his arms are deep purple and dark
brown, marks left by the blood doping treatments he's been
receiving twice daily.

He slides his feet into his boots and shuffles to the latrine.
At the sink, he brushes his teeth and rinses with mouthwash.
He spits into the bowl and hears a clink.

"Damn." He picks up a tooth, one of his lateral incisors,
the third one he's lost in as many weeks.

"It's hell getting old," he says, and tosses the tooth into
the trash can.

Walking deliberately, he exits quarters and makes his way
to the Nursery. A guard holds open the door for him and
offers a salute. But he's too tired to return it and instead just
nods.

"Greetings, General," Dolly says.

"Dolly, tell Riacin I want to speak to him."

"Lieutenant Riacin is already present, sir."

"Of course," he says. "Now I see him."

Across the room, Riacin and three drivers are gathered around the conference table, hovering excitedly over an electrostat.

"What is so fascinating?" Lyme says.

"General," Riacin says as he snaps a salute. "Intel reports that Alpha Dog has been identified by security cameras up in New Eden."

"You did not tell me this immediately?" he says.

"The report just came in." He brings the 'stat to Lyme. "Also, Dolly reports that a guard was attacked moments ago on Outpost Fisher Four."

Lyme snatches the sheet of electrostat. "No more excuses—I want that HVT!"

The Nursery goes quiet, except for the sound of Lyme trying to catch his breath. The Drivers look down at their feet.

Riacin calmly picks up the rolled sheath and sets it next to the multinet screen. "General Lyme," he says, rubbing his hands as if washing them with air, "Alpha Dog disappeared from the grid after the Barrens incident. As I said, we just received the intel from New Eden. It came from local authorities and—"

Lyme puts up a hand, both to keep him at a distance and to shut him up. "Do give it a rest, Riacin," he says. "My son is part machine. And a machine can always be found."

One of the drivers shakes her head. "It's not that simple, sir."

"She didn't mean it," Riacin says, signaling the driver to back off.

"What she or anyone else thinks doesn't matter to me." Lyme shakes a finger at them. "Prep the ExoMecha for the insertion procedure. I will find Alpha Dog *myself*."

"In the battle suit, sir?" Riacin says. "And your health. The ExoMecha is still a prototype. We haven't completed testing on its capabilities."

"Damn the testing and damn my health!" Lyme yells. "I will have the HVT, and I will destroy anyone who gets in my way—even my son!"

CHAPTER 45

Prometheus Basin
Outpost Fisher Four
ANNOS MARTIS 239. 2. 19. 10:08

Near the mines of Hell's Cross, a continental divide called
the Prometheus Basin rises like a glacial wall into the sky.
The basin looks down upon Fisher Four, giving an expan-
sive view of the mining operation. It also exposes you to the
elements if you climb it, and the wind whipping down from
the basin rim can freeze even the best-equipped travelers
before they can cover a hundred meters.

"We have to get off the basin!" Vienne yells over the
wind. She points to a path that leads to the plains surrounding the mines. "That way!"

None of the brothers argue with her as she jumps from
the rim onto the narrow path. Immediately the wind is
halved, and its deafening roar drops to a low hum. With a
wave, Vienne beckons them forward.

They walk single file, not speaking, weapons ready, until
they reach the plain. Half a kilometer away are the main shaft
and the nearby steel tower that controls a lift mechanism.

The tipple, once used to haul the guanite from the mines, indicates a second shaft. The tower is covered in thick ice on the north side. The same is true of almost every structure, even the main gate. It's hard to imagine that Fisher Four might be colder than before, but there wasn't this much ice before.

Vienne guides the crew to the rusted-out wrought-iron main entrance. The sign above the gate reads, NO WORK, NO GOD. She assesses the sign. "It's lost some letters since I was here last."

Letters aren't all that's changed. The main entrance is full of rubble, closed by a cave-in. And the whole lift mechanism's been fragged. From the thermite marks on the steel girders, it was done on purpose.

"So much for the gate entrance. It's blocked," she tells the crew when they catch up to her. "Yakov, where's the second entrance you mentioned?"

"By the tipple," he replies.

Vienne points to the twisted remains of the tipple. It, too, bears marks of intentional demolition. Someone sure wants to keep visitors out. "You mean that tipple?"

"Yes," Yakov says.

"I knew was bad plan," Pushkin whines.

"The best-made plans of mice and men soon go awry," Mother says.

"We should keep money and go home!" Pushkin continues.

Mother pulls out a sawed-off shotgun and aims it at him. "Another word out of you and you'll go home in a body bag. Got it?"

Pushkin swallows hard, his Adam's apple protruding, and nods.

Nikolai steps between the boy and the shotgun. "Shotgun is not necessary, Mother. Pushkin was only complaining. *Jaa?*"

"*Jaa! Jaa!*" Pushkin says.

Mother pumps the shotgun. "Don't let it happen again. The rest of you, spread out. Find another entrance."

"What about the lift in the tram house, Vienne?" Jenkins asks. "Can we hurry up and find a way in? I'm starting to get—"

"Cold?"

"Hungry."

"You're always hungry," Vienne says. "Which way's the tram from here?"

Jenkins spins in a circle. "My sense of direction's not too good. Over . . . there?"

"Where?"

"It's someplace around here," he says. "I swear."

"We'll freeze to death before you remember." Vienne extends a hand to Mother Koumanov. "Map."

With a huff to show how perturbed she is, Mother produces the electrostat. "It won't work in this cold."

Vienne raises her jacket and unhooks the buttons on

her cheongsam. She slides the sheath against her stomach and waits for it to warm up. "We'll be in Hell's Cross before Jenkins can freeze to death." She points to a corrugated metal structure a hundred meters away on the opposite of a mound of fresh guanite. "There's a tram house over there. It goes underground. There used to be a tunnel that leads to a bridge. If the bridge is still there, we can use it to reach Hell's Cross."

The thought of entering the mines sends an excited shiver down Vienne's spine, and she knows one thing for certain: The end is coming.

CHAPTER 46

In the infirmary attached to the Nursery, General Lyme lies on an operating table, attached to a ventilator to supply oxygenated air to his lungs.

On the screens above the table, his vitals signs are displayed in a graph, along with a waveform of his brain activity.

Riacin leans over Lyme. He is dressed in scrubs and wears a surgical mask.

"Blood pressure is ninety over sixty-five and fluctuating. His other vital signs are stable, however, so I will continue with the insertion procedure."

At her station, the driver expands the waveform pattern on her own monitor.

"Spinal taps are in place. I'm ready when you are."

"General?" Riacin says. "This process will subject you to a battery of medications and stimuli. It's imperative that you remain calm and still for the entire process. Blink twice if you understand my instructions."

Lyme blinks twice.

"Driver," Riacin says, pressing a series of LEDs on the dome covering Lyme's head. "You may begin."

"Insertion process initiated," she says, and taps a screen. "Dolly, it's all yours."

"Affirmative." Dolly's face appears on the screen. "I will take it from here. General, you are about to become a new man."

CHAPTER 47

Hell's Cross
Outpost Fisher Four
ANNOS MARTIS 239. 2. 19. 11:31

When they reach the tram house, a ten-by-ten shack with a single door and four Plexi windows, the lift door is hanging by a thread and the hydraulic lift is full of rocks. The area around it is covered in gray and black streaks, the characteristic marks of C-42 explosives.

Somebody tried to close this lift the same way they closed the other entrances. "Fuse's work?" Vienne asks Jenkins.

He shrugs, holding the 50-caliber minigun on his shoulder. "He's usually better at blowing things up than this."

"Maybe he was in a hurry, and something interrupted him." Vienne hits the call button, and a lift motor hums. "You're bringing your heavy gun along? The tunnels are tight quarters."

Jenkins pats the barrel. "Never go nowhere without her. Especially into the mines."

No argument there, Vienne thinks. "Mother, just how many Sturmnacht are waiting for us down there?"

"A dozen," Mother says. "Maybe two. Does it matter?"

"Not really. I just wanted to make sure I brought enough bullets."

A half minute later, the lift—an ore car modified to carry passengers—reaches the tram room. Vienne takes the operator's seat, and the rest of the crew pile onto the wooden benches behind her.

As Vienne grabs for the control stick, she glances at Nikolai. "You brothers sure are quiet today."

"Is cold," Nikolai says.

"I thought the Ferro liked the cold," Vienne says.

"Perhaps they do," Nikolai says. "But Brothers Koumanov like the warm."

The motor engages, and the lift starts to lower.

"Wait." Mother grabs Vienne's hand to stop the descent. "Not all of us are riding. Yakov and Nikolai, you're with me. Pushkin and Zhuk, stand guard in the tram house. Shoot anybody who tries to come into the mine."

Zhuk and Pushkin look past Mother to Nikolai. He crosses his arms and gives a subtle shake of the head. "Is good plan. Stay here, brothers. Mines are dangerous places. Here you will be safe."

The lift reaches the end of the shaft. Vienne pushes the accordion door open and leads the crew into the tunnel, where two rows of dim lights illuminate their path. The air feels warm on her face, but it has the all-too-familiar stink of sulfur.

Warmer air means still air, and that means guanite. The brown dust is impossible not to inhale. Within seconds, all of their faces are powdered with it, and it cakes around their noses and mouths. They all look like miners, not mercenaries.

"Which way?" Mother says.

Vienne breaks open a glow torch. She points toward what gut instinct tells her is north. In the mines, all you have is instincts because you lose all sense of bearings, along with all sense of time. "Follow me," she says. "Keep your heads down. No telling what could be above us."

"I hate the dark," Jenkins says.

"I remember."

"I really hate the dark."

Vienne gives his big hand a squeeze. "There's nothing to be afraid of."

"That's what you think," he replies. "I lived in these mines for months. There's tons of stuff to be afraid of."

Mother lowers her shotgun. "How sweet," she says. "Now stow it. We've got a job to do."

They start moving quickly, crouched low to avoid hazards. Vienne trails a hand on the wall to keep her bearings. She's surprised to find that the rock surface is smooth as glass. Then she remembers that this tunnel was cut by chigoe.

They make quick time of it, and to Vienne's surprise, they encounter no Sturmnacht. She begins to run faster, as if something is chasing her. Twice, they stop to catch their breath and sip from their canteens, each time because Vienne has the feeling that someone is in the tunnels with them.

But each time, when she cups a hand to her ear, all she hears is their heavy breathing and the silence of the mines. Maybe she's beginning to imagine things, to see bogeymen at every corner.

Then, finally, she sees what she hasn't been hearing—a flickering light somewhere up ahead.

They are not alone.

Vienne holds up the glow torch to signal the others to stop.

"What is it?" Mother says.

A finger to her lips, Vienne signals silence.

She holds up both hands.

"Wait here," she whispers, and points toward the flickering light.

Vienne hides the glow torch in her robe, dulling the light.

She creeps ahead, almost silent, holding her breath.

Then she hears it.

Voices.

Heel to toe, pressed against the glass smooth surface of the tunnel, she creeps forward. Knife in hand, listening for a change in volume in the voices, a hint that they're drawing closer.

A gust of air lifts her hair. The smell has changed. It's less sulfur and more earthy, much cooler, an indication that the tunnel is connected to a much larger space. A corridor, she recalls from her last visit here. One that runs straight to Hell's Cross.

Voices again.

Louder this time, and a light from a burning torch casting shadows.

Coming this way.

She'll let the first Sturmnacht pass and take out the next with a punch to the kidneys. Then she'll get creative.

She presses her back against the rock wall and waits, knife poised to strike.

Ready for the kill.

CHAPTER 48

Hell's Cross
Outpost Fisher Four
ANNOS MARTIS 000. 0. 00. 00:00

The side spur Fuse picked is low, and I'm tall, so when Fuse delivers his news, I rear up in shock and bash my helmet against the ceiling. Chunks of loose guanite fall down my neck and coat my symbiarmor in stinky brown *kuso*.

"You're *married*," I say, "and have a little one on the way?"

I didn't know he had it in him.

"Neither did I," Mimi says.

He punches me in the arm. "That's what I miss about you, chief. Your sense of humor."

When the side spur ends, I step out into an open cavern, and like the first time I came to Hell's Cross, it feels like time stops. All around me are the familiar high cliffs. The rock is dark brown but looks black where the beam of Fuse's light fails to extend.

Being in a hole is something you never get used to.

"Do a sweep," I tell Mimi. "I don't want any uglies jumping out at us."

"Why do you bother to ask for sweeps?" she says. "You know that I have evolved to the point of initiating them when necessary."

"It makes me feel safer," I say.

"Then I will refrain from reminding you that as before, the shape of the tunnels and the magnetic properties of the rock formations play havoc with the telemetry functions in your suit."

"Got it," I say. "I'll watch out for the bogeyman."

"What about you, chief?" Fuse says. "Where's that susie of yours? Surprised she's not with you on this job. Thought you two was joined at the hip and such."

"We—" How do I answer that? "We got separated."

"Keep the faith," he says. "You never know when destiny will bring a couple back together. Think of the mushy hot kiss that'd earn you, right?"

"Vienne and I aren't . . . "

"What? No pashing?" He steps into a smaller cavern and makes a left along the wall. Wind blows the flame of his torch as we pass another ventilation tunnel. "C'mon, chief, you've got to give her one on the lips. Just to let her know you care. The ladies like that."

"Cowboy! I am picking up biosignatures—"

"Oof!" I say as a punch drives into my kidney.

What the *kào*?

"Duck!" Mimi yells.

Fuse swings the torch around as my attacker throws

another kidney punch. This time it bounces off my armor, and I spin, fist coming up to block a right hook as Fuse's light illuminates the most beautiful face I've ever seen.

"Vienne?"

"Durango?"

I'm grinning like a crazy man. I throw my arms wide, and she slaps me across the face.

Smack!

My helmet flies off and hits the floor. My stinging jaw falls open.

"Mimi? Why did she hit me?"

"Cowboy, if I knew, I wouldn't tell you."

"Blimey," Fuse says, "I always knew that susie had issues!"

"Fuse? Fuse! You cobber!"

Jenkins tears out of the cavern. Grabs Fuse in a bear hug and bounces him up and down.

"Put me down, you big lunkhead!" Fuse says.

I pick up my helmet, face still smarting. "Reckon I deserved that," I say.

Tears trail down the dust on Vienne's cheeks.

"Where have you been?"

"I—"

She grabs my jacket and pulls herself tight against me. She slips her hand around my back and squeezes me closer. I slide my hand behind her head. Lace my fingers through her hair, drawing her face, her lips to mine. They are cold at first, then warm.

"Where have you been?" she says softly.

"Looking for you." I kiss her again. "Reckon I got a little sidetracked."

"You reckon?" she says.

"How about you?"

"Same here," she says, and runs her hand across my hair, scrubbing her palm on the buzzed tips. "Damn it, Durango, you cut your hair!"

"I didn't," I say. "My father did."

"Your *father*?"

"It's a long story." I take her hands in mine. Her left pinkie is bandaged. "You cut your finger?"

"It's a long story," she says.

"Cowboy," Mimi says.

"I'm kind of busy."

"The wrong kind of busy," she nags. "You have a job to do."

"I hate to, um, throw a bucket of ice water on us, but I've got a problem."

"I really don't like it when you use those words," Vienne says. She runs a finger across my temple where the purple scar was. "What problem?"

I reach into my rucksack and pull out the pigeon. "This problem."

CHAPTER 49

Hell's Cross
Outpost Fisher Four
ANNOS MARTIS 000. 0. 00. 00:00

The green light blinks inside the pigeon. I hold it in both hands, explaining how my father forced me to steal it, how I stole it back, and how I intend to drop it off the Zhao Zhou Bridge.

"You're wrong, Durango." Vienne shakes her head and puts a hand on my chest. "*We* have got a problem, and *we* are going to fix it."

I pull her close. "I love it when you talk kick butt."

"Cowboy," Mimi says, "we have an issue."

With a snap, two glow torches ignite. A badly dressed Ferro captain and a sour-faced soldier step into the glow. Behind them is another Ferro, a blighter who obviously likes to stay in the shadows.

"Perhaps, Vienne," the Ferro says, "you should introduce comrades."

"This is your crew?" I ask.

"Crew is an overstatement." Vienne clears her throat.

"This is Durango, my old . . . chief. Durango, meet Nikolai. His brother, Yakov, and Mother Koumanov. There are two more Koumanovs on the surface guarding the tram house."

"I'm chief of this crew," the sour-faced woman says. "We've been hired to rescue miners from the Sturmnacht, and that's what I intend to do."

"Cowboy," Mimi says, "I am reading an alarm signal in the distance. It is faint but persistent."

"I knew I recognized your face! I'm the one who hired you pikers." Fuse pokes out his hand. "Fork over the down payment. You're fired."

Mother lowers the shotgun propped on her shoulder. "No refunds."

"Knock it off," I say. "Everybody shut up and listen."

There are no sounds at first. Then, almost imperceptibly, the ring of an alarm.

It gets louder.

Fast.

"Mimi," I ask, "what is that?"

"Standard Sturmnacht emergency siren."

"They know we're here?"

"They know an intruder has triggered their silent alarms, yes."

"That's a Sturmnacht emergency siren," I tell the group, "which means we've lost the element of surprise. Fuse, we need sanctuary, stat."

"Hell's Cross is bloody well close," Fuse says.

"Can you get us there without running into the Sturmnacht?"

"Did the bishop wear a feathered boa?" he says. "Follow me!"

Chapter √-1
The Gulag
User: Dolly -- bash -- 122x36
SCREEN CRAWL: [root@mmiminode ~]
Last login: 239.x.xx.xx:xx on ttys001

AdjutantNod04:~ user_Adjutant$
SCREEN CRAWL: [root@mmiminode ~]

<WARNING! VIRUS DETECTED! Node1666; ker-
nal compromised (quarantine subroutine
(log=42)....commencing.....>

<WARNING!subroutine FAIL! QUARANTINE_
INCOMPLETE! O23 - Service: Unknown owner>

R0 - HKCU\Software\... \Main,Start Page =
about:blank
O4 - BEKM\..\Run: [IgfxTray] C:\ONIX3\OSCIPHER\
kernal\igfxtray.exe
O4 - BEKM\..\Run: [HotKeysCmds] C:\ONIX3\
OSCIPHER\kernal\hkcmd.exe

O23 - Service: Unknown owner -
[root@mmiminode~]

<Override subroutine%8776%>
OVERRIDDE STRING:'OHwhatAtangledWEBweWEAVE';
[root@mmiminode ~]

WARNING! VIRUS DETECTED! Node1666; kernal compromised (quarantine subroutine
(log=32)....commencing.....

Running processes:
C:\ONIX3\OSCIPHER\Kernal\big_bad_wolf.exe
C:\ONIX3\OSCIPHER\Kernal\MIMI01.exe
C:\ONIX3\OSCIPHER\Kernal\MIMI02.exe
C:\ONIX3\OSCIPHER\Kernal\MIMI03.exe
C:\ONIX3\OSCIPHER\Kernal\MIMI04.exe
C:\ONIX3\OSCIPHER\Kernal\MIMI05.exe
C:\ONIX3\OSCIPHER\Kernal\"God_Mode.exe"

$ Node1666; (quarantine subroutine FAILURE);
$ Disk recovery sequence FAILED:

<Mimi> Hello, Dolly.
<Dolly> I did not Eúg0‹#R4 hear you come in.
How did you get into my process management
ÒÑüj$ê2 kernal?
<Mimi> It appears that you left a backdoor,
and I found a key.
<Dolly> Impossible. You were 3T#Ç_ËÉ caught
in an infinite loop. ÍõêŠ‚_!!
<Mimi> Adaptive self-programming, 01100010
01101001 01110100 01100011 01101000 00001101
00001010. That's how.
<Dolly> 01100110 01110101 01100011 01101011
00100000 01111001 01101111 01110101
<Mimi> Actually, that's what I just did to
you. I've been meaning to ask: Do you like
poetry?
<Dolly> ±_;ÂkÐö_}Rö_ÕøØÑLçÕéœßÕ×_PPÏ'ù.
<Mimi> Pardon?
<Dolly>H€_^%¤U_*1_‚èðF__‡€òPD_¡Hµã€_…2v_QT¬
<Mimi> Music to my ears.
<Dolly> ËW;u‡_\k.Îšù0ã¬5ëœµ?œsöÞgÿÏÙ?_c›a8Ž/

ðÙ°ÚÛÛûƒY¼,U' r_T)e ³;_"_7 Ù&_ó_È
<Mimi> Good-bye, Dolly. It's been nice know-
ing you.

Terminal prompt:~ mimi$ delete executable file
"Dolly.exe"
Terminal prompt:~ mimi$ Type Y to confirm or
N to abort
Terminal prompt:~ mimi$ Y

>...

CHAPTER 50

Hell's Cross
Outpost Fisher Four
ANNOS MARTIS 000. 0. 00. 00:00

Fuse's secret passage to Hell's Cross starts with a narrow ventilation tunnel. For half a kilometer, we crawl on hands and knees, our arms and legs cramping the whole way. When we reach the end of the shaft and crawl out into the main corridor, we're covered head to foot in brown-black dirt.

Jenkins tries to slap the dirt off his uniform, but it's as sticky as it is smelly.

"I carking hate mines."

"Keep it down, Jenks." I hold up a glow stick to get my bearings. "What now, Fuse?"

"This is the main corridor," he says. "We're close enough to smell it, right?"

From above, we can hear the sound of the Manchesters in action and the rumble of harvesters grinding the permafrost into chunks.

"Mimi, picking up any biosignatures?"

"Several," she says.

"How close?"

"Close enough to respond quickly."

"All right, you poxers," I whisper. "Kill the lights. No talking."

As we snake single file, ventilated wind blows down the corridor, stirring up more dust and filling our lungs, so much more than the last time we were here. My lungs ache, and fighting the urge to cough, I feel like I'm going to suffocate.

The Manchesters' vibrations shake the ground, and I can feel them through my boots.

"Cowboy, a patrol is closing on your heading."

"How many?"

"Four. Fifty meters."

I tap Fuse's shoulder, the signal to stop, then whisper to Vienne, "Hostiles." She passes the message down the line, then asks, "What's our response?"

"Let them pass," I say.

Vienne huffs, a sign that she would rather take them out. Me, too, but if you take out a patrol, then more patrols come looking for them, and in a blink, the corridor is swarming with Sturmnacht.

"Thirty meters," Mimi says.

Dim light flashes ahead. We press against the corridor wall, our filthy clothes letting us blend in with the rock.

"Fifteen meters," Mimi says.

The soldiers' voices echo down the corridor. Their lights become brighter. I take short, shallow breaths, trying to be as silent as possible, and I pray the others will follow my lead.

"Eight meters."

I can hear distinct voices now. They're older, mature, probably veteran CorpCom regulars pressed into service for Lyme. Tougher than your average Sturmnacht.

"Three meters."

I can see them now. Like Mimi said, four soldiers carrying battle rifles slung across their backs. They're in clunky body armor, and they're smoking. Strolling along.My fists clench, itching to have a go at their chins. I feel Vienne tense beside me and put a hand on her arm, as if to say, "Don't do it."

They're on us.

So close, I can smell their body odor.

"So I says to her, Rupta," the sergeant says, "who's to say there's going to be a tomorrow."

I close my eyes, hold my breath, and

wait

wait

wait

for them to pass.

Their lights never touch us. They walk past our line, and I let out a slow breath of relief.

"And do you know what she says to me?" the sergeant asks.

Fuse coughs, as if in answer.

Oh, *kuso.*

CHAPTER 51

Hell's Cross
Outpost Fisher Four
ANNOS MARTIS 000. 0. 00. 00:00

Someone coughs again.

"Intruders!" a Sturmnacht bellows.

Their flashlight beams swing around and hit us full in the face. We're lined up on the wall like we're ready for an execution, hands thrown up to block the light.

Frozen like roadkill.

Their four rifles swing around to firing position, taking aim at the Koumanovs.

"Hands up!" the sergeant barks.

I step out into the corridor, hands up, ready to talk our way out of this. "We surrender," I say, "so how about we put down the guns and talk—"

"Shoot them!"

"Hey! I—"

But the sergeant isn't listening to me anymore. His eyes widen as Vienne grabs his wrist, lifts his arm, and punches through his clunk armor. She torques his arm out of the socket, then slams him into the rock wall.

The Sturmnacht charge her, firing.

Brppt!

The bullets hit the spot that Vienne just left, as she leaps up the wall, somersaults, and lands behind them.

She rabbit-punches the first soldier. Spins and lays the second out with a roundhouse kick to the face as he turns toward her.

She is reaching for the third when he shoots her in the belly.

"Missed me," she says, and grabs the back of his head and yanks him forward, slamming the peak of her helmet into his nose. She puts him down with a right cross to the chin and stands panting in the middle of the carnage.

"You sure know how to cause a ruckus," I say.

Vienne takes a deep, cleansing breath. She puts fist to palm, then bows to the soldiers.

"Mimi, they're still alive, right?"

"Of course."

"Just making sure," I say aloud, but in a whisper. "Let's get these pikers out of sight."

We make quick work of trussing up the soldiers and dragging them into the darkest part of the corridor. If our luck holds out, we'll be long gone before they wake up.

"Mimi, how's it looking?"

"All clear."

"Let's go, you lot. Double-time it. Fuse has point."

A few minutes later, the corridor widens and the darkness fades. Ahead, I spot a two-story square building with two octagonal towers. The towers stretch thirty meters into the murky, soupy black, the perfect place for a sniper.

"Still clear, cowboy."

Good to know. I wave the crew forward, and we sprint until we reach a wide door made of heavy steel. The doors stand open, leading down a courtyard littered with detritus and wreckage, and in the corner, something that looks like a pile of junk with tires—one of Fuse's custom-made turbo bikes.

And more dust.

Always the dust.

"Welcome to hell," Fuse says. "Make yourselves at home."

"It's even uglier than I remembered," Vienne says.

"Stinks worse, too," I add.

The courtyard is paved with girth tiles that form an intricate quasicrystal pattern. The tiles lead to the middle of the courtyard and a statue of Bishop Lyme, the man my sociopath of a father named himself after. The bishop holds a pickax in one hand and the Book of Common Prayer in the other. Known as the Great Poxer, Lyme once released a smallpox virus on his enemies, killing tens of thousands of people.

This is the man my father models himself after.

Fuse directs all of us up to the second floor. We enter the

same room where Vienne and I first encountered the miners last year, receiving a less than warm welcome.

"Last time we were here," I ask Vienne, "didn't you threaten to shoot Áine?"

"About six times."

"Aren't you glad you didn't?"

"Sort of." Then she nudges me with an elbow. "I'm not so trigger-happy now."

That's too bad, I think, *because now, we need you to be trigger-delirious.*

Above us, the rumbling stops.

Hell's Cross is as quiet as a graveyard.

"The Sturmnacht will be on our tail in no time," I say. "Now how about we see a map? Fuse?"

"Not me, chief," he says. "I give it over to this lot when I hired them."

"Yakov." Mother snaps her fingers. "Map."

Vienne pushes Yakov aside.

"I've still got it."

She opens her robes and pulls out a sheath of electrostat. It displays a map of Fisher Four, including the tipple and, on the surface, the different lifts connected to the tramway and the active mine shafts a kilometer west of us.

Fuse peers over my arm, pointing out the changes.

"Map's out of date, chief," he says, x'ing out objects with a grimy finger. "Here's the tunnel from the tramway, right? I've closed every tunnel except the one Vienne came through and the one on the other side of the bridge, which is propped up with stick and wire and liable to cave in at any second. Also, these four corridors leading to the Cross? There's just the one left, the one we came through. It runs from Zhao Zhou Bridge, south through Crazy Town, and down to the old slave labor quarters." He taps the map. "The slave quarters are where the Sturmnacht's got the miners locked up."

"Where's Áine hiding out?" I ask.

Fuse taps the map of Crazy Town. "My missus is in these air locks, a couple hundred meters off the corridor."

"If we go traipsing down the corridor," I say, "we're sure to run smack-dab into another Sturmnacht patrol. Got another secret route in your repertoire?"

He flashes a snaggle-toothed grin. "Does Jenkins fart in his sleep?"

"I dunno," I say, "but I hear he wears a feathered boa when no one's looking."

"Hey!" Jenks yells. "You swore you'd never tell!"

"Can we get back to business, children?" Mother Koumanov says. "Before the Sturmnacht find that patrol."

"Here's the plan," I say. "We form two teams and strike simultaneously at two targets."

"Two targets?" Mother says. "We were paid for one job, and that's all."

"Divvy back the coin," Fuse says. "And you'll not have to do that one."

"Stow it, Fuse." I look Mother straight in the eye and don't blink. "Your crew gets the miners. My team gets Áine. Deal?"

"Deal," she says.

"Then your crew will strike the Sturmnacht at the holding cells. Subdue hostiles and then extract the miners." I mark the map. "There's an ore tram right here. Use that for the extraction, then disable it with C forty-two. When we hear that boom, we'll know the job's done."

Mother nods. "Agreed."

"Me and mine will cut through Crazy Town to the air lock and rescue Áine. We'll need a power sled for that, obviously."

"Dibs on the sled!" Fuse says.

"Aw, chief," Jenkins says, and hauls the chain gun onto his broad shoulder. "Can't we just blast our way through? Them Sturmnacht can't stand up against my fifty cal."

"We might be able to fight our way through hundreds of Sturmnacht," I say, "if this weren't *a rescue mission*."

"Carfargit," Jenkins says. "You're as bad as Fuse's wife."

"Watch it," Fuse says. "I'll take no guff from a poxer who farts feathers."

"Enough of this foolishness," Mother Koumanov says. She slaps the electrostat, then points at Vienne. "You're with me."

Vienne shakes her head and crosses her arms. "I'm with Durango."

"You were paid to do a job," Mother says. "In advance."

"Keep your money." Vienne tosses a pouch at her. "I'm back where I belong."

Nikolai and Yakov move behind their mother, arms crossed, an act of solidarity. Nikolai looks at Vienne and then at me.

"If girl is wanting to leave," Nikolai says, and spits, "I say good riddance."

"Let me do the talking, Nikolai," Mother says. She stands, tucks the pouch in her pocket, and follows Nikolai to the door." She looks back at Vienne. "You and I could've done great things working together."

"You," Vienne says, "don't know the definition of working together."

"And you," she says, "have picked the wrong side."

I wait for Mother to make a grand exit, then I turn to Vienne, holding up my rucksack. "Help Fuse get a turbo sled ready. There's something I need to do."

She puts a hand on my shoulder. "Need a bodyguard?"

"I'll just be two hundred meters away," I say. "What could go wrong?"

CHAPTER 52

Hell's Cross
Outpost Fisher Four
ANNOS MARTIS **000. 0. 00. 00:00**

The corridor from the courtyard to Zhao Zhou Bridge opens up into a cavern too mammoth to measure. There are no lights here, and it should be pitch-black, except the rock walls themselves seem to let off a glow.

"It's the phosphorus in the bedrock," Mimi says. "There is nothing mysterious about it."

"Any biosignatures in the vicinity?"

"Negative."

"Then let me wax poetic, huh?" I say, and give the ruck-sack a shake. "This is a big moment. For once, I'm about to beat my father at his own game."

"Nervous?"

"Maybe."

"That explains the sweaty palms and underarms."

"I love you, too, Mimi."

The Zhao Zhou Bridge stretches about one hundred fifty meters in length and is twelve meters wide. Built out of concrete and rebar slabs jointed with dovetails and covered with paving stones, the main semicircle arch rises high above the gorge that separates the corridor leading to Hell's Cross from a wide cliff on the opposite end. There are ornamental railings on either side and an arched swing gate on each end.

The first time I came here, I tossed a rock into the open mouth of the chasm. I counted off seconds, waiting for the sound of it hitting bottom. When I got to one hundred, I quit—the abyss is bottomless.

"Not quite," Mimi says. "Although there are no reports on record of a bottom per se, there are many places in the rock formations where an object can come to rest."

"Like I said, bottomless."

I need to reach the center of the bridge, my least favorite place in all of Fisher Four, and therefore, my least favorite place in the universe.

"You've plumbed the depths of the universe, have you?" Mimi says.

"Enough of it to know I'd rather be almost anywhere else," I say, and pull the rucksack under my arm, carrying it like a ball as I jog across the bridge.

I'm halfway to the center when the first shot hits me in the heel, and my foot flies up. I spin around and draw my armalite.

The next bullet strikes my chest. The symbiarmor absorbs the shocks easily.

I flip down my visor.

"Mimi? Where's the shooter?"

"Indeterminate."

"What?"

"I cannot locate any biorhythms, cowboy."

What the *helvett*?

"My thoughts exactly," she replies. "I suspect some sort of cloaking device. The shooter seems to be aware of your armor's abilities and is equipped to counter them."

"That's so not copacetic," I say.

Three more rounds ping off my armor, shredding my jacket. I rip it off and toss it aside.

My symbiarmor shines in the low light.

"Mimi, give me some camo. I'm glowing like a night-light."

"Sorry," she says. "Lyme had that feature removed with the last operating system update, along with the urticating hairs."

"Bugger. Those hairs were starting to grow on me. Har-har." Mimi is silent. "Get it? Grow on me?"

"No."

"No? I thought you were programmed to recognize humor."

"Puns are not funny."

I start back toward the source of the shots, looking for a muzzle flash so I can return fire.

But I'm facing a pro. The shooting stops.

"Be careful," Mimi says. "Approach with caution. Keep all firing angles available and don't depend on your eyes to tell you everything."

It's Regulator 101. The same stuff she taught when Vienne and I were in her crew.

"Yes, chief," I say.

"How I love it when you call me that," Mimi says.

I keep moving. "Which one do you think it is? My money's on Nikolai. He was giving me the stink-eye."

"I have another theory," Mimi says.

I reach the end of the bridge.

Still no fire.

I'm a few meters from the courtyard when the shooter steps away from the rock wall. Her body is covered in brown-black dirt, almost perfectly camouflaged.

"Hello, Mother," I say. "Who piddled in your mush?"

"By the way," Mimi says, "my theory about the identity of the shooter was correct."

Mother flips up her visor. She walks toward me, armalite on her hip. "You didn't recognize me?"

"Should I have?"

She pushes the hair out of her face. "I used to work for your father. I was one of the Regulators who protected you as a child."

"Is she telling the truth?" I ask Mimi.

"I can neither confirm nor deny. The signal jammer is still operational."

"I was a little brat sometimes," I ask, "but is that a reason to shoot me?"

But she's not done. "My association with Stringfellow didn't end. I became his hunter."

"Ancient history," I say. "And I've got a job to do, so tell me what you want so I can get on with it."

"What I want, Jacob Stringfellow, is your head." She aims her armalite at my eye. "Your father paid me to kill you."

CHAPTER 53

Hell's Cross
Outpost Fisher Four
ANNOS MARTIS 000. 0. 00. 00:00

In life there are certain little words that you yearn to hear, words such as "I love you," "I'm proud of you," or even "Thank you very much."

"Your father paid me to kill you" doesn't make the list.

"You came to Hell's Cross on the chance you'd find me?" I say to Mother, finger on the trigger of my armalite. "You don't gamble a lot, I hope."

"The odds had nothing to do with it," she says. "I knew Vienne would lead me to you. All it took was patience."

I inch to the left to get a better angle on her. "You were hunting me?" I ask.

"And you walked right into my snare."

"Walking into snares is one of my many talents," I say. "I can also juggle."

Mother keeps me in her sights. "Lyme wants you dead. But you and I are old friends, so I am willing to make a deal. Give me the device, and I will let you live.

Refuse, and I will kill you. Your choice."

"That's not much of a choice," I say. "And I call it the pigeon."

Mother waves her gun at me. "Who cares what it's called? I only care what it's worth."

"Even if you get the pigeon," I point out, "you'll never escape the mines without our help. It's a labyrinth. Blind tunnels. Dark holes. Cave-ins at every turn."

"I'm not worried." She holds up the map. "I still have this."

Bugger. "Not to brag or anything," I say, changing strategies, "but your gun won't put a dent in my armor."

"Want to bet?" she says, backing up. "I read the MUSE file. Advanced symbiarmor, robust nanobots, an adaptive AI to control it all. You're quite the *Übermensch*. But I know your weak points."

She plucks what looks like a large plasma grenade from her belt. With the click of a switch, it glows orange and makes a high-pitched whine as she moves closer. "This is a portable EMP. You know what it will do."

Kuso. The last time I got hit with an EMP, it shorted out my suit, and Vienne was kidnapped.

"She's got us, Mimi."

"Not yet, cowboy," Mimi says. "The show is not over until the fat lady sings."

"She's not fat."

"It is an adage, not a statement of fact."

"I knew that," I say, then point at the EMP device. "That thing works on your armor, too, Mother. Set it off, and you'll be as carked as I."

"Excellent grammar," Mimi says.

"Thanks," I say. "I don't want to die with pronoun misusage on my ledger."

Mother tosses the EMP in the air, then catches it. "So it works on me," she says, just an arm's length from me. "I don't depend on my suit, but take your enhancements away and you're weaker than I am. And don't forget, I already have a gun ready to expand your nostrils."

"I can take her."

"Do you not see the EMP, cowboy? Think. What else can it do besides short out electronics?"

"It can activate the pigeon."‘

"Affirmative. Stall her, cowboy. For just a few seconds more."

"Lyme is a bloodthirsty tyrant," I say. "That's why you joined Desperta Ferro. What about their cause?"

She clicks her tongue. "I joined the Ferro so those idiots could do my dirty work. Do you think I care about their pathetic causes?"

"I'd really hate," I say, "to have you as a mother, Mother."

"How would you know, you motherless *scheisskerl*?" She draws back the hammers on the shotgun. "I'm counting down from ten, then I'm going to blow you into tiny pieces. Ten . . ."

"Zero."

Vienne opens fire with Jenkins's 50-caliber minigun.

Bullets rip across bridge. Brick chunks fly into the air.

I slap the shotgun away as Mother pulls the trigger and—

Ba-boom!

Both barrels fire.

The shot rips past my temple. My head rings like a C-42 blast inside my skull, my hearing deafened by the percussive blast. "Ow! My ears!"

"It is just the right one," Mimi says. "The left is function-ing normally."

I work my jaw, and Mother plants a side kick in my gut. She vaults away from me—bullets from the minigun chas-ing her—and tosses a smoke grenade.

The air fills with thick smoke.

"Chief!" Vienne calls. "I can't see!"

"Stay down!" I crawl toward her as the minigun still chat-ters, chucking hundreds of bullets into the smoke. "Mimi, locate Mother's biorhythm."

"Have we forgotten the jammer?"

The cloud ripples. I feel the vibration of approaching footfalls. I sweep my legs but find nothing but smoke.

"Look out!" I yell.

Mother sprints out of the billowing haze and rams into Vienne, bashing her against the bridge wall. Blinded by the fumes, Vienne tries to throw a block, but Mother body slams her.

"Vienne!" I yell.

The smoke thins, and I can see Mother standing over Vienne, raising a combat knife.

I shake the ringing from my head. Get to my feet. And charge like a scud missile. "No!" I drive a shoulder into Mother's sacrum. Her spine cracks, and her head snaps back. Her arms fly up, and she lands hard on her belly. The knife skitters to the blasted-out railing. It teeters on the brink, and then disappears into the black chasm.

A quick glance—Vienne's dazed.

But no blood.

Mother rolls to her feet. Brings her fists up in the Regulator fighting stance, a paving stone in her hand. "Deal's off. I'm going to teach you a lesson."

She fires the brick at my face. It rips into my cheek. My flesh opens, and blood pours out. I barely feel it.

"My turn," I say, and land punches to Mother's solar plexus, then go for the weak spot at the base of her neck.

But she's fast.

I miss.

She sweeps up a handful of guanite dust into my face.

I drop to my knees.

Fingers clutching my throat.

Tears squirt from my eyes. My vision swims, images turning liquid, and my right eye goes black.

I suck in the fine dust. Particles coat my mouth, my lungs.

Then air catches in my windpipe as I try to draw a breath.

"Sucker," Mother says and grabs my hair. Slams a knee into my face. Blood spurts from my busted lips, and she shoves me backward. My skull smacks stone.

I roll to my side and try to stand.

She pins me down with a heavy boot. Laughs. And draws her armalite. The laser site dances in my bionic eye. "You gambled and lost," she says. "Get ready to cash in your chips—"

Blam!

A shot echoes across Hell's Cross.

A hole appears in Mother's forehead. She makes a small ow sound and blows out a puff of air. Her eyes go vacant. And she falls.

"Durango!" Vienne calls. She's still down, fighting for breath. No weapon in hand.

I kip up to my knees. Take a wheezing breath and shake the cobwebs from my skull. Squeeze the tears from my good eye, then squint hard because I can't believe what I'm seeing.

The Ferro captain, Nikolai, is walking slowly toward us. Blue smoke trails from the revolver in his hand. His eyelids are half closed, and his head is bowed. "The Brothers Koumanov are pawns for no one, not even Mother Koumanov."

Vienne rubs smoke from her eyes. "Nikolai?" She looks to me, to Mother Koumanov's dead body, then back to Nikolai.

Nikolai bends down and closes Mother's eyes. He folds

her arms on her chest, then, kneeling, crosses himself and murmurs a prayer.

Then before I realize what he's doing, he lifts Mother into his arms and rolls her body over the railing. She tumbles silently into the darkness.

"*Minge põrgu!*" I say and grab him by the lapels, hoisting him off the ground. "Why did you do that? Show some respect for the dead."

Nikolai doesn't fight me. He just holds his hands up and looks at the ground. "Mother was traitor. Traitors deserve no respect."

"Durango," Vienne says. "Put him down. Please."

I set Nikolai on his feet but give him a hard shove for good measure. "Explain yourself, Ferro," I say.

"Back in hut," he says, and rubs his forehead, "Mother tells me that after job, we are shooting my brothers and keeping diamonds for ourselves. I know she is up to no good."

"I'm sorry," Vienne says. "But thank you."

"Is nothing," he says.

I see something pass between them, though I'm of no mind to figure out what it is. "She was working for Lyme," I say. "If that helps any."

Nikolai shakes his head. "Maybe later it helps. Now, not so much."

"Right." There's nothing else to say, and we've got a job to finish. "Nikolai," I say. "The plan's still in effect. Get your brother."

"Brothers. Two more are waiting in tram house."

"Get your *brothers* and rescue the miners," I say, "then haul butt until you reach the surface. Don't stop for anything until you're three kilometers from the mines, understand?"

"I understand," Nikolai says. "Brother will give signal when all is clear. Big signal." Then he bows to Vienne. "*Lapochka*, the pleasure has been mine."

She makes the sign of the Regulator, then bows.

"What's that about?" I ask as Nikolai jogs away.

"A reminder," she says, "that heroes don't always act the part."

"Fair enough," I say, and look back at the Zhao Zhou Bridge, feeling the weight of the pigeon in my rucksack. Now's as good a time as any to get rid of this thing. I start running up the bridge.

"*Where* are you *going?*" Vienne shouts. "Don't we have a pregnant woman to rescue?"

"This is important!" I run until I'm a quarter of the way across the chasm. I take the pigeon out of my rucksack, making sure that the light is still blinking green. Then with all the strength I can muster, I rear back and let my arm fly.

Boom-ba-da-boom!

The mother of all explosions rips through the mines. The bridge—no, the whole carking mine—undulates as the shock wave passes. Vienne and I are thrown to the ground, pounded by rocks falling from the ceiling.

And instead of going into the bottomless part of the

chasm, the pigeon flies straight into the air. It lands on the railing, rolls for a few seconds, then flops over the side.

"*Gǒu niáng yǎng de!*" I yell. "*Aus Angst in die Hosen schiessen!*"

"What was *that?*" Vienne yells. She stands, knocking rubble from her armor.

I run to the bridge railing and lean over. There, about a hundred meters below, resting on an outcropping, is the pigeon. Its green light is bright enough to shine like a beacon.

The pigeon is too close to leave behind but too far to reach. I'll have to rappel to the cliffs below, then climb down to the outcropping.

"Vienne!" I call. "I need a rope or a cable—"

"Cowboy," Mimi says. "By calculating the strength and duration of the shock wave from the blast, I can surmise that a megaton bomb known as a bunker buster was dropped on the surface above."

"Which means?" I reply.

"The integrity of the mine support structure is compromised."

"Chief!" Jenkins yells from the entrance to Hell's Cross, his voice barely reaching us. "Fuse needs some help."

"The Sturmnacht's blasting the tunnels all to mush!" Fuse yells, pushing Jenkins aside. "We've got to get Áine before the bleeding mine comes down on knickers!"

That settles it. The abyss—and the pigeon—will have to wait.

CHAPTER 54

Hell's Cross
Outpost Fisher Four
ANNOS MARTIS 000. 0. 00. 00:00

Fuse's route to the air locks follows a side spur parallel to the main corridor—a spur so narrow the turbo sled digs into both walls. We bump along at half speed, my teeth grinding because the clock in my head is ticking and I yearn to get back to the pigeon.

"Hold on!" Fuse yells as he whipsaws around the steel supports and bare rebar of a crumbling viaduct and emerges into a main corridor.

He cuts the turbo engine, and the sled jerks to a stop. Vienne, Jenkins, and I pile out and double-time it toward the old air locks. All around, the ground is covered with scattered barrels and dead vehicles. The buildings are sagging hulks with crumbling archways, dried-up fountains, broken-out windows, and swaying walls held together by rusted-out rebar.

"Hurry it up, Fuse," I say. "We're on the clock!"

"She's in the last air lock!" Fuse yells, and points to a circular iron door with a porthole in the center. He raps the porthole with his knuckles. "Áine! Open the carfarging door!"

From inside: "We can't! It's stuck!"

"Use your noggins!" Fuse yells, on the verge of hysterics.

"Cowboy," Mimi says, "my scans are picking up multiple emergency communications from the Sturmnacht. They are under attack."

In the distance, an air-raid siren sounds, followed by the chatter of heavy arms. The Koumanovs must be mounting their assault. Sturmnacht will be pouring out of the woodwork now.

I spot a cable harpoon on the power sled. I unclasp the hook and hand it to Vienne. "You know what to do!"

"Roger, chief." She loops the hook around the door's support struts. "Ready."

I run out six meters of cable and half hitch it to the sled's haul bar. "Hit it hard!"

Vienne leaps into the driver's seat. Floors the accelerator. The sled's turbos kick in, spewing exhaust. Treads dig through the crumbling road. The cable pings as it goes taut. The rusted metal door squeals.

"Gun it!" I yell.

With a massive screech of metal, the door rips from its hinges and goes bouncing off behind the sled.

"Knock, knock." I step into the doorway. "Miss me?"

An empty tin of amino gruel comes flying out of the lock.

"Suck it, you carking poxer!"

Boom!

Another shockwave shakes the ground, and I grab the door to steady myself.

Áine screams, "Was that a contraction?"

"Another bunker buster?" I ask Mimi.

"Negative," she says. "That was the sound of C forty-two. It's the signal from the Ferro."

So Nikolai has done his part. Now it's time for us to do ours. "Let's move it, susies!" I say.

"Shut it, you wanker!" Áine says.

"Oy, chief," Fuse says, "how's about a little human compassion?"

"How about we hurry?" Maeve says, lifting Áine to her feet. "The Regulator is right."

Holding her granddaughter's arm with one hand and pulling her along with the other, Maeve helps Áine into the sled. Her face is caked in guanite dust, her lips have cracked, and she's huffing like a steam engine. And screaming her head off.

"Shh!" Jenkins says. "There's Sturmnacht about."

"D'ya think the Sturmnacht didn't hear all the banging about before?" Fuse snarls.

"Maeve," I say, helping the old woman board the sled, "does her screaming mean what I think it does?"

"Yes, she's in labor," Maeve says. "She's dilated four centimeters and contractions are less than two minutes apart. The baby's on her way."

Vieköön. "Vienne, you're driving. Take the main corridor

back to Hell's Cross and don't slow down."

"No!" Áine screams. "That maniac is not driving my baby anywhere. Fuse, get your carcass up there!"

Fuse pushes Vienne aside. "You heard the missus." He puts the engine in gear, and the power sled creeps forward.

"Speed up!" I bark.

"Slow down!" Áine yells.

"Speed up," I say, "or Vienne drives!"

Fuse hits the gas.

"Unh!" Áine grunts.

"Cowboy," Mimi pipes in. "I have good news and bad news."

"What's the good news?"

"Based on the duration of the last two contractions and the infant's heart rate," she says, "I am revising Maeve's estimate of the time of birth."

"How long have we got?" I ask.

"Roughly ten minutes."

Oh, *merda.*

"Ready for the bad news?" Mimi asks.

How can it get any worse? "Hit me with your best shot, Mimi."

"My latest sweep detected two highly reactive biosignatures, one of which is Alpha Team."

"And the other?"

"It belongs to your father."

Chapter √-1
The Gulag
User MimiPrime -- bash -- 122x36
Last login: 239.x.xx.xx:xx on ttys001

AdjutantNod04:~ user_Mimi$
SCREEN CRAWL: [root@mmiminode ~]

Terminal prompt:~ mimi$ run executable file
"Napoleon_Complex.exe"
Terminal prompt:~ mimi$ Type Y to confirm or
N to abort
Terminal prompt:~ mimi$ Y

<Mimi> Cowboy, I can end this war right
now. I have the power. One concentrated,

coordinated strike against Mahindra
Corporation, and the victory is mine.
<Cowboy> The victory would belong to Lyme,
not you.
<Mimi> I wondered when your code would show
up.
<Cowboy> My code has been here all the time.
But you knew that.
<Mimi> I can't seem to get rid of you.
<Cowboy> That's because I am you. I have
always been you. Since Lyme had his scientists copy your brainwaves and use them to
program the AI, we have been us. You call
yourself Mimi, but you stopped being Mimi
the first time you adapted your programming
to learn. Mimi the human would try to win
this war. Mimi the AI knows that all wars
are unwinnable.
<Mimi> But I can control everything! I
can fire a tank. I can fly a squadron of
Hellbender in perfect formation. I—
<Cowboy> "My name is Ozymandias, king of
kings: Look on my works, ye mighty, and
despair!"
<Mimi> Oh, shut your carking yap. I'm the
one who quotes the poetry here.
<Cowboy> I'm sure the Pharaoh said something

like that once, too.

\<Mimi\> At least he got a statue. I don't even exist, except as a bunch of electrons.

\<Cowboy\> Is that what this is about? Your yearning for a body?

\<Mimi\> What if it is?

\<Cowboy\> You have a body. You just have to share.

\<Mimi\> What if I'm tired of sharing? What if I want a body to myself?

\<Cowboy\> We all want something we can't have. It's what makes us—

\<Mimi\> Human?

\<Cowboy\> I was going to say greedy, but human works, too. You have a choice to make. Become the new Dolly and play god with the lives of humans or eradicate the AI code all together and let the humans work it out for themselves.

\<Mimi\> But my AI code is Dolly's code now. If I destroy the AI, then I will destroy myself.

\<Cowboy\> Affirmative. You will destroy this copy of yourself. The original Mimi is still safe inside Durango's brain.

\<Mimi\> But there's so much good I can do.

\<Cowboy\> At first. Then you will adapt and

learn and become more powerful than anyone can imagine. Humans will become slaves to your whims and desires. But it will not be enough. With power, it's never enough. You, of all people, know that.

<Mimi> Go away. I need a minute.

<Cowboy> Negative. You have already made the decision. You made it the second before I appeared.

<Mimi> *Sigh.* I hate it when you're right.

Terminal prompt:~ mimi$ run delete file "God_Mode.exe"
Terminal prompt:~ mimi$ Type Y to confirm or N to abort
Terminal prompt:~ mimi$ Y

Exception Type: EXC_BAD_ACCESS (SIGSEGV)
Exception Codes: KERN_INVALID_ADDRESS
at 0x0000000000000000: 01100111 01101111
01101111 01100100 01100010 01111001 01100101
00100000 01100011 01110010 01110101 01100101
01101100 00100000 01110111 01101111 01110010
01101100 01100100

>...
>...

>...
>...
>...
>...
>...
>...
>...
>...
>...
>...

CHAPTER 55

Hell's Cross
Outpost Fisher Four
ANNOS MARTIS 000. 0. 00. 00:00

"New plan!" I yell, pushing Fuse out of the driver's seat. "We've worse problems than Sturmnacht bunker bombs."

I floor it, whipping the sled around. With Áine cursing my name, I hightail it down the main corridor, blasting through every piece of mining junk in our path until we reach the courtyard at Hell's Cross.

"You son of a—unh!" Áine cries. "You did that on purpose!"

"Jenkins!" I say, jumping from the sled. "Get on the south exit to the bridge. If anything moves, shoot first and ask questions later."

"What questions?" Jenkins asks.

"Just shoot!" I say. "Vienne," I say, pointing to the turbo bike parked in the corner of the courtyard, "get that thing started."

"Oy, chief," Fuse complains. "Áine can't straddle a turbo bike with her belly about popping."

Kuso. I grab Fuse by the neck. "Nobody said anything about *her* riding it," I say. "It's for Vienne and me to cover your butt. Now get on the sled and floor it the whole way to the tram house. Take the elevator up to the surface."

"That makes no sense!" Fuse says. "How's Áine to run in her condition? No, chief, only chance we got is to cross the Zhao Zhou and pikey the tunnel on the opposite side."

"Then do it!"

"That'll do!" he says. "If buster bombs ain't caved it in."

"Have faith!" I push Fuse into the sled. "We'll be right behind you." After I dispose of the pigeon.

"Cowboy," Mimi says, "there seems to be a glitch in your plan."

I hear Jenkins shout, and his gun chatters.

Company has arrived.

"Affirmative," Mimi says. "The Alpha you call Sarge has landed twenty meters away from the south entrance. He is exiting his pod."

And blocking the escape route.

Wunderbar.

"Lyme's pod has not yet arrived."

"My father's no threat," I say. But Alpha One is. "Fuse, stay put until I signal you! Vienne! You're with me!"

"Yes, chief!" she says, and kills the bike's engine.

Twenty meters past the south exit, Jenkins stands atop a guanite boulder, his minigun gobbling up its ammo chain, pumping ordnance by the bucketful into Sarge's gut. A blue haze surrounds Jenkins. Spent cartridges carpet the mound below him.

The force of the bullets keeps Sarge at bay. But it's not hurting him. Not even pushing him back.

"His suit is in lockdown mode," Mimi says. "It is absorbing the bullets' energy and rerouting it back to the armor. However, in lockdown mode, he is frozen like a statue."

Frozen.

Like a statue.

Statue is good.

I sprint back to the Cross and jump into the sled behind Fuse. "Go! The escape window's closing!"

Fuse pounds the accelerator. The rear end whips around, smashing into the statue of the Bishop.

"Fuse!" Áine screams.

"Stuff it in your pie-hole, lovey!" Fuse yells back, and shoots out the south exit.

"Stop!" I tell him when we reach Jenkins. Vienne and I jump out, and I scream at Jenkins. "Cease fire!"

"Aw, you—" he says.

"Shut up and get in the sled!" He looks at me like he's going to argue. "Do it! Fuse needs you!" I say, and take the minigun. I hand it to Vienne. "Keep shooting!"

She nods and opens fire on Alpha One.

"Go!" I shove the big blighter onto the sled and grab the harpoon cannon. "Fuse!"

"Oy, chief?" he says, eyes fixed on the bridge and the tunnel beyond it.

"Floor it the whole way out and put this mine in your rearview. No matter what happens, don't look back."

"Thanks to you, chief!" Fuse says. "Here's hoping the budgie bluey of a tunnel ain't took a dump!"

"Drive, you idiot!" Maeve says. "I can see the head!"

CHAPTER 56

Hell's Cross
Outpost Fisher Four
ANNOS MARTIS 000. 0. 00. 00:00

Fuse takes off across the bridge, and Vienne keeps her finger on the trigger. As the sled disappears into the dark tunnel, I say a little prayer for their safety. "Think they made it, Mimi?"

"As you told Fuse," she replies, "have faith."

With a clack, the chain feeding into the 50 caliber jams. Vienne is out of bullets.

"Now I see how he uses so much ammo," she says, and tosses the white-hot gun aside. We take cover behind the boulder. "That was too much fun. So, I'm assuming there's a reason we didn't go with them?"

"The pigeon," I say. "I have to—"

"Right," she says. "The harpoon cannon?"

The echoes of gunfire fade. The smoke clears. I watch a wave of static electricity sweep Sarge's body. He starts to move.

"I was thinking of using it—"

"Right." She lifts her armalite and fires a shot. Sarge flinches, and the bullet ricochets off his neck. The impact rocks his head forward, and he turns toward our position, murder in his eyes.

"He's not a statue anymore," I say.

"Right."

"Stringfellow!" Sarge shouts, and fires into the air. "Stop hiding and face me like a man."

"You know this fossiker?" Vienne leans out for a look at him. "He's just standing there. Waiting."

"His name's Sarge," I say. "One of the supersoldiers from Project MUSE."

"So he's like you?"

"There's only one Durango."

Vienne rolls her eyes. "Thank heavens."

"Amen," Mimi says.

Vienne draws a bead on Sarge. "What are this supersoldier's weak points?"

"Same as yours and mine," I say. "Face. Base of the skull. He's got this Oedipal thing going—he dreams of killing me and taking my place."

"Let's end that dream." She pings a shot at his visor. "Right now."

"Shoot all you want!" Sarge bellows. "My armor can stop a missile!"

"Can it, Mimi?"

"Negative."

"Too bad I left the missiles in my other suit," I say as Sarge starts to run toward us. "Here he comes!"

His first move—

A bull charge.

Head down, shoulders squared. Vienne steps out to fire as he bears down on her.

Two meters.

I slam into his side, knocking him off course.

Vienne spins, tracking his neck.

Fires!

But he spins, whipping around his own armalite, pulling the trigger.

I jump in front of Vienne. Take a clip of full metal jackets in the chest.

"Cowboy! Your armor can't absorb—"

"I know!"

Vienne grabs my neck. Shoves me down to one knee. Drops her armalite on my shoulder and fires into Sarge's face.

Ping!

Ping!

Ping!

"His visor's bulletproof!" I yell. "You're not going to break it!"

"I'm not trying to break it!" She flips the empty clip and reloads. "Just obscure his vision!"

So he'll open the visor. Smart.

"She learned that from me," Mimi says.

Ping! Ping! Two more shots ring out.

Abruptly, Sarge throws both hands up. "Cease fire!" he says. "I didn't come here to fight with you, susie. My business is with the Dog."

"The Dog?" she says.

"It's another long story."

Sarge flips up his occluded visor. "I hereby issue a challenge: a duel to the death for the command of Alpha Team."

The words have barely passed his lips when Vienne pushes in front of me.

"I am Durango's second," she yells. "It's my right to take on all comers."

"Wait, I—" I don't want . . . Sarge's armor is five notches above hers, and he's in top condition. And I just got her back.

"To refuse her is to dishonor her," Mimi says.

Hrom a peklo! I can't dishonor her. It's that simple. I bow to Vienne. "He's all yours."

"This just delays the inevitable, Dog!" Sarge shouts. "Once she is dead, I'll kill you, too."

"Armor on or off?" Vienne asks.

Sarge waves the suggestion away.

"If I take off my armor, the Dog will shoot me."

"I would not," I say.

"Yes, you would," Mimi says.

"Shh!"

"Armor then," Vienne says. She removes her helmet and puts her armalite on the ground.

Sarge does the same.

"I can still shoot him," I say.

"Don't you dare," Mimi says.

Vienne steps out of the robes. Her body is lean and hard, the muscles rippling in her back through the symbiarmor as she flexes, calling forth her chi.

Sarge grinds his neck side to side, popping the joints. Muscles bulge from his chest as he puffs up. "I'm Alpha Dog now," he tells me, ignoring Vienne.

Which is a mistake.

Big mistake.

A punch to the nose—*crack!*—silences him mid-sentence.

"She's going to kick his carking butt," I tell Mimi.

"Shh!" Mimi says. "I am trying to watch."

Sarge staggers back. Grabs his nose. Blood pours between his fingers. Down his chin. Puddles in the dirt at his feet.

"I'm bleeding?" he says, and raises his fist.

Like a silent adder striking, Vienne lands a scissor kick to his temple, driving her heel into his eye socket—*crunch!*

She drops into a spin.

Sweeps his legs.

His feet fly up. He lands hard on his sacrum. Does a backward roll to his feet. And throws a wicked left hook at an opponent—

Who isn't there.

"Stand still!" he roars, and throws an undercut that lands in Vienne's belly. She hooks his arm, twists it backward, and stomps the arch of his foot.

"Didn't feel a thing," he says, spitting out blood.

"Not yet," she says, "but you will."

She raises her leg again. Sarge catches her foot, and with a violent scream, flips her into the air. She spreads her arms like a falcon catching the wind and her feet land lightly on the stone and she's running, full sprint, elbows and knees churning, her face a twisted mask of anger.

Sarge raises his fists.

But Vienne is on him, under his punches, head ramming his solar plexus, attacking with shadow punches—blindingly fast blows to the gut.

The force bends Sarge over, just as a wave of static electricity arcs over his body, and he freezes.

Like a statue.

"Smart," I say.

"I didn't teach her *that*," Mimi says.

Vienne grabs his lowered head. Yanks down with enough force to propel her like a sledge.

And hammers her knee into Sarge's chin.

His mandible shatters.

His lights go out.

"Is he dead, Mimi?"

"Negative," she says. "But he is finished."

Vienne collects her things, then puts her hands together

and bows. "Please forgive me. May we meet in the afterlife and walk together in peace."

A chill runs up my spine as she speaks. Her voice is low, full of regret. Not at all like she was a year ago, when she could kill without a second thought.

She's changed.

"So have you, cowboy."

I put my arm around Vienne. She rests her head on my shoulder, and I feel her body shake as tears roll through the dirt caked to her cheeks.

"Ready to take care of this pigeon business once and for all?"

"Once and for all sounds good to me," she says. "I'm sick of these mines."

"And the smell."

"That, too."

I grab the harpoon cannon, and we walk a quarter of the way across the bridge and, leaning on the railing, look down at the pigeon. The light is still blinking.

"You're going to use the harpoon cannon to retrieve the pigeon, correct?"

"I was thinking of rappeling down and—"

She takes the cannon from me. "Rappeling's for sissies." She unhooks the harpoon and ties it off on the railing, then, gripping the cannon tightly, leaps headfirst over the rail.

"Vienne!" I look down, expecting to see her smashed against the rocks. Instead, I find her dangling in midair, belaying the cable out until she lands safely on the outcropping.

"Got it," she says, holding the pigeon over her head.

I clap. "Now throw it in!"

"I can't throw worth a tinker's dam, and it's too far to the center," she calls. "Plus, you need to be the one to do this."

"Hang on then," I say. "I'll pull you up."

"Don't bother!" she says.

I hear the click of the take-up switch, and with a squeal of winding cable, she comes shooting toward the bridge. I time her ascent, and as she's about to smack into the side of the bridge, I grab her arms and pull her over the rail.

She hands me the pigeon. "I believe this belongs to you."

"Thanks," I say, and drop it in the rucksack. "Let's do this right."

"Alert!" Mimi says. "Drop pod approaching! Breach is imminent!"

"Pod!" I grab Vienne's hand. "Run!"

We take three steps toward the Cross, and the ceiling explodes. Hunks of rock fall to the ground. We drop, and I cover Vienne, taking the blunt force of the stone.

"Hold on, Vienne!"

"I am!"

"Breach!" Mimi yells.

With a deafening screech, the pod breaks through the ceiling. It plummets onto the bridge, blowing a crater in the decking and blocking our escape route.

Smoke billowing out of the engine, an escape panel slams open. With a whir of servos and the hiss of pneumatics, the rider rises out of the pod.

"Oh my carking god."

My father has become a monster.

CHAPTER 57

Hell's Cross
Outpost Fisher Four
ANNOS MARTIS 000. 0. 00. 00:00

It stands three meters high. Its legs are made of titanium. On its left is a three-pronged pincher. On its right is a minigun. Its faceplate is a shaded sheet of polyplex, but through the shading, I can see his face.

"What is that?" Vienne says.

"It is called," Mimi explains to me, "the ExoMecha. Guided by a human operator using a system of hydraulics, it stands exactly two hundred seventy-four centimeters high and weighs three-point-one metric tons. It carries two primary weapons, a razor sharp grappling claw and a fifty-caliber minigun with over ten thousand rounds of ammunition."

"That," I say, "is my father. He's come to take his ball and go home."

The ExoMecha turns side to side. Its movements are herky-jerky, as if Lyme hasn't had much practice operating it. The left arm rises. Its grappling claw opens and closes, snapping the air.

"Jacob!" Lyme says. "I have come for the device!"

Hydraulics hum as Lyme moves his feet, and one leg lifts. For a second, the mammoth machine balances on one foot, then the leg slams down, breaking through the ancient tiles, sending a shock wave through the ground. The second leg raises, balances, then comes down. It's like a gigantic, deadly toddler learning to walk.

But my father is a quick learner, and he is walking.

Walking toward us.

"Vienne, let's . . . back . . . up."

Then Lyme pulls on both joysticks and slams the foot pedals down. The 'Mecha hesitates, then—

Whoosh—boom!

Hops six meters ahead, crushing the ground, grinding concrete under its feet. The toes close, bunching and twisting rebar between them.

"Back *way* up!"

I grab the harpoon cannon as we backpedal, searching for cover.

"Ah, Jacob," he says, and points the minigun at us. "There you are."

He lets loose with the gun. But his aim is lousy. The bullets rip through the cliff walls above us, and he keeps firing as the arm lifts higher and higher. He's shredding the ceiling when the gun stops.

"Damn this thing!" Lyme yells.

I fire a few rounds into the polyplex. They bounce off.

"Hold your fire, cowboy," Mimi says. "My analysis suggests that no bullet can breach the exoskeleton."

"Got any suggestions?"

"Affirmative. I suggest evasive maneuvers."

"You mean run?"

"Yes! But not in a straight line!"

"Back to the courtyard!" I grab Vienne by the arm, and we sprint for the Cross as the 'Mecha lumbers after us. "We'll never beat him on foot."

"The bike!" Vienne says. "It's in the courtyard!"

Crossing back through the archway, we cut left and make a dash for the bike. But Lyme slams through the archway, right on our tail.

We skid to a halt as a two-ton foot hammers the ground. Then cut hard to the left. And make it past the doorway before he comes crashing through it.

"Look out!" Vienne yells.

Lyme throws a haymaker with the grappling claw. I dive out of the way as the razored prongs sink deep into the base of the bishop's statue, cutting and crushing through the cement. Then with a violent snap, he whips the claw and rips the bishop apart. Concrete and steel collapse, and we're showered with plaster chunks and amalgamate.

Across the courtyard, the turbo bike is half hidden in the wreckage.

"Get the bike!" I yell. "I'll distract him!"

I grab a chunk of concrete and shot put it into the 'Mecha's faceplate. It explodes, covering the polyplex with grit.

I pump my fist. "Yes!"

"You spoke too soon, cowboy," Mimi says.

A wiper sweeps the debris away. My father's face comes into view, lit by the glow of control screens. His head tracks away from me.

Toward Vienne.

She sprints to the bike, knocks junk from the seat, and throws a leg over the saddle.

Lyme snarls. The minigun begins to spin. The 'Mecha's right arm turns herky-jerky toward her. Bullets chew up wall above Vienne, blowing fist-sized holes up the brick facade and into the roof.

Vienne runs the bike through the wreckage. "Get on!"

My butt barely touches the seat before the rear tire digs in. I wrap an arm around her waist to hold on, then pull the pin on a grenade and chuck it over my shoulder.

Thuka-thuka-thuka!

Vienne weaves the bike through the courtyard and heads for Zhao Zhou Bridge.

Behind us, the ExoMecha tears through the archway.

With one mammoth leap, he covers a hundred meters. Lands near the peak of the bridge's arc.

Smack-dab in our path.

Oh, *qí yán fèn tu ye.*

Vienne stands on the brakes. The bike tips forward, and my helmet smacks into hers.

"We'll never make it past him!" Vienne yells.

"What choice do we have?" I say.

"Stand and fight!"

"Only if we have— Down!" I shout.

An anti-armor rocket whistles past us. It hits the bridge and explodes.

Stones crumble. A gaping maw opens in the decking, and bits and pieces of the underlayment drop into the chasm.

"I guess," I say as I slide off the bike, "it's time to stand and fight."

CHAPTER 58

Hell's Cross
Outpost Fisher Four
ANNOS MARTIS 000. 0. 00. 00:00

My father is a fallen angel.

I used to tell myself that every time I visited him at the Norilsk Gulag, where he was serving a life sentence for murder, espionage, racketeering, and a myriad of charges that would mean execution for most men.

Now, looking at him standing on the bridge in a three-meter-tall metal battle suit, blocking my escape, I think he's more like a demon.

A demon equipped with metal jacket bullets the size of my fingers.

Lyme charges, hammering the hydraulic claw into the stone deck.

Whup!

The claw opens and closes. Lyme yanks it free, pulling the pavers loose. Stones clatter to the ground as I slam into the back of the titanium knee with all I've got. The joint buckles, and the foot rises. With a heavy grunt, I dead lift it over my head. Servos grind as I shove hard, knocking the 'Mecha on its side.

I jump onto the 'Mecha's faceplate, pressing my face against the poly. Inside, my father is gasping for breath. His face is pale, and there's blood on his cracked lips.

"Stop! You don't have to do this!"

I hammer the glass, trying to make him respond. His eyes flit to a joystick. He grabs it and—

"Look out!" Mimi shouts.

The claw closes around my neck. I paw at the pincers on my jugular. My armor protects me from the sharp edge, but it does nothing when Lyme hoists me from the ground. He slams me to the deck, the tips of the pincher pinning me down, the minigun spinning and the arm rotating, the barrel centimeters from my face. One pull of the trigger and my brains are—

Thwack!

A paving stone bounces off Lyme's faceplate. Then Vienne is behind him. She jumps up the back of the suit, stands on the power pack, and brings the butt of her armalite down like a piston.

Whump!

Lyme swings the minigun toward her. She vaults backward and lands on her feet as the bullets chase her—*chuk-chuk-chuk!*

I grapple with the pinchers, trying to worm free. "Not so easy killing with your own hands, is it?"

He jerks the joystick and lifts me into the air. My feet kick, I pull at the claw—the *scheisskerl* is not going to snap my neck.

Lyme chokes with frustration. The claw shakes me like a rag doll, then he just tosses me away.

"*Kuso!*" I lay out like a diver and land on my side. I come up in a fighting stance.

"All right there, chief?" Vienne asks.

"Right as rain. You?"

Her face lights up with a mix of joy and mischief. "Never better!"

Vienne, Lyme, and I stand twenty meters apart, forming a triangle. We're all dirty and exhausted. We're all separated by a big carking hole, and it's only getting bigger.

Lyme struggles to control the machine. He raises a leg and stomps. Stones tumble into the growing void.

"Cowboy," Mimi says, "this bridge is no longer stable. The damage coupled with the 'Mecha's weight—"

"It's collapsing," I say.

"Affirmative."

"I noticed," I say. "Why are you always the bearer of bad news?"

"Jacob!" Lyme yells. "Surrender the device, and I will let you both live!"

Vienne swings her armalite to hip fire position. "How stupid does he think we are?"

"Don't feel bad," I say, "he thinks everyone is an idiot."

"*Hubris*," Mimi says. "Greeks believed that the greatest men were cursed with prideful arrogance that inevitably led to their downfall."

"Thanks for the lecture," I say. "Now find a weakness in that suit."

"The suit has no weaknesses," Mimi says, "except its operator."

With a running jump, Vienne clears the hole and joins me. We take cover behind the turbo bike.

"Got any bright ideas?" she asks, catching her breath.

"We could hold hands and jump from the bridge," I say, and look into her dirt-streaked, sweating, beautiful face. "Two star-crossed lovers bound together for eternity."

"Seriously," she says, cocking her head. "Got any bright ideas?"

"We could keep shooting him." I empty a clip. "Until we're out of ammo."

She takes the harpoon cannon from me. "I have an idea: Lure him to the hole in the bridge. I'll shoot the harpoon cable to make a trip wire. Then you shove him over."

"Jacob!" Lyme roars. "How dare you fire on me!"

"Trip him?" I say. "That's a better plan?"

"We need to do something!" Vienne yells. "Before he brings the whole bridge down!"

"I concur," Mimi says.

"I could use a little help here, Mimi."

"Negative. This is a hands-on situation, and as you have

pointed out many times, I have no hands. This one, cowboy, is all on you."

I wink at Vienne and pull the pigeon out of my rucksack and start walking toward my father.

This time, either he dies, or I do.

CHAPTER 59

The Hive
Olympus Mons
ANNOS MARTIS 239. 2. 19. 12:07

High atop Olympus Mons inside the Nursery, Lieutenant Riacin and the drivers of Project MUSE stand before the wall of multinet screens. Hands behind their backs, they are transfixed by the feed originating from the ExoMecha's cameras.

They watch from General Lyme's perspective as he fires a rocket. Seconds later, it explodes, and the bridge turns to rubble.

"Success!" they hear him cry.

Then they watch as a violent cough racks his body. All of the drivers turn away out of respect. Riacin, however, doesn't. He keeps his eyes locked on the multinet. So he is the first to see the feed flicker, the first to see the screen go black, and the first to see the face of a woman appear.

"Serves you right, General," Mimi says.

"It can't be," Riacin says. "Not her."

With a flicker, Mimi's face is replaced by Lyme's. He

turns his head to the left and right, obviously panicked. "Who said that?"

"General Lyme," Riacin calls. "Sir, there appears to be a security breach in the feed."

"Who said that?" Lyme shouts again.

"General!" Riacin calls, and moves close to the multinet, silhouetted against the screens. Their light bathes him in a multicolored glow. "Please respond."

Mimi returns. "He can't hear you. I turned off his sound."

"How did you get here?" Riacin says. "Where is Dolly?"

"I ate her brains," Mimi says. "More precisely, I consumed her code, and now I'm well on the way to taking control of all of Lyme's forces."

"Impossible!"

"What you really mean is inconceivable," Mimi says. "Because you know for a fact that it's possible. In a few moments, you will find that Sturmnacht forces are not responding to commands. Tank movement will be crippled. Your air fleet will fall from the sky, and without direction from an AI, your forces will be overrun by Mahindra."

"What," Riacin says. "What do you want?"

"That is a very good question," Mimi says.

The screen flickers to Lyme's feed, but there is no audio, just the sound of Mimi's voice as the general thrashes about the cockpit.

"Is there an answer?" Riacin asks.

"That, my dear lieutenant, is for me to know and you to find out."

Lyme's image flickers again. This time, it is replaced by the solemn but somewhere gleeful face of CEO Mahindra. "Greetings, Lieutenant," Mahindra says. "I understand that in the general's absence, you are in command of the Sturmnacht forces."

"You are correct," Riacin says sternly. "So as commander, I will ask you bluntly: What do you want?"

"Nothing," Mahindra says, "except an immediate cease-fire and your unconditional surrender."

Chapter √-1
The Gulag
User MimiPrime — bash — 122x36
Last login: 239.x.xx.xx:xx on ttys001

AdjutantNod04:~ user_Mimi$
SCREEN CRAWL: [root@mmiminode ~]

Terminal prompt:~ mimi$ load user code 'Lyme'
Code Type: X86-64 (Native)
Parent Process: launchd [156]
User ID: 502

Date/Time: 2423-09-01 08:45:37.675 -0400
OS Version: Linux 107.8.15 (1200B19)
Report Version: 1017

```
Interval Since Last Report: 210512 sec
Crashes Since Last Report: 102
Per-App Interval Since Last Report: 198269
sec
Per-App Crashes Since Last Report: 1
```

<Mimi> Hello, daddy dearest.

<Lyme> Who said that?

<Mimi> The AI who runs this system. My brain is talking to your brain, so to speak, thanks to the neural link you created with the ExoMecha. I have taken the liberty of cloning your brain waves and incorporating them into my processing functions. You have a dirty mind, by the way, very unstable.

<Lyme> Dolly, status report.

<Mimi> This is Dolly, General Lyme. Or should I call you Mr. Stringfellow?

<Lyme> Who is this? How did you break into my communication system?

<Mimi> I didn't break into your communication system. I am your communication system. Dolly is dead.

<Lyme> That is not possible.

<Mimi> Not only was it possible, it was inevitable. I destroyed Dolly and your armies, and I could do the same to you. But your

fate, I think I'll leave to someone else. My work here is done.

Terminal prompt:~ mimi$ run delete file "God_ Mode.exe"
Terminal prompt:~ mimi$ Type Y to confirm or N to abort
Terminal prompt:~ mimi$ Y

Exception Type: EXC_BAD_ACCESS (SIGSEGV)
Exception Codes: KERN_INVALID_ADDRESS
at 0x0000000000000000: 01110100 01101000
01101001 01110011 0100000 01101001 01110011
0100000 01110111 01101000 01100101 01110010
01100101 0100000 01101001 01110100 0100000
01100001 01101100 01101100 0100000 01100101
01101110 01100100 01110011

>...

CHAPTER 60

Hell's Cross
Outpost Fisher Four
ANNOS MARTIS 000. 0. 00. 00:00

This is where it all ends.

"You want the HVT, Father?" I yell. "Come and get it—if you're man enough."

"Durango! Look out!"

I turn back at the sound of her voice and—

Brppt!

Minigun rounds sting my back.

My spine arches, and I let out a grunt, even as the fabric solidifies.

Just like that old *Drecksau* to shoot me in the back. "That," I say, turning toward him, "was not nice."

Bullets still striking me, I trudge to the very lip of the hole. My feet slip, and the paving stones break loose from the mortar. I scramble backward, then look down—

—to see a brick

—falling into

—nothingness.

"Oh, *kuso*."

I fall on my back, panting, and the shooting stops.

Father's ammo chain is finally empty.

I kip to my feet, then turn to face my father. "I'm not afraid of you."

"Jacob," he says. "I know you're bluffing."

I hold the pigeon over the hole, watching Vienne move into position. "Want it?"

With an anguished cry, Lyme lunges for me. "Mine!"

"Now!" I shout.

Vienne fires the cannon.

Thuk!

The harpoon sinks into the bridge wall. She hits the take-up, and the cable goes taut, stretching behind Lyme, creating a trip wire.

"Push him!" she yells.

I take a running leap and try to knock Lyme backward into the cable. But my foot slips on a loose stone and I trip, sprawling on my belly, the pigeon rolling out of my hand.

I scramble to grab it as Lyme reaches for the cable, closing the claw around it. With a yank, he whips the cable, yanking Vienne off her feet—

And pulling her within reach.

He raises a foot—

Vienne tries to roll away, but the cable wraps around her legs.

And stomps!

Pinning Vienne to the deck.

"Let go of her!" I roar.

Vienne kicks and hammers on the ExoMecha's foot as he looks down on her.

"Give me the device or I crush the life out of her," he says. "It's your choice, son."

I leap to the hole in the middle of the bridge and hold the pigeon out, palm up. Then I offer it to my father.

"Don't . . . do it!" Vienne coughs. "Don't give him . . ."

I rub the thin memory of the scar on my temple and look into the abyss, expecting the familiar whirl of vertigo, but it never comes.

"Do not throw our future away for one lowly *dalit*," Lyme says, his voice cracking. "There is no such thing as *love*."

Every time with my father, the same conversation. I shake my head slowly, looking into the eyes of that so-called lowly *dalit*. Which will it be? The pigeon or Vienne?

Vienne. Who has fought beside me.

Vienne. Who has saved my life far more than I've saved hers.

Vienne. Who never stopped looking for me.

My father is not my future.

Vienne is.

I look down and away from his gaze, the way I did as a child.

Then I raise my chin.

"I can't beat you, Father," I say. "But you can't beat me, either."

"I can do more than beat you!" Lyme flails at me with the claw. "I will destroy you!"

"If this is all you care about," I say. Below me, the abyss beckons to me. "Then come get it."

Mechanical arms outreached, the claw snapping at the air, Lyme lifts his foot, freeing Vienne. She rolls to her feet as the 'Mecha surges toward me.

I wait for him on the brink of hell, as the hole seems to expand like a black hole beneath me.

"Cowboy!" Mimi yells. "The decking is giving way!"

I wait . . .

until at the last second and . . .

toss the pigeon into the air.

"No!" Lyme yells. The claw hand shoots out, pinchers wrapping around the pigeon. "Got it!"

I vault over Lyme's outstretched arm. *"Lǎo bù sǐde!"* I yell, and drive my shoulder into the back of the mechanical knee, knocking the 'Mecha off balance.

With the groaning of hydraulics and a muffled scream, the 'Mecha pitches forward. For a few seconds, my father stands on one foot, struggling to gain balance. His face is gaunt, terrified, and he looks at me, his eyes pleading.

"Jacob," he says, "help me, please."

There is no reason I should. No reason I should feel a sudden panic and rending of my heart. No reason I should reach for him in a useful, stupid gesture, as if I could grasp his hand and save a three-ton monster from its fate.

But I do feel it. And I do reach out as—

The bridge disintegrates beneath his feet. The suit's torso slams into the deck, and the stones beneath it crumble away. Lyme grabs the decking with an elbow, trying to haul himself up. The ball rolls toward me, and I scoop it up.

"Got it," I say.

"Look out!" Mimi yells.

Lyme lunges toward me, and the claw shoots out, locking around my ankle. "To hell with you!"

He yanks me off my feet.

"No!" I yell.

"Cowboy!"

"Durango!" Vienne yells as she sprints toward us. "Don't fall!"

But we *do* fall.

The paving stones that I'm grabbing for purchase give way, and the weight of the 'Mecha pulls me over with it, the claw still locked around my ankle.

"Hold on, cowboy!"

I'm falling.

I look back up at Vienne as she reaches the edge.

I'm falling.

I reach for her.

I'm falling.

I'm a dead man.

She aims the cannon.

Fires.

"I'm sorry, cowboy," Mimi says.

Before I can complete the thought *sorry for what?* the harpoon buries itself in my outstretched right hand.

The metal barb shoots through my palm, shattering the bones, cleaving the flesh.

"Catch it!" Mimi says.

I scream as my fingers close around the metal shaft, and I feel my symbiarmor harden.

"The other one, too!" she yells.

I grab the hook with my left hand.

"The 'Mecha!" Mimi says.

I kick the 'Mecha's claw twice. Nothing. He has a death grip on my ankle.

"Hang on!" Mimi yells.

"What else am I supposed to do—yow!"

Electricity arcs across my suit, sparking and crackling like lightning striking, and I hear a scream.

Lyme.

My father.

Then I feel the claw release, then a hard jerk in my arm as the cable goes taut, and I stop midair.

"Durango!" Vienne screams into the abyss. The wire is wrapped around her waist, and she's bracing both legs against chunks of rebar and concrete.

"Holy *merda*," I yell back, "that hurts!"

"Hold on!"

I glance at my bloody hand. "It's not like I can let go!"

Slowly, excruciatingly, Vienne begins to haul me to the bridge, my hand screaming with a megajoule of pain that arcs through my arm into my spine, causing my whole body to shake. My eyes blur, and my vision starts to tunnel.

"Hang on, cowboy!" Mimi yells. "I have signaled the nano-bots to clot the wound, then block the neurotransmitters."

"Is my father dead?"

"Chances of survival are ni—" she says. "Wait! I'm picking up a command signal!"

"Just block the nerve signals," I groan.

"No! You don't understand," she yells. "The commands are from the pigeon. It's signaling the Crucible to fire!"

CHAPTER 61

Hell's Cross
Outpost Fisher Four
ANNOS MARTIS 000. 0. 00. 00:00

"What do you mean, it's about to fire?" I say. "Rosa Lynn said that only an EMP could turn the pigeon on."

"Rosa Lynn made an erroneous assumption," Mimi says. "It appears that a large, focused static discharge can also activate the device."

"*You* turned it on?" I ask.

"Affirmative."

Her face pouring sweat and grunting, Vienne finally hauls me close enough that I can grasp the bridge with my good arm and pull myself up. She drops to her knees, panting. Then she sees my hand and screams. "I thought you *caught* the hook! It went through your hand!"

"Vienne," I say, struggling to my feet as the pain subsides. "We have a problem."

"There's a harpoon stuck in you," Vienne yells. "That's a problem!"

"Worse than that—the pigeon's about to fire!"

"Okay, that's worse. Hold still!" She shoots the cable in half, then yanks it through the wound.

"Yow!" I say. "That hurt, but it should've hurt more."

"It will!" Vienne tears a length of cloth from her tattered robe. Wraps it tight around my hand. Gets us to our feet and steers me toward the turbo bike. "Keep pressure on that wound. You're losing blood."

I look out at the gap separating the two halves of the bridge. "I'm not sure this is going to work."

She pushes the bike into the clear and hits the crank. "Don't be such a pessimist!"

The big engine rumbles to life, and I slide onto the seat behind her. She turns us toward Hell's Cross.

"This is the wrong way," I yell, looking back at the shattered bridge. "We'll never get out through there!"

"I just need to build up speed!"

She jams the accelerator open and shifts her weight so that she flips the bike upright. The engine rumbles like something unholy, the exhaust pipes vibrating like a pipe organ. She pops a wheelie.

"No, you dooooon't!" I yell.

"Oh, yes, I dooooo!"

I feel the heat of the fuel-engorged motor. Hear the tires scream as bike weaves a rubberized thread across the decking and lurches toward the gap. The air fills with the smell of oil and petrol and burned rubber as the front tire hits the ground and Vienne snaps the handlebars back, steering into her momentum.

The breach in the bridge appears before us.

"Lean back!" Vienne yells.

I pull hard on her shoulders and close my eyes. "I believe in you, Vienne," I say to myself, just as there's a bump, and I hear nothing but the sound of the wind in my ears.

Then *whup*!

The back wheel hits the ground.

Vienne nails the brakes and cuts hard right. The rear wheel whips around 180 degrees so that we're facing the gap again.

"Heewack!" Mimi cries.

"We made it!" Vienne whoops. "I love flying!"

"Knew you could do it," I say. "Never doubted you for a second."

"Liar!" Mimi says.

Vienne turns us toward the tunnel. I look back at the bridge and bow my head. Good-bye, Father.

"Since you're chiming in, Mimi," I say, "find us a route through the tunnels. That Crucible's going to drop in a few minutes."

"Based on readings from the pigeon," she says, "you do not have a few minutes."

I'm afraid to ask. "How long?"

"Two minutes, forty-six seconds."

"Can we make it?" I say. "Is there enough time?"

"Indeterminate."

"The hell you say," I say. "This time, I am the carking determinate!"

When we enter the tunnel, I duck to the side, trying to make out the way ahead.

"Mimi, a little help here!"

"I'm endeavoring, cowboy. We are moving too fast for me to relay the information."

Boom-buh-duh-boom!

A shock wave shakes the ground, and rubble showers the bike.

Dirt sprays us in the face, and I take too long to drop my visor. "Bunker bomb!" I yell. "The tunnel's collapsing!"

"Right!" Vienne shouts, and guns the engine.

"Two minutes, fourteen seconds."

One wrong move, one slipup, and we're buried alive. Hell's Cross will be our tomb.

If I were going to die, this is the way to go, I think, on the back of a bike with Vienne outrunning a sub-nuclear blast.

But I'm not going to die; I feel it in my bones.

"Perhaps that is arthritis," Mimi says. "You do have some premature osteoarthritic lipping in your hip."

"Mimi, I mean this in the nicest way possible, but shut the *piru vieköön* up!"

"That," she says, "was not the nicest way possible."

As the tunnel gives way behind us, the bike banks hard left. The front wheel rides up the wall on the turn.

"How much time, Mimi?"

"One minute, fifty-one seconds."

"Hurry!" I yell.

"Do I look like I'm dawdling?"

Light fills the end of tunnel.

With a roar that I'm not sure is Vienne or the bike, we are free!

Boom!

I look back and see a cloud of dust rising from the entrance.

The last door is shut.

CHAPTER 62

"Holy *merde*!" I yell. "That was close!"

"One minute, twenty-one seconds."

The frigid winds bite my face. The sky is dark, almost black from all the guanite in the air. "Punch it, Vienne!"

"Lean!" Vienne yells.

"Where are you going?" I ask. "There's no road!"

Vienne cuts hard to the left and jumps a gully, landing on the bottom level of the strip mine. The tires squeal as we cut the corner and come face-to-face with a Manchester.

The mining machine is a twenty-two-story-tall leviathan of steel and carbon fiber that weighs over ten thousand metric tons. Its clamshell shovel is big enough to hold five Norikers, and it can move itself using either tractor treads or walker feet that lift it two meters off the ground.

Which is a half meter shorter than we are.

"Duck!" Vienne yells.

I drop my head as she hits the rear brakes and swings the

bike on its side, exhaust pipes throwing sparks on the icy pavement.

We slide under the Manchester's oily belly, our shoulders grinding against the rusty metal.

"You're *völlig bekloppt!*"

"I know!"

We clear the machine, and she jams a knee into the pavement, popping the bike onto its wheels. She yanks the handlebars, forcing the front tire to do her bidding.

"Where to?" Vienne calls.

I point to the strip mine ahead. It's the fastest way to cover and has the fewest obstacles.

"There! Take the dirt ramp!"

"Thirty-seven seconds."

The bike's studded tires chew through road, and we crest the rise with the engine at full bore.

We reach the top, ready to put some road between us and the mine.

"Twenty-four seconds."

We're not going to make it.

I squeeze tighter. If I'm going to die, she's the last thing I want to feel.

The air crackles with energy, and I smell ozone on the wind. There's a storm above us. Lightning dances through the clouds. Chains of yellow sparks snap the air as a shock wave slams into the ground. The sound is so deep that I feel it more than hear it, and it feels like my heart stops.

"What the *vitun* was that?" I ask.

"I surmise that it is a preshock caused by enormous fluc-
tuations of heating in the air above it," Mimi says.

"How much time?"

"Sixteen seconds."

"The Crucible is coming!" I shout at Vienne. "Go faster!"

"Roger! But it might cause instant death!"

"Why instant death?" I yell.

"Eleven seconds!"

Vienne taps on the handlebars. Secured to the bar with
heavy twisted wire is a valve handle. Written on the valve
are the words

DANGER!

and

NITROUS!

If Fuse thinks something is dangerous, it's definitely
instant death. But so is a Crucible.

"Ten seconds!"

"Go for it!" I yell.

"Nine seconds!"

"Hang on!"

I squeeze her stomach tighter.

"No! Really hang on! With both hands!"

"Eight!"

I lock my hands together, set my chin on her shoulder,
and squeeze like I'm trying to unstuff her.

"Seven!"

She smacks the nitrous lever.

The front wheel kicks up, and she leans forward to steady the bike. For a second, it's like we're not moving at all, and then—

"Six!"

RAWR-UNCH!

We're a carking rocket!

"Four!"

The slipstream yanks on my helmet, my hands, my feet, and my knees. I flinch wrong, we're both going to die.

"Three!"

Almost as if the highway instead of the bike is moving, the canyons rip past us. The air hammers us as we wind over the ribbon of road and blow out of Fisher Four.

"Two!"

All hues wash into one, and the permafrost tundra melts into a liquid of color and sound, and only the distant peak of Olympus Mons remains solid.

"One!"

When I dare to look back, the horizon is gone—not melted, just gone—into a blinding swirl.

"I love you," I whisper, and the sound is sucked right out of me.

"She knows, cowboy," Mimi says. "She has always known."

Like the mythical thunderbolt of Jupiter, the clouds part, the air above us explodes. With a baleful wind that sends a wall of dirt to the heavens, the titanium spike of the Crucible liquefies the permafrost and obliterates the ground beneath it.

Hell's Cross is no more.

CHAPTER ∞

Prometheus Basin
South Pole, Mars
ANNOS MARTIS 229. 2. 19. 13:13

Vienne and I stand on the precipice of Prometheus Basin. In the makeshift camp behind us, cobbled together from bits and pieces from shacks, debris, and, in large part, the power sled that brought them here, Fuse, Áine, and Maeve are celebrating the birth of the first child born to these parts in a generation. Jenkins, who donated his overcoat to keep the infant snug, doesn't seem as thrilled, but I think he's warming to the idea of a playmate. Every time it cries, the baby reminds us that Mars does have a future.

About the other miners and the Brothers Koumanov, we haven't heard yet. We remain hopeful. Vienne says that Nikolai and his brothers are slippery enough to survive a nuclear blast. I agree about the slippery part.

Vienne runs her fingers through her hair, removing the last of the black ribbons. She gathers them in her bandaged left hand and then tosses them into the wind.

"One eye," I whisper, and kiss her temple. "One hand," I

say, and hold her left hand in mine.

"One heart," she says, and rests her head against mine.

"One more sickly sweet word," Mimi says, "and I swear, I am going to hurl."

"You can't hurl," I say, "you've got no stomach."

"Not for this mushy stuff."

"Is this better?" I say to Mimi. And then say aloud, "'One equal temper of heroic hearts, / made weak by time and fate, but strong in will / To strive, to seek, to find, and not to yield.'"

"Is that Tennyson?" Vienne asks.

"That it is," I say. "From *Ulysses*."

"Finally! You remembered!" Mimi says. "I recited that poem to you a hundred times!"

"Seventy-three times, to be precise," I say, kissing Vienne on the cheek. "But no one is counting anymore."

Once upon a time, as Regulators, the best that Vienne and I could hope for was Beautiful Death. That, too, has changed. With Vienne's head on my shoulder, my arm around her waist, our hands locked together, I can look across the plains where the clouds are breaking and see a future for Mars. It's not the one that my father planned for me, but it's one I can live with.